THE LEAKY ESTABLISHMENT

Other Books by David Langford

Fiction

An Account of a Meeting with Denizens of Another World, 1871
Earthdoom! (with John Grant)
The Dragonhiker's Guide to Battlefield Covenant at Dune's Edge: Odyssey Two
Guts (with John Grant) *
He Do the Time Police in Different Voices *
Irrational Numbers
A Novacon Garland
The Space Eater

Nonfiction

A Cosmic Cornucopia (with Josh Kirby)
The Complete Critical Assembly *
Critical Assembly
Critical Assembly II
Facts and Fallacies (with Chris Morgan)
Micromania: The Whole Truth About Home Computers (with Charles Platt)
The Necronomicon (with George Hay, Robert Turner and Colin Wilson)
Pieces of Langford
Platen Stories
The Science in Science Fiction (with Peter Nicholls and Brian Stableford)
The Silence of the Langford
The Third Millennium: A History of the World AD 2000-3000 (with Brian Stableford)
The TransAtlantic Hearing Aid
The Unseen University Challenge
Up Through an Empty House of Stars: Reviews and Essays 1980-2002 *
War in 2080: The Future of Military Technology
The Wyrdest Link

As Editor

The Encyclopedia of Fantasy (with John Clute, John Grant, and others)
Maps: The Uncollected John Sladek
Wrath of the Fanglord

* In Cosmos Books

THE LEAKY ESTABLISHMENT

David Langford

Introduction by Terry Pratchett

Cosmos Books • 2003
An imprint of **Wildside Press**

THE LEAKY ESTABLISHMENT

Published by:

Cosmos Books, an imprint of Wildside Press
PO Box 301, Holicong, PA 18928-0301
www.wildsidepress.com

For more information, contact Wildside Press.

ISBN: 1-59224-125-5

Dedication

To those who put up with me in and around A70
(1975-1980)
with gratitude, nostalgia, apologies

Acknowledgements

This book should not be forced to shoulder the entire blame for its crimes. It is, after all, the product and victim of its environment. Not it but Society stands condemned. We are all guilty. Knowing and unknowing accomplices include Katie Cohen, who encouraged the author to babble; Maxim Jakubowski, who put him on the tube to Wimbledon; Catherine McAulay, a mean woman with a photocopier; *New Scientist*, who arranged Roy Tappen's print debut; and Christopher Priest, to whom thanks for many close-typed pages of wise advice (1977, 1980) and one tactful silence (1982).

Later: Additional thanks to Ben Jeapes of Big Engine for reissuing this 1984 novel in 2001, to Terry Pratchett for generously writing the introduction which first appeared in the Big Engine edition, to Sean Wallace of Cosmos Books and John Betancourt of Wildside Press for this new edition, and to Juha Lindroos for the jacket design. Geo Parkin created his cover painting for *Frontier Crossings*, the souvenir book of the 1987 World Science Fiction Convention (Conspiracy '87) in Brighton, where I was one of the guests: I'm delighted to have it appear at last on the book it illustrates. Some welcome help in tracing this painting came from Rob Jackson, the editor of *Frontier Crossings* – who among other things diligently searched his attic for the original Parkin artwork which was, as it turned out, somewhere else.

Introduction: Terry Pratchett

I hate Dave Langford for writing this book. This was the book I meant to write. God wanted me to write this book.

For a large part of the 1980s I effectively worked (which was definitely not the same as worked effectively) for the civil nuclear industry, or at least that part of it that produced cheap, clean nuclear electricity, if I remember my facts correctly, in South West England.

Reactors hardly ever exploded. I was a Press Officer, so you can trust me on this. But they didn't have to explode. Some little known component of nuclear radiation made certain that life for anyone involved with the public face of the industry became very weird. And I worked with Dave Langfords all the time. I had to. I knew about words, they knew about uranium. They were a fine body of men, with a refreshingly different view of the universe.

When a member of the public turned up at a nuclear power station and was found to be too radioactive to go near the reactor, they advised me. When I had to deal with the news story about the pixie that shut down a nuclear power station, they advised me again. Scientists with a twisted sense of humour can do wonders for your education, provided you believe only fifty percent of what they tell you. (Er ... perhaps thirty percent, come to think of it – I never did actually use the phrase "The amount of radiation released was so small that you could hardly see it.")

They'd produce figures to show that the Sun was an illegal emitter of laser light and under Health and Safety regulations no one should be allowed outdoors, or that the natural background radiation in granite areas meant that registered nuclear workers should only be allowed to go on holiday in Cornwall if they wore protective clothing. And I can no longer hear the words "three completely independent fail-safe systems" without laughing.

The job was also my introduction to the civil service. Yes, there really was the man who came around ever six months to check that I still had the ancient four-function calculator that I'd signed for on joining, and was probably worth 10p. Yes, some of the Langfords upstairs brought in their own word-processors to write their reports and then, because of the regulations,sighed and sent the print-outs down to the typing pool to be re-typed. And then there was the guy who actually went onto a nuclear reactor and ... but I'll save that one, because you'd never believe it. Or the one about the lavatory.

It's no wonder that this clash of mind-sets produced something like *The Leaky Establishment* (which of course deals with an entirely different kind of nuclear establishment to the ones I worked in, where things were not actually *intended* to blow up.) The book is practically a documentary. I read it in horror, in between laughing. This man had sat in at exactly the same kind of meetings! He'd dealt with the same kind of people! He'd been at the same Open Days! The sheer *reality* of it all leaked from every page! It was just like the book I'd been planning to write one day! How could I ever write *my* book now?

And then I got to the end and ... well, Dave Langford's garden would probably bear examination by the Health and Safety Executive, that's all I'll say.

I'd rank this book alongside Michael Frayn's *The Tin Men*, another neglected classic. I've wanted for years to see it back in print. It is one of those books you end up buying several copies of, because you just *have* to lend it to friends. It's very funny. It's very real.

I hope it's as successful as hell, and will happily give up any plans to write my own nuclear book. After all, I'll always have my memories to keep me warm. And, come to think of it, the large, silvery and curiously *heavy* mug they presented to me when I left....

Terry Pratchett

Author's Note

There is of course barely a grain of truth in this book. All the characters are quite fictitious, as are the Civil Service eccentricities and peccancies inserted for the sake of the plot; even the technology has been slightly blurred to protect the innocent. I state the obvious because it's been suggested to me that my fantasy research establishment could be taken as a portrait of the real one where I chased neutrons in my carefree youth. Perish the thought.

The book *An Experiment with Space* does exist, as to the best of my knowledge does its author Robert Kingsley Morison, to whom apologies for the attitude of my bigoted rationalist hero.

Younger readers should ask Mummy and/or Daddy before trying to construct the interesting scientific apparatus described close to the end of the book. The materials are in any case rather expensive and hard to come by. Perhaps you could organize it as a class project at school!

We shall never get people whose time is money to take much interest in atoms.
    – Samuel Butler, *The Notebooks*, c.1880

It is necessary for technical reasons that these warheads be stored upside down; that is, with the top at the bottom and the bottom at the top. In order that there may be no doubt as to which is the bottom and which is the top, it will be seen to that the bottom of each warhead immediately be labelled with the word TOP.
    – British Admiralty, 1960s

One

Roy Tappen was always mildly amazed when the security police passed him through the high steel gates into the tightest of all Britain's research establishments, the Nuclear-Utilization Technology Centre, whose inmates alternately pronounced the acronym Nuts or vilely anagrammatized it. Not that he felt a suspicious character; indeed, he regarded himself as startlingly handsome and distinguished, tastefully average in height, appropriately kempt of hair and generally British through and through. The trouble was his security pass, with a photo labelled R TAPPEN SSO, but in fact showing an unshaven homicidal lunatic and child-molester with a crippling hangover and at least one glass eye, photographed after forty-eight hours' strenuous axe-murdering. How unfair that each morning the Ministry of Defence police acknowledged this apparition to be unmistakably Tappen, and agreed that his pleasant light brown hair was identical with the photograph's, which appeared to be plaid.

He passed on into the sinister hinterland of NUTC. Its scatter of buildings, no two alike and not one of them likeable, huddled in a dingy corner of Robinson Heath resembling a cut-price setting for *Macbeth*. First came shiny new office blocks for administrators and typists. Then gaunt buildings like crematoria which were laboratories, workshops, plutonium-handling facilities or the canteen, until he reached the decaying wooden huts which looked like the worst and most squalid of post-war "temporary" accommodation, and were. These were the offices reserved for the highly trained scientists like Tappen who were the brains of NUTC.

The four-mile-long outer fence was electrified, bugged with microchip miracles which could very possibly detect a Trotskyist tendency a hundred yards off, and patrolled by guard dogs of

11

amazing ferocity and incontinence. Security was so theoretically strict that there'd once been a move to have senior personnel wear standardized hats, in case Soviet spy satellites could spot their characteristic hair-partings and relay information about highly confidential movements within NUTC.

Later that day, at the heart of the establishment, a crumbling Terrapin hut (protozoic ancestor of today's Portakabin) which was the inner sanctum of Britain's nuclear research, protected from the general public by layer on layer of top security and barbed wire, Roy Tappen glumly leant back from the desk and picked his nose.

There were a dozen folders piled on the battered worktop. The most important concerned the major project which aimed at replacing all the warheads in British missiles with new improved Chevalines ("the latest super-duper ones with ten-year guarantee and built-in Space Invaders facility," as Llewellyn liked to say). As a long-term project, it was at the bottom of the stack. On top were the far more urgent draft minutes of the Nuclear Public-Image Working Party, which met every Tuesday. A warm, muggy, Thursday afternoon, and one page to go on the first draft ... With a sigh Tappen bent forward to the highly illicit apparatus on his desktop, and there was a tap on the door. His heart jumped. He flipped a wad of old computer printout over his guilty secret just before the Security man stepped in.

"Afternoon just a routine inspection records say you are in charge of a valuable piece of electronic equipment subject to regular inventory checking under regulations ..." said the unwelcome visitor all on one note. Tappen sighed, hunting out the decrepit calculator which must be worth all of fifty pence; the almost equally decrepit Security man noted its serial number on three forms and had Tappen sign each one twice. Thus a jealous government guarded its funds against the wanton ravages of greedy scientific civil servants.

Alone again, Tappen uncovered the incriminating portable typewriter and began to tap out that last page. "The Press Officer proposed again that since public hysteria and apprehension are too easily inflamed by scare-words like 'plutonium', this element be renamed, e.g. as 'Element 94', 'Ingredient X' or 'Superfuel' ..."

Knock. Knock.

"Afternoon just a routine reminder records say you are in charge of a cupboard with security lock and it's time for you to change the combination and notify Security of the new one if you can just spare a minute please." The safe-and-cupboard Security policeman was even more withered and ancient than the electronics one, and his neck stuck out of the dark-blue uniform collar like a well-dried Bombay duck. Tappen breathed deeply, stood, and manipulated the cupboard lock for several minutes. All he usually kept there was the typewriter and his supplies of tea and coffee; the combination switched regularly between his wife's birthday and – if only to see if Security would ever notice – Josef Stalin's. 21-12-18-79, he wrote on the proffered form, twice, and signed, three times.

As the door slammed and neatly bisected a lackadaisical "Thank you Sir," the typewriter emerged from cover again.

"An alternate proposal was to classify the word 'plutonium' under the Official Secrets Act and to make knowledge or use of the word illegal. The Chairman pointed out that the name appeared on every copy of the Periodic Table of the Elements and that it might not be politic to classify this document. The Press Officer asked why not, and ..."

Knock.

"Afternoon just a routine inspection records say you are in charge of a valuable piece of calculating equipment subject to regular inventory checking under regulations if you could spare a moment please."

Tappen had almost forgotten that on moving in he'd inherited, along with the cupboard, the desk, the woodworm and the cockroaches, an elderly slide rule possibly used by Isambard Kingdom Brunel. After some research in dusty corners he produced it, and there was a further dispiriting rustle of forms. "Thank you Sir ..."

With sinking heart Tappen eventually finished typing the draft minutes, locked away the machine (diverted in defiance of regulations from the NUTC scrapheap), and began the grimmest stage of the afternoon's work: copying out the draft legibly in longhand. The fluency and ease of typing were only for Tappen's early drafts;

his entire section of NUTC would be blacked by the unions if a mere scientist did typist's work, so a longhand version was needed for the typing pool to redo in their own idiosyncratic way. It had been a great moment for everyone when the phrase "unclear syntax in minutes" had one day come back as "nuclear attacks on Munich".

Where was he? The tie-in with the forthcoming royal visit, yes: "The suggestion that individual missiles be named after members of the Royal Family to promote empathy and good public feeling was felt to merit further consideration," he painfully wrote. The door crashed open and a nuclear weapon came in.

"Hello Joe," Tappen murmured.

"Hi Roy," said young Llewellyn, making yo-yo motions with the string bag dangling from one hand. Inside was a dull metal sphere, not as big as a football. "Could I just dump this here a minute, nip into the Gents? I know it's all psychological but I don't like unzipping my fly with 200 kilotons in the same room, know what I mean?"

"Could you imagine that thing being called Prince William? Or maybe one would address it as Your Royal Highness."

"What?"

"Never mind. Stick it in the wastebasket, then it won't roll round the floor."

"Your wish is my command ... Don't throw any lighted fags in there, that string bag's mine and it cost money ... Oh, 'lo Roger."

Dr Roger Pell had fifteen years' seniority over Tappen and nearer twenty-five over the still university-scarred Llewellyn, but seemed too vague and woolly either to notice this or ever to be promoted again. He towered cadaverously in the doorway as though rank were measured in inches: Pell, Principal Scientific Officer, six-four; Tappen, weary Senior SO, five-ten; Llewellyn, a mere SO all bones and joints, five-eight-and-a-half.

"I brought the new pamphlets," said Pell, staring absently into the wastebasket. "Any word on the reactor business?"

Tappen stuffed the proffered sheet (MAKE ROBINSON HEATH A NUCLEAR-FREE ZONE! BURN THE WARMONGERS OF NUTC!) hastily into a drawer, and shook his head. "Don't push your luck,

Roger. One day they'll finish the thing and try some of those experiments you spend your life inventing, and then where will you be?"

Llewellyn burst into his favourite Ministerial Publicity Office impersonation: "Very soon Dr Pell's five-years'-overdue project to discover whether nukes are harmful to the health will be completed, thanks to the Advanced British Test Reactor, another superb triumph of British Technology! Soon as the Americans deliver the bugger, that is. Then once again Britain shall be strong. Let the smelly wogs tremble. R-u-u-le Britanniaaa ... Oh God, my bladder's reached critical mass."

He left. Pell stared after him. "Do you suppose the US outfits at, ah, Oak Ridge and Los Alamos have people like him?"

"Why not?" said Tappen glumly. "They probably even have people like you, handing out embarrassing flyers which would get us pissed on from a great height if we left them on our desks. Can't you just stick them through my letterbox at home?"

Pell and Tappen were next-door neighbours in the town of Redbury ten miles away.

"It seems best to, er, *bore from within*," said Pell. "That's what I always say," he added with the tedious assurance of a man who always said it. "... Did you notice that in your wastebasket ...?"

Knock. Knock. The familiar knock which gave one a sense of Security.

Tappen tidied the top of his desk with a sudden, convulsive motion which accidentally sent two stacks of computer printout off the edge and into the bin, closely followed by the telephone.

"Afternoon just a routine fire safety inspection did you know that having papers on your desk is a fire hazard a clean desk is a safe desk ... Eh, what's this?" The navy-uniformed man picked the telephone from its nest with the disdain of a chef discovering fruit-bats in the *ananas au kirsch*. "Electronic apparatus should never be disposed of through the waste paper collection service, could cause serious hazards. Shouldn't leave those inflammable pencils on your desktop either, Sir." With a curl of the lip he retreated, making ostentatious black marks on a clipboard.

"That reminds me," said Tappen. "Half a second." He bent

again over the unloved and unfinished minutes, and wrote: "In accordance with NUTC fire safety policy it was decided that at future meetings, smoking will not be permitted while working papers are on the table."

"Really?" said Pell, squinting over Tappen's shoulder.

"Well, nobody remembers what's been said at those meetings, so why not try it on? If all the seniors there would stop puffing their bloody fags and cigars, it might be less like Auschwitz in there and my lungs might hold out till retirement."

"Good luck to you," said Pell, who smoked a curious herbal mixture which burnt with a smell of old compost heaps subtly laced with condoms. "Now what did I come to see you about?" His bewildered eye fell on the wastebasket again.

"To tell me we should all be hung, drawn and quartered in the name of peace and goodwill?"

"No, that's just politics. It was something important. Ah, filing cabinet, that's what. There's one in Hacker's old room next door, er, going begging, and I naturally wondered ..."

Hacker had once worked with Tappen, but proved so inept that he was promoted into the much dreaded Laser Project, a stagnant Sargasso where all the Ministry's scientific no-hopers drifted to rest at last. In the midst of life, etc. Even this sombre memory didn't stop Tappen saying, quite automatically, "I had my eye on it; already made arrangements to have it shifted in here tomorrow, actually. Terribly sorry; if only I'd known ..."

This was the only possible answer under the rules of NUTC office power-play. Pell grunted and meandered towards the door, perhaps cheered by the thought that Tappen would now have to shift a heavy filing cabinet all by himself, perhaps satisfied by a successful feint because really he wanted Hacker's old desk. At the door he turned, tugged at his skimpy beard, and said, "Oh yes –" Then he lurched sideways under the impact of the returning Llewellyn, who carolled, "Knocking-off time, knocking-off time! Lay down your instruments of toil!"

"Good night," said Pell as he escaped.

"Oh God," said Tappen, scrawling another token line of minutes before abandoning the effort. "It'll have to go off in the morning now." He wrote CONFIDENTIAL/ATOMIC across the handwritten sheets, converting them at a stroke from mere scrawl to a classified document defended by the awe-inspiring majesty of the Official Secrets Act, and headed for the security cupboard.

"Fancy a drink at the Mushroom Cloud?" said Llewellyn, sitting on the edge of the desk, swinging his legs and looking as much a member of the scientific intelligentsia as Bertie Wooster.

"No joy for me, I've got a bus to catch," Tappen twiddled the combination lock through the familiar numbers of Lizzie's birthday. It failed to open. He tried again; more slowly.

"Give you a lift. Car's just outside."

"Well ... yes, thanks. *Bugger* this cupboard."

On the fourth attempt he remembered that not a million years ago the combination had been changed. It was Stalin's birthday today – in a manner of speaking. He shook the cupboard in annoyance, misdialled the numbers in an attempt at haste, and angrily gave up. The cupboard pulled away from the wall quite easily, and it was no trouble to shove the highly classified papers through the hole where someone else not good at remembering numbers had once kicked the back in.

"I saw that," Llewellyn observed.

"Mine's a pint," Tappen replied cleverly, seizing his briefcase and making for the door. "Come on."

Then, in the corridor: "No, I'll get *you* a pint. Just give me a hand with this tiny, streamlined, featherweight filing cabinet next door."

Actually there were two cabinets in Hacker's ex-office, only one of them a desirable property; the other appeared to have been mugged several times. Half a dozen dents in its side made up a pattern like a grinning face, and two of its drawers were jammed. The overall effect of battered antiquity reminded Tappen of Polaris.

They concentrated on the good cabinet, emptying out what seemed like several tons of old teacups, clapped-out radiation sources, lead shielding blocks, dusty lab coats and papers from forgotten TOP SECRET projects. Even when largely gutted, the thing's weight made Tappen grunt and groan, while Llewellyn muttered, "Two pints. No, three. Ouch. Three pints and a free truss is the least I deserve.... Your office is supposed to be next door to Hacker's, not five hundred miles away –"

At last Tappen was able to close his office door on a feat which made them both consider the erection of the Great Pyramid to have been something of a doddle.

They were the last to leave the tottering Hut of Usher; a grumpy Security man locked the door after them; they hurried across the alternating NUTC landscape of crumbly concrete and wildlife sanctuary. The establishment fences protected and encouraged the local rabbit population: great drifts of rabbit turds lay everywhere like filthy marbles, and on Spring days the scientists could hear the squeaking and thumping of rabbit production lines right under the floors of their huts. Tappen and Llewellyn watched where they trod.

Several thousand people were trying to use the main (North) gate at the same time, restrained by security police who prowled like overweight sheepdogs and had sadistically opened only one of the double gates. One touched Tappen on the arm despite his efforts to be inconspicuous. "Search, Sir," he said, and pointed to the dismal little booth like a public lavatory to the left of the gate. It was the last straw.

Long afterwards, Tappen blamed everything on that moment.

Two

The Mushroom Cloud had unofficially been the Mushroom Cloud for so long that any NUTC worker would have had to think long and painfully to identify its weathered sign as a Wheatsheaf. Sinisterly close to the Robinson Heath establishment, it was precisely the sort of place against which Security men warned you, where alcohol-gimballed tongues could spill the secrets of the nation's defences to unfriendly ears all over the wallpaper. Five minutes after opening time it was jampacked with NUTC scientists talking shop at the tops of their voices. Tappen was hunched morosely in a corner, staring at the Fairey's Bitter beermat he'd torn into thirty-two small pieces, and wondering whether to go for sixty-four.

"... really hilarious," someone next to him was saying. "We hadn't cleaned out the reactor inspection tube in eight *years*, and so this bright lad tried to do it with compressed air last week, connected up a big cylinder and *whoosh!* Radioactive dust all over the reactor hall, and the staff, and the party of VIPs they were showing round, *including* the Ambassador from Zimbabwe ... Laugh? We thought we'd die. No, it was all right, we hoovered them down and sent them on their way rejoicing. Think the Ambassador was quite *flattered* when we told him the decontamination routine was for really special people and put him in a bath of –"

"Two pints of Fairey Liquid," said Llewellyn cheerily. He dumped the horridly foaming glasses and sat down.

"Ugh," said Tappen, reaching out.

"Cheers ... Look, you're not going to sit looking like Count Dracula just because you drew the short straw, got a spot-search? Happens all the time."

"I loathe it," said the glum Tappen, gulping too-fizzy beer and moved to frothing eloquence. "They get you in the little hut, and it's always this wally who looks like one of the Hitler Youth, and he smarmily says, 'Can I check there's nothing classified in your briefcase?' ... as though you'd be allowed to say No. So he fumbles ineptly through these handwritten notes and he's got no idea what's classified and what isn't, and anyway he probably can't read in the first place, and then he wants to turn out your pockets, and then the horrible little pervert starts feeling under your arms and between your thighs, looking for suspicious lumps of plutonium I suppose, and when he's gratified his lewd longings he gives you this tolerant little smile as though he was doing you a favour letting you go at all...."

"Well: random checking. All got to put up with it."

"Bloody hell, it's randomly happened to me four times in four evenings. They've got it in for me. They fancy my strong young scientist's thighs, or something like that. Blah."

"Perhaps they're feeling stroppy," Llewellyn said tolerantly. "Heard someone pulled their leg for ages, going in every morning with a picture of Rasputin pasted over their own on the site pass, took them three weeks to notice. That must have really got up their noses."

"It wasn't Rasputin. It was Mao Tse-Tung. And that was weeks ago, and I'm a reformed character now. Whose round is it?"

"Ask a silly question."

After a confused interlude at the bar, Tappen found himself delivering another gloomy lecture. "I know what's behind it all. Security is just an excuse. Ha, if you or I wanted to sneak the secret plans of Trident over the fence we'd memorize them bit by bit, not superglue them to our thighs. Or we'd saunter out with them at lunchtime. Big Chief Fortmayne explained it to me once, he said the whole security scare is a bit of a joke and the real reason they have the searches is to stop the industrial workers nicking electric drills and suchlike. So, the reasoning is, you don't have to have searches at lunchtime because industrials are working class and haven't got cars and can't go home until the site bus takes them in the evening. Q.E. bloody D."

"But you catch the bus," Llewellyn noted. "Me too, usually. Only PSOs and up can afford to run a car every day ... them and the industrials."

Tappen shrugged. "Who says their theories have to be in touch with reality? It's like ... like ... your computer simulations for Pell."

"Look, my computer-modelled reactor gives a bloody sight better test results than the real ones ever do."

"Quite." Tappen stared with distaste into the dregs of the aptly nicknamed beer. "Why do we ever come here anyway?"

"There's nowhere else. And the security indoctrination films made it look so tempting ... remember? 'Avoid gathering at public houses close to your place of work, which may be watched.' Oh, the pictures that went with that. The days I came here hoping I'd get bought double vodkas by big men in fur coats, or slant-eyed temptresses ..."

Together they looked at the barmaid, graded her at approximately 0.6% on the internationally agreed slant-eyed temptress scale, and sighed. The only thing to do in the face of such odds was to order more "Fairey Liquid", which Llewellyn promptly did.

"I bet you," he said after a while: "Bet you it's not so simple as you think. Your idea is, you can sneak anything you like out of Nuts come lunchtime, but just you try it. Get you by the goolies before you had that electric drill halfway through the gate. They're not so stupid."

Tappen swayed wisely on his stool. "You haven't been here long enough to know, you miserable product of an inferior university." (A couple of years ago Llewellyn had graduated from Cambridge.) "If I put one of the reactors on wheels and towed it out, they'd only wonder why they didn't recognize that particular make of Ford van."

"Go on then. Go on. I bet you."

"Not a reactor," Tappen said hastily. "How about a screwdriver? I'll triumphantly smuggle out a screwdriver tomorrow lunchtime, a really big one, and you can buy me another pint, say, now."

"Listen to the man. Daring international espionage master, no security fence can stop him, and he raves about screwdrivers. Think big! Think ... you get that filing cabinet out of the place without being sat on, and I'll buy for you all Friday evening. Or if you're nicked, you buy for me."

As a sane, responsible, pessimistic scientist, Tappen had no difficulty in formulating dozens of entirely reasonable arguments against such a ludicrous proposal. It was with a sense of deep betrayal that he heard his mouth say, "Yes, it's a deal." He peered accusingly at his glass.

Dreamily Llewellyn said, "Think of the memoirs you'll be able to write. 'I Was a Prisoner of the Official Secrets Act'. 'Fifty Years for a Filing Cabinet'. 'Tappen at the Prison Bars' ... that one's got class."

"What a good thing my accomplice will be helping me haul the forbidden treasures into the car," Tappen said dourly. A look of deep thoughtfulness spread over Llewellyn's face, barely distinguishable from a look of deep indigestion.

"Excuse me, gentlemen, but I believe you're Nuclear-Utilization Technology Centre scientists," said a sandy-haired and chubby man as he squeezed himself into the formerly nonexistent space between them. As one who used the establishment's full name, he was plainly an outsider, beyond the pale, not to be encouraged.

"I'm Steve Green from the *Redbury Evening Chronicle* – and I'd like a quick word – but first let me fetch you a drink."

In such cases one could make allowances even for outsiders. Tappen and Llewellyn nodded. When three generous halves of Fairey's stood on the table, the reporter insisted on first names: Steve, Roy, Joe. "I'm preparing a local-colour piece on the Centre. It's amazing to see you scientists – people we think of as remote white-coated men in laboratories – unbending and knocking back beer when the working day is over ..."

A grey vision of the coming story seeped like rising damp through Tappen's mind. "BOFFINS ONLY HUMAN. When work is done, atom-base men like their pint like you or me ..."

"Actually," he said in a depressed tone, "we have to drink this beer for health reasons."

Llewellyn blinked, and then became unnaturally straight-faced.

"Could you explain that?" Green asked, notebook suddenly

prominent.

"Well, as you know, we work in the middle of deadly neutron contamination, and these neutrons can build up in our bodies, causing obesity and proctalgia. Fortunately they're soluble in alcohol, so every so often we flush out the contamination with beer. It's very unfortunate for those of us who don't like the stuff."

"Twelve pints, I've had already today," said Llewellyn tragically. "Otherwise I'd simply keel over with radiation sickness. What's really grim, the NUTC Health Physics lot keep dosing us with drugs. Stops the alcohol having any effect. Have to force myself to drink all day but I can't ever get drunk. Hic."

"Well, it's been nice having this chat with you," the reporter said casually over his shoulder as he sprinted for the door. "Goodbyeee ..."

"Sometimes," Llewellyn said, "I feel like one of those fantastically irresponsible Mad Scientists you used to get in the SF magazines. Look at me, manipulating major organs of the Press with just the tiniest twitch of my brain."

"I told one of them last year that heavy water was good for plants, you know, and reams and reams about it turned up in the gardening column. 'Snow is good for your strawberries because it contains Deuterium Oxide which refreshes the parts no other water can reach.' Oh, speaking of being fantastically irresponsible, didn't you leave a warhead core somewhere in my office?"

"Oops, yes I did. Remind me to pick it up tomorrow. It's got to go back into the plute store."

"If the cleaners didn't throw it away, of course," said Tappen indulgently.

"Some hope. Won't even take away my teabags. Can't imagine 'em *lifting* a ruddy great lump of plutonium ... Well, better go. Tomorrow it's Operation Filing Cabinet!"

"Ssshhh," said Tappen repressively as he rose and trod on a stray security man's foot.

Three

As Tappen eased his battered Volvo towards the western NUTC entrance in the sickly morning light, he was struck by a thought that perhaps, like dogs, cars grew to resemble their owners. Like his liver, the Volvo had this morning developed a curious knocking; like his complexion, its paintwork looked grimy and unwell; even the holes in the body seemed uncannily like his own eyes, being vacant with red rims. When he pulled in to the entrance queue, the engine instantly coughed and stalled. Massaging his chest nervously, he decided not to take the analogy too far.

The usual subjective hours of stopping and starting flashed by like mere hours, while Tappen stared dully at the fascinating landscape of identikit gorse bushes and NUTC's endless tall wire-link fence. At the gate at last, he flashed his site pass with confidence and sat fuming as a particularly bestial and atavistic security policeman stared at it from numerous angles with a look of agnosticism, perhaps muttering the riper sayings of Mao Tse-Tung under his breath. Eventually Tappen was permitted to drive in. Everything felt hostile and threatening, everything from the painful circulation of his own blood to the malignly staring rabbits at the roadside.

When he'd parked, the empty tailgate space seemed hideously, blatantly filing-cabinet-shaped. The first door inside the Terrapin hut was fraught with hidden menace, as though about to disgorge a battalion of triumphant security men; and it was only a broom cupboard. Tappen couldn't face looking at the cabinet in his office, and went for a quiet pee: the hand of the Establishment followed him even there, for the Health Physics department had provided a gigantic polythene sample bottle with his name on it. He had three days in which to provide a full gallon to be boiled down and examined for nuclear warheads ... which meant three days of drinking far too much coffee and tea while hearing colleagues say (the level of achievement being clearly visible through the translucent plastic) things like "Creative juices not flowing too well today, eh, Roy?" As usual when faced with this particular challenge, Tappen dried up altogether and retreated to the office.

He'd never before thought that a mere filing cabinet could loom and dominate a room, like Centre Point planted amid suburbia. He turned his back on it and hauled out the Nuclear Public-Image Working Party minutes. Only a few lines to go, date of next meeting, tum-ti-tum, circulation list, tra-la-la, remember not to include the Kremlin here because Fortmayne said that wasn't funny, not since one of the clericals took it seriously and mailed the relevant copy ... He slid the handwritten sheets into the desk drawer as a feeble scratching sounded at the door, as of withered and bony fingers scrabbling futilely at the inside of a coffin lid.

"Come in," he called, anticipating the coming performance.

Llewellyn entered on all fours, tongue protruding, emitting febrile, tortured coughs while clawing the air with one palsied hand. In the accents of a traveller who'd crawled thus across the Sahara and the Gobi and was now well into Death Valley, he croaked: "Tea ... Tea ..." Tappen sighed and went to plug the kettle in.

When he turned back, Llewellyn was sitting on the edge of the desk again. "Your bin's empty," he said accusingly.

"So it is. I think, Joe, that you're probably old enough to learn certain facts of life. It's like the bees and the flowers; there are those creatures called *cleaners*, and at certain rare times of the year they ..."

"Stuff that. What about my string bag, and the whatsit?"

A shrug. "Just knock at the door of the Big Hive, I mean the lost property office up at Security, and ask. No doubt they'll give you a ticking-off too, but that's what you have to put up with if you *must* leave two-hundred-kiloton nasties in people's bins. Tell you what, ask for the string bag and casually pretend to be surprised when you find there's something in it."

When dull metal spheres not as big as footballs were forever passing across one's desk, in and out of the labs, or being stowed under canteen tables during lunch, it was difficult to take them as seriously as some would prefer.

The kettle puffed and clicked off.

"Tea ... milk?" Tappen asked.

"Lots, please."

"Sugar?"

"Two."

"Paracetamol?"

"Three."

"Brilliant high-flying young scientists shouldn't get pissed in low pubs like the Mushroom Cloud. Try Dr Tappen's famous course of therapy, helping carry filing cabinets out into the backs of cars."

"Oh shit," said Llewellyn, choking over the tea. "I'd forgotten that."

"We could both forget it if you like," Tappen said rather too hastily.

"Not on your nelly. What sustains me when I grovel at the lost property lot is going to be a picture of you hauled in chained to that cabinet by one ankle ... sentenced to fifty years' hard labour as Sec. of the Plute Resources Working Party."

Tappen raised an eyebrow, something he liked doing because Llewellyn couldn't. "I thought the PRWP was no trouble. Just stocktaking, isn't it?"

"Stocktaking, he says. Jesus. Yeah, and World War II was a minor police action. Let me tell you, plute workers don't know a decimal point from a tadpole. Last year our records had 3,789,412 million tonnes of plute until we checked. This year it switched to computer ... first printouts said we were proud possessors of 0.02 micrograms of the stuff. OK, maybe I exaggerate, but even bloody government economists notice this sort of thing ..."

"Not my problem," said Tappen insufferably. "But that reminds me, time's wingèd chariot is hurrying near." He wrote URGENT, TYPING POOL, BLDG 69 on a giant envelope, fumbled out the despised minutes and sealed them inside. At once the door opened and one of NUTC's internal messengers looked in: "Any post?"

"Great biological clock you've got there," Llewellyn said as the messenger carried off the spoils. "The way you can predict knock-ing-off time long in advance and make your preparations to go home with hours to spare. Psychic Research Society ought to do an article on you."

"Filing cabinet," Tappen said sternly. "Here Fido. Fetch."

Despite feeling horribly conspicuous as he and Llewellyn manoeuvred the big metal box from the hut through the jungle of 334-area buildings, Tappen found that no one took any notice. Once or twice people passed by, but at a cautious distance, alarmed by the prospect of being asked to help. At last the thing was in the car, lying full-length in state and reverently draped with old lab coats.

"If all else fails," Llewellyn advised, "I should strew flowers round it and drive very slowly."

The morning wore on in a flurry of scientific research. Five members of NPIWP rang Tappen to ask that particularly brilliant remarks of theirs be properly quoted in the minutes, whether or not actually made at the meeting. Little Fortmayne, whose every whim was theoretically law for Tappen despite heroic Gandhiesque resistance, fussed in and out of the office with a crackle like ball lightning, continually removing and replacing his glasses as he delegated new, ambitious projects each requiring 30,000 hours of computer time and each likely to be forgotten by the following Tuesday. The Ancient of Days, a white-bearded technician called Munt who was believed to have been lab assistant to the Curies and/or Isaac Newton, came pottering from room to room to make his Friday joke. "Arr, it's Poets' Day!" Glum silence from Tappen. "Piss off early, tomorrow's Saturday!" Wan attempt at smile from Tappen. "He he he he ..." and Munt was ambling to the next office.

All the same, Tappen took the ancient sage's advice. The master plan required a lunchtime getaway and preferably no return – and at twelve noon Tappen came down with a severe attack of Friday-Afternoon Fever, possibly caused by nuclear contamination and possibly not. The symptoms were restlessness, inability to cope with paperwork and a sudden, overmastering need to travel. In addition Tappen found himself suffering from shortness of breath, sweaty palms and palpitations all over. He diagnosed typhoid, radiation sickness, epilepsy, malnutrition and schizophrenia before it occurred to him that this could be simple terror. It was what came of having a naturally gloomy nature.

It took six tries to start the sinisterly burdened car. "They never stop you at lunchtime," he repeated under his breath until it sounded like a litany. "Blessed are the pure in heart: for they shall never be stopped at lunchtime. Blessed are the meek: for they shall never be stopped at lunchtime ..." Then he was coming up to the open gate, and in a few seconds it would all be over, and a man in a blue uniform walked out onto the roadway before the gate, holding up a hand to stop him. At lunchtime.

Any self-respecting hero in Tappen's favourite literature would have run the enemy down, or lured him close and despatched him with a straight left to the jaw, or perhaps allowed a mocking smile to touch his cruel lips before pressing the button to activate the disintegrator beams in the headlights, the invisibility screen, the vertical takeoff jets. What Tappen found himself doing was rolling the window down and saying to the youthful security policeman:

"Ah, I don't suppose you've been here very long, officer, or you'd know that the standard policy is never to stop people at lunchtime."

"Oh," said the neophyte, moving uncertainly to the car's side.

"Well, many thanks. Glad to see you boys so keen," said Tappen with repellent heartiness, and let in the clutch.

"But we were testing ..."

What they were testing became suddenly apparent as an automatic barrier swung down in front of Tappen's car while an appalling clangour of sirens and bells began to sound on every side. Blue-uniformed men poured from the small huts on either side of the gateway. It was like the bad parts of a Colditz-escape film. Tappen wondered about fainting and refusing to be revived until stowed in some comfortable bed in the prison hospital.

"... NEW DETECTOR SYSTEM," the young-looking symbol of fascist repression was bellowing over the shrieks and jangles.

"CAN'T YOU TURN THE BLOODY THING OFF," Tappen roared back, into an echoing silence as the alarms were stopped halfway through his first word.

"Aha, if it isn't our practical joker, caught in the net," said a new voice. Sergeant Alf Rossiter was the only security man Tappen was on speaking terms with: he affected a Hitler moustache and was irritatingly good at squash. "Just testing, Roy ! Still getting these here false alarms, but when the wossname's tuned up right it'll spot a gnat's whisker of your actual naughty substances being smuggled out, and blow the whistle. Ah, you should have seen your face!"

"It's a fair cop, Sarge," Tappen muttered with an effort. From the inside his face felt as though it must be the grey-white of NUTC notepaper, with the same burning red highlights provided by the paper's CONFIDENTIAL or SECRET markings. "Let me out on parole now?"

"Right you are. Just this once we'll let the desperate criminal slip through our fingers. Up with the barrier, Jock!"

Tappen let in the clutch again, too quickly, and the car stalled, and Alf Rossiter guffawed repulsively, and Tappen twisted the ignition key so hard it nearly Gellerized, and somehow the engine didn't quite –

"Eh, what's that you've got in the back there?"

Fighting off a simultaneous stroke and major heart attack, he looked over his shoulder. The cerements of ancient lab-coats had slid away to reveal the filing cabinet in its glory.

"It would appear to be a large briefcase," he said at random.

"Don't suppose you've any classified papers in it, eh lad?"

"No, no, none at all. Want to look?"

"Suppose I ... ah fuck. It's lunchtime. Off you go."

The Volvo lurched erratically forward. Had Rossiter winked? Tappen drove homeward as fast as he dared, feeling a bit like the legendary peasant on the Hungarian border. Each day he'd crossed with a wheelbarrow full of straw, and each day the baffled Customs officials had searched the straw with increased frenzy, trying to find what the devil this peasant could be smuggling. He was, of course, smuggling wheelbarrows.

Tappen was still breathing hard when he pulled in outside the semi-detached hovel in Rutland Gardens, Redbury, where he and Lizzie had lived ever since he became a world-shaping nuclear physicist at Robinson Heath. (Roger Pell had moved into the other half of the semi later, an uncomfortable neighbour for whom Tappen now scanned the horizon in case Friday-Afternoon Fever was endemic in building 334d.) Here, besides winning him the odd drink, the filing cabinet would be useful for storing his back numbers of *Nature* and *New Scientist* and *Aviation Week & Space Technology* and *Private Eye*. A mere matter of lugging it upstairs ...

Twenty perspiring minutes later he'd got it into the front hall and felt like a near-terminal muscular-dystrophy case. Worse, the cabinet had grown: though it submitted to being squeezed into the hall, it plainly had secret ambitions to dominate the New York skyline or fill the Grand Canyon. At this point, with one of those brilliant strokes of scientific insight which he tended to have after the project in question had been written up and filed away forever, Tappen realized the millstone weight would be easier to get upstairs if he removed its drawers. (Sternly he repressed the Llewellynesque quip which occurred to him.)

The top drawer came out easily. So did the second and third. There was still something in the bottom one, wrapped in more of the ubiquitous lab coats which scientists used for everything but lab work. A note was pinned to it, scrawled in round, menacing handwriting. *Mr Tappen. Please do not leave heavy things in the baskets as we aren't responsible. Thank you kindly.*

He stared at this for a long while and moaned. As he unwrapped the thing, he already knew what the thoughtfulness of the cleaners had brought him in the privacy of his own home. Nestling there in a convenient string bag, a dull metal sphere not as big as a football, was the important part of Britain's Independent Nuclear Deterrent.

Four

Lizzie Tappen leant forward over the cleared table; the candle burning in its red glass chimney evoked sexy highlights from her long blonde hair and huge owl-glasses.

"Roy," she said softly, "that was a lovely treat. Now tell me, darling, have you burst the overdraft barrier again, or caught herpes, or simply lost your job?"

Tappen turned an ornate porcelain teacup round and round in his fingers. "Well," he riposted. "Um. Don't know where you get these ideas."

She snorted faintly. "When you bashed in the front of the car, we went for a takeaway kebab and a few pints of Directors before you told me. When Barclaycard started breathing down your neck, you subtly led up to the news with a tandoori and some plonk. When you failed that first SSO promotion board, it was haute-cuisine at L'Escargot Jaune plus vintage wine." With awful wifely precision she ticked off the indictments on her fingers, one by one. "So when we have a nineteen course Peking-style feast washed down with champagne ..."

"He, ha. I can't keep anything from you, my love."

"You had better not," she said ominously.

Tappen raised a finger to call for the bill, and by this stratagem caused all four Chinese waiters to vanish mysteriously from sight. Then, in a furtive undertone, he explained.

"I don't believe a *word* of it. A *syllable*. A ... oh God. The one thing I liked about your job was that it was so secret you couldn't bring work home with you."

"I'll take it back on Monday. Don't *worry*."

"And in the meantime ..." She reached her thin hand across the table to touch his. "My husband. What a man. Single-handedly he makes 33 Rutland Gardens a prime target for the first strike of the Soviet nuclear attack. Do I have to sign the NATO treaties now?"

"How about if we move on to the pub?" said Tappen feebly.

"But our tongues might be *loosened* by the beer, and we might start spilling terrible secrets everywhere – the landlord at the Woodcock is a National Fronter, I'm sure, and you wouldn't want *them* to become a nuclear power. And the house could be burgled, too. No, darling, you'll just have to stay in all weekend, and watch over your little egg like a broody hen till Monday."

"Can I have the bill, please?" Tappen called, as a distressed sailor might cry *Mayday!*

"No Saturday visit to the Woodcock. No Sunday lunchtime visit to the Ferryboat. No Sunday evening pint with your bloody boring computer pals ... Never mind, dear. What your social life loses your liver will gain."

"With a radiation hazard in the spare bedroom I think we need to spend *more* time in pubs," Tappen wanted to say, but couldn't because of the waiter who materialized with a toothy smile and a slip of paper inscribed with the amount of the National Debt. Tappen's credit card seemed to wilt, Dalí-fashion, as he signed the chit.

They made their way through the garishly grotty streets of Redbury to the car, a light rain falling on them to add to the general depression. Tappen took the wheel and delivered a short, husbandly lecture on nuclear nasties as he drove: how the hollow plutonium core was safe as houses and probably safer than a subsiding home like the Tappens', and how the aluminium jacket kept the naughty parts as securely locked away as a nun's, the whole thing unable to do anything antisocial unless one inadvertently surrounded it with quantities of erupting plastic explosive to collapse it and make it go, er, supercritical ...

"Oh, and what happens *then*?" Lizzie asked suspiciously, if not supercritically.

"About two hundred kilotons," quipped Tappen in as offhand a tone as he could manage, whereupon the light of his life fell silent, perhaps wondering whether to insist that the unwelcome guest be lodged out of harm's way in the garden shed.

Somehow Tappen's shaken reflexes missed the turning home but instead brought him accidentally and accurately to the Woodcock, where they managed to chatter nervously about shoes and ships and sealing wax, and numerous related subjects forgotten by closing time. They might have sat morosely silent, but this was risky in the Woodcock, where the slightest lull could lead to the landlord's playing his conversational Pawn to King Four: "Of course I'm not one of those *racialists*, but –"

Eventually Tappen drove home with that species of unnatural care and attention which usually alerts the suspicion of every policeman for miles. Lizzie said nothing en route except, once or thrice, under her breath, the bitter imprecation, "Filing cabinet."

The evening ended with Tappen saying hopefully. "You're looking really nice tonight," whereupon Lizzie tucked her thin arms under the duvet and announced that *this* would infallibly be the night on which the pill failed, and that the plutonium thingy was undoubtedly leaking neutrons (which she pretended to believe were small, scurrying things like woodlice), and on the whole children were awful enough anyway without her being lumbered with one having three heads and a scaly hide like Margaret Thatcher's. Tappen raised his eyes to the ceiling and delivered an eloquent speech on radiation, genetics, superstition and non-sequiturs, to be silenced at last by a faint but firm snoring. He muttered black things under his breath as he turned over.

About thirty subjective seconds later he woke to find Lizzie prodding him, the doorbell ringing and cruel shafts of morning sunlight slipping between the curtains and under his eyelids like slivers of bamboo. His mouth felt like the testing ground for some appalling, new form of biological warfare, or worse, the gum on Civil Service envelopes. Summing up the situation, he said "Urrr," seized his dressing gown and headed downstairs. Halfway down he remembered the events of Friday and groaned; by the time of reaching the front door he'd persuaded himself that large unsympathetic Ministry of Defence police were clustered outside, waiting to fall on him and beat him about the head with warrants for gross naughtiness, rank insolence and high treason. He felt he should shout conciliatory things through the letterbox before coming out with his hands up.

It was Roger Pell from next door, holding a black box sprouting knobs and dials in unlikely profusion.

"Good morning," he said cheerfully. "I thought I'd come right round and tell you."

"Good morning," Tappen lied.

"Now this is really most, ah, interesting ... oh, I'm forgetting my manners. How is Lizzie?"

"Asleep."

"Eh? Good heavens, it's after eight ... Well, I was doing my morning scan of the house and garden –" he displayed the black box proudly, as though it were a set of encyclopaedias and Tappen a likely prospect – "and I found the local background radiation has, you know, *risen* overnight. Especially upstairs. Only a teensy bit, nothing to worry about, but ... you know."

Tappen knew. Specifically he knew that the famous filing cabinet with its famous contents was upstairs, right against the dividing wall between the two houses. He produced what he hoped was an intelligent, perceptive grunt.

"Anyway ... where was I? The Campaign, you know. Good political, er, capital in this; plainly there's been a leakage and we're getting fallout on the roof. I can hardly, um, wait till the Campaign boys verify my readings, take up the whole issue in the press ... could be very embarrassing for NUTC, very embarrassing ..."

"You work there," Tappen reminded him for the hundredth time.

"Oh, well, yes, but of course they'll never actually *close* the place. You know. Now where was I ... oh yes. If I could come in and check my reading in your, mmm, upstairs rooms, quickly ...?"

Tappen shut his eyes at the mere thought. "Maybe later on," he managed to say without actually fainting. "Lizzie's probably wandering round naked up there."

"Oh, but I wouldn't mind ... mmm, quite. I'll drop round later, Roy."

He left, pausing at intervals along the front drive to point his radiation meter at such plants as (Tappen supposed) looked unusually deviant and scraggy. Which was most of them.

Tappen had never quite been able to understand Pell. There were two main schools of nuclear physicist at NUTC, the wolves and the ostriches. The former, like Fortmayne, were on the whole keen on the notion of testing their toys in action, and spattered their conversation with technical terms like overkill, second-strike capability, terminal defence and Ronald Reagan – like the people who know about cars or computers, and take great conversational pains to ensure everyone knows they know. The ostriches, like Tappen, contrived not to think about end results, or convinced themselves that nobody was going to let one of the bloody things off really, so in the long run it didn't matter. (Anyway, as Keynes said, in the long run we're all dead.) Pell, though, was hard to fit into any group: in a scientific world divided into sheep and goats he would be something exotic like a giraffe, a creature he vaguely resembled.

Pell was the only person Tappen knew whose garden boasted a fallout shelter and also a thirty-foot vertical-axis windmill tower which – if only the prevailing wind hadn't been nearly blocked by Pell's and Tappen's houses – would have made Southern Electricity's profits shrivel to nothing. Atop the roof were solar panels resembling dirty old radiators; for three days each summer these delivered relentlessly tepid water which the neighbours were invited in to admire. Two years before, Pell had even experimented with a gadget called a heat pump which warmed his house by refrigerating the shared loft, and thus – owing to a disparity in loft insulation – the Tappens' bedroom. This had produced what could only be described as a slight coolness between the neighbours.

A slight coolness greeted Tappen upstairs now. "I heard all that, my love," said Lizzie to the ceiling. "Congratulations on blowing your guilty secret the morning after sneaking it home."

"I couldn't do anything else. Roger might get all suspicious."

"Ugh. Creepy-crawly Roger. Letting him come and sniff round the house, dear, is a guilty reaction and *deeply* suspicious. Anyone with an unspotted conscience would have told him to push off, in the same hearty, ringing tones you keep for the Jehovah's Witnesses."

"Pell's all right really," Tappen mumbled, nervously taking

down the liberated DANGER NEUTRON RADIATION sign which for months had hung over their bed.

"There you go again, leaving a trail of guilt behind you everywhere, like a slug. Let's face it, darling, before your breakfast you have the practical common sense of a pebble. Do you think you could put the kettle on without setting fire to yourself, now?"

"I hardly even dare turn on the stove – in case the great Roger Pell bursts in with an infra-red detector and a theory that the Thatcherite junta is contaminating decent folk's kitchens with deadly heat radiation. Anyway, coffee coming ... at my usual slug's pace." Tappen slouched down again, feeling like a rough beast, and vainly tried to shake the morning fog from where it clung inside his skull.

At ten o'clock Pell and his talismanic Box returned, to be greeted with false smiles by the now-presentable Tappen, while at the back door Lizzie slipped out on a reluctant errand to the shed at the bottom of the garden, carrying a medium-sized suitcase. It had begun to drizzle. At ten-fifteen Pell apologized profusely for having caused inconvenience, seeming slightly relieved by the lack of sinister radiation levels anywhere.

"If I could, um, just check the garden?" he said diffidently. "You know, while I'm here ..."

They were still upstairs, looking out over the back garden, and Tappen pointedly pulled the curtains to and fro a few times ("Just shaking out the woodlice") before ushering Pell downstairs once more. In the hallway he invented a most unsavoury rumour about the Health Physics division – "You mean you haven't *heard* why Dr Buckmaster gets through three times as many test rabbits as they budgeted for?" – thus giving Lizzie time to sprint round to the front door before Pell opened the back one and started sniffing suspiciously towards the shed.

While Pell braved the drizzle, Tappen watched from the back door, puzzling over occasional mysterious wisps of smoke rising (not for the first time) from the gooseberries next door. In the event, Pell only made desultory investigations of a single clump of forget-me-nots near the dividing fence before losing interest. When Tappen slipped back to let Lizzie in at the front door he found Pell close on his heels, and before he could invent more ingenious distractions and fibs Lizzie apparently lost patience. The doorbell rang. It rang again.

"Aren't you going to open it?" Pell said mildly as Tappen quivered this way and that, like a luckless particle exhibiting Brownian Motion or caught in the indecisive grip of the Uncertainty Principle. The doorbell rang a third time. Pell seemed to be peering at the dials of his detector; with desperate inspiration Tappen broke into violent coughing spasms with overtones of epilepsy. The outbreak prolonged itself unnaturally until his flailing and uncontrollable elbows had succeeded, on the fourth attempt, in dashing the Box to the ground; instantly recovered, he dived for the door and let in Lizzie, who said "About time –" before performing a doubletake and whizzing upstairs like a startled grouse.

"Er, sorry," said Tappen. "Time of the month, you know. Lizzie doesn't like visitors to see her before she's put on her lipstick," he added inventively.

"That's a very, erm, impressive make-up case she was carrying," Pell observed as he picked up his gadget and nursed it gently. "Oh dear, I'll have to recalibrate this."

"Good! I mean, nothing like taking care of your tools. I mean, a recalibrated detector is a happy detector ..." With suchlike cheery babble he propelled his guest out into the drizzle. Weekends were always too short, but this one planned to be an exception, he could see.

Lizzie came downstairs with damply glistening hair, still breathing hard. "Time of the month, eh? You'll pay for that, husband of mine." Lizzie never wore lipstick. Before Tappen could reply, her thin hand snaked out and ungently tweaked his nose. Definitely it looked like being a long week-end, when what he needed was a lost one.

Five

Driving along on the crest of the wave, teetering on the threshold of relief and an end to all his worries, Tappen could hardly keep himself from whistling. The house had not been burgled nor struck by a meteorite. The SAS had utterly failed to repossess the booty in a shower of stun-bombs. The Volvo had brought him and his medium-sized suitcase to within sight of the NUTC fence without once breaking down or exploding. The Sun had risen, the Earth continued to move in its orbit, and it was a wonderful, glorious Monday morning. (Offhand he couldn't remember when he'd last used those adjectives of a Monday.) He pulled over to the left and joined the crawling queue at the western gate, reflecting that never, never, never were people searched on the way in.

Without the least premonition of impending doom, he happily contemplated the thin trickle of vehicles coming out of Robinson Heath. These would be people who'd briefly called at work before moving on to carry confusion and excuses for uncompleted projects to Culham or Aldermaston or Harwell or wherever; others off to breathe the heady air of power at Ministry HQ in Whitehall, where decisions about physics were taken at terrifyingly high level by cobwebbed men who'd long forgotten all their physics; and, no doubt, a few who'd reached their desks and at once fallen prey to the ravages of Monday Morning Malaise, an affliction as baffling and incurable as Friday Afternoon Fever. For a too-brief moment, Tappen wondered whether the sight of these select few travelling in the opposite direction should remind him of something. Then another ripple of movement travelled up the queue, as though along a narcoleptic caterpillar, and he moved a little further forward, and at once stopped wondering.

"... when the wossname's tuned up right it'll spot a gnat's

whisker of your actual naughty substances ..."

The appalling clangour and wail of bells and sirens seemed twice as loud as it had on Friday. The automatic barrier swung relentlessly down and crunched into the bonnet of a quite new-looking Alfa-Romeo three cars ahead. Callously ignoring this, the security police descended like a swarm of locusts on the four vehicles currently queuing to get out. Bonnets were flung up and boots wrenched open, tyres and upholstery probed, while the drivers were hustled off to have their nostrils fluoroscoped and fillings removed for security inspection. With the kind of lightning insight which kept getting him almost promoted, Tappen deduced that the long-rumoured detector system had gone into full operation at last. Luckily, what was being detected wasn't slipping out but failing to sneak in: after a moment he eased the Volvo out into the road and drove on, clockwise round the NUTC perimeter, with half-a-dozen other cars following like a retinue of ducklings. The Alfa-Romeo was not among them.

The followers peeled off towards the next NUTC entrance, the north-western one; Tappen had had time to deduce that this might not be wise. Briefly he felt like the Flying Dutchman, doomed Vanderdecken sailing forever in a storm-tossed Volvo Estate, never permitted to halt until the Day of Judgement came or the petrol ran out.

Onward: past the Establishment's supposedly impressive main gate, which had all the technocratic glamour of a British Rail goods yard; past more gates, a final angle of the perimeter fence and downhill to the grubby village of Bogley. Bogley had been there long before NUTC, the sort of village which the inhabitants of Cold Comfort Farm would shun as too sleazy, where the grimy inn's clientele sported a knife in every other sock and nasty things happened by dead of night in the marshes, if not in the woodshed. Latterly the place had sprouted Establishment housing estates like patches of loathsome fungus, leaving the degenerate locals baffled and outnumbered. Now there were shops like Bogley Surplus Stores, selling ex-government desks, filing cabinets, bookshelves, dozens of other exotic wares incomprehensible to the old Bogley-folk, like subscriber trunk dialling to Cro-Magnon man.

Tappen parked by the post office and sidled towards a call-box, watching the car nervously from the corners of his eyes. Amazingly, he could remember both the direct-dial-in and extension numbers.

Pip-pip-pip-pip-pip-pip-pip ...

"Hello, is that Building 334 Admin? ... Hello, Carol. Roy Tappen here. I just wanted to say I was a bit groggy this morning, and I'll be in late ... No, only a touch of radiation sickness, ha ha ..."

Carol was the Admin Officer in Building 334, an awe-inspiring being whose powers ranged far and wide, who ruled Superintendents and Principals with a whim of titanium-steel concealed by a voice of saccharine, and who from time to time even consented to regulate the low affairs of the dry-rot sanctuary where Tappen furthered the cause of pure science (this didn't even boast a number of its own and was merely 334d).

The sweet voice said: "I suppose it was delirium, Roy, that took you from your sickbed all the way down the street to a pay phone?"

Oops, thought Tappen, inwardly cursing the pips. Bloody old-fashioned phones, that was Bogley for you. He broke into paroxysms of theatrical coughing. "Be along as soon as I can," he gasped in accents suited to last words on the deathbed, and put down the receiver.

In the car he assumed the attitude of Rodin's *Thinker*, slightly deformed by the presence of the steering wheel, and conjured up vivid newsreels of the immediate future. With a violent effort at optimism he imagined casually bringing in the Thing – "found it by the roadside" – no, better, "I wrested it from this man in an astrakhan hat who was furtively creeping along the ditch, heading east" – applause and processions and promotion! Only he promptly lost control of his own fantasy, which sprouted unpleasant growths of questionings and courts of inquiry and dungeon cells, Llewellyn and himself surrounded by a hollow square of security police and formally divested of their pocket calculators before being hurled into outer darkness with the word UNEMPLOYABLE forever tattooed on their foreheads...

After all, people had been reprimanded, and as it were

tattooed, and even exiled to the doldrums of the laser project, for such lesser crimes as trying to go home with an MoD-accredited screwdriver sticking from some pocket.

Drawing on the experience of six long-ago months as a Boy Scout (survival of the fittest, nature red in tooth and claw, etc.) he visualized a cunning use of woodcraft and knots. One of the scrubby, gnarled trees of Robinson Heath would be hauled back level with the ground by ropes under incredible tension, and a dull metal sphere laid carefully in a woven rope cradle between two upper branches. With one swift slash of his Swiss Army penknife the tension would be released, the payload sent arcing through the air over the NUTC fence, coming safety to rest in, er, something soft.

At once a new sequence of images appeared, with ballistic errors or improperly calibrated trees hurling it not far enough or too far, and the weapon core splitting open against a rock or something harder like a stray security man's head, shattering in a spray of tinkling plutonium shards which contaminated great tracts of land and were spread by birds and earthworms in the pay of the Kremlin until half Britain was a reeking radioactive wasteland ... He managed to turn off the newsreel in his head before it ran too far along the well-worn paths of questionings, courts of inquiry and trials for treason.

Start again. Llewellyn would help. Nothing could be simpler than to throw the thing like a medicine ball, curving gently over the twelve-foot fence and into the waiting arms of his old drinking buddy.

In every version of this sequence that he could imagine, Llewellyn dropped it.

Mentally he swapped places with his colleague. A phantasmal Llewellyn swung the sphere dextrously into the air and (a) it overshot and Tappen lurched backwards trying to catch it and fell over and it hit him in the teeth; (b) it bounced neatly as a squash ball from the springy wire fence, to break like an egg at Llewellyn's feet; (c) it went straight up and as Llewellyn stared after it came straight down again on his puzzled head.

Tappen mused that somehow his subconscious didn't appear to

repose total trust in his old, or rather young, drinking buddy. Now why should that be? The question was wiped from his mind by the most likely scenario of all, as the sphere soared over the fence and tripped some species of detection apparatus, and whether or not the fielder achieved a neat catch he vanished three seconds later under a vengeful mound of blue uniforms and toothy guard dogs.

So much for the synthetic power of the scientific imagination. That was the trouble with places like NUTC: after a year or two your genius and originality began to wither and you found it easier to curl up like a dormouse in your snug nest of reports, minutes, printouts, r/a (radioactive) material movement documentation ... Tappen's eyebrows rose in turn and did a little dance before they could be persuaded to calm down. He rolled the luscious thought about his mind for a minute or two, decided he was an unsung scientific genius after all, and set it out in properly scientific form:

- If x is a shipment of r/a supplies entering Robinson Heath,
- and y is a detector-tripped barrier blocking the way to the sound of bells,
- then x implies an absence of y,
- and therefore there exists a time t equal to ten o'clock each Monday morning at which they have to turn off the bloody alarms to let the lorry in, Q.E.D.

Possibly the Regius Professor of Mathematical Logic would have quibbled over the exact phrasing, but Tappen felt this was brilliant enough to warrant his streaking past Bogley General Stores with traditional cries of *Eureka!* Almost.

At thirty seconds before time t the Volvo was casually drifting past the main entrance and visitors' car park. Nothing in sight. A minute later Tappen casually drifted past in the other direction. Still nothing. He wondered whether there were hideous penalties for such obviously enemy-inspired reconnaissance of NUTC comings and goings. The Ordnance Survey had been politely instructed to piss off and put a white patch on their maps, so where did that leave mere amateurs like Tappen? After several pints of sweat and petrol and what seemed like enough casual drifting to last the average vagrant most of his life, Tappen succeeded in turning off the Queen's highway exactly behind the huge khaki supplies lorry as it arrived (t plus twenty-two minutes).

The lorry barely paused as it entered. No alarms sounded. Tappen felt that the sun was shining again, as he followed close on the grimy behemoth's tail, as close as he dared to the little sign CAUTION AIR BRAKES, and held his site pass to the window as the gate came near ...

A terrific bang sounded on the roof of the car. He'd been struck by a meteorite after all. No, he realized as reflexes slammed him to a halt, it was blasted Alf Rossiter, who'd come up on his blind side and slapped the roof. Aggrieved, he wound the window down.

"Oi, mate, that suitcase in the back ..."

Tappen closed his eyes wearily. This can't be happening, he told himself. This can't be happening.

"We're tightening up all round, Roy me boy – thought I'd give you the tip, only fair. As of next week we'll even be sealing the gates ten minutes either side of this delivery – never thought of that, did you, stuff slipping out with the detector plugs pulled? Tightening up, see? Take that there case in, and on the way out they'll likely strip the lining, chop up the handles, proper Customs stuff. Thought I'd give you the nod, eh? Bloody silly thing to bring in anyway."

"Thanks, Alf," Tappen said with a sickly smile. He had a dreadful feeling he knew what was coming next.

"Give it me now and I'll shove it in the police store – that's what you ought to of done straight off. OK?"

There was a small brick hut inside the main gate, looking as though it should be labelled GENTS. If you brought something you needed after work but shouldn't take into NUTC, a camera for example, or a party of Romanian friends, you were supposed to deposit it there and yield it up to the tender mercies of Security for later collection. Right by the gate. So when he collected it ... A broken man, Tappen engaged reverse gear.

"Glad you gave me the tip," he said without sincerity. "Didn't know I was carrying it – my wife's, er, make-up case. I'll catch hell if I don't get it right back to her now. This just isn't my lucky day!"

(And inwardly: God, if you happen to exist, why not him? Thunderbolts are cheap. Are you there, God?)

Rossiter looked puzzled as the Volvo crashed into reverse, but he failed even to show signs of becoming a pillar of salt. The words Tappen pronounced aloud as he swerved back onto the road and hit the accelerator should by rights have converted all Robinson Heath to a fire-licked dustbowl ringed with bleached bones – but of course there was no justice. The amateur Flying Dutchman lurched on his doomed course back to Redbury, not merely accursed but forever manacled by one leg to a dull metal sphere not as big as a football.

Fortunately Lizzie was off doing whatever it is that social workers do on Monday mornings, and Tappen was spared unfavourable comparisons of his organizational ability with that of the average meths-drinker or glue-sniffer. Meths, glue, why hadn't he taken up a career in these rewarding fields? He carefully stowed the suitcase in the loft, between the broken chair and the cardboard box of Christmas decorations. Despite wild plans to crash the car "by accident" through the NUTC fence and absent-mindedly drive at 90 mph to building 334d, there to conceal the suitcase dextrously before turning to confront (apologetically) the hitherto unnoticed pursuit of fifty armed security police with rabid Alsatians and armoured cars ... despite this tentative plan, Tappen had decided he would have to work from inside and do what Pell always claimed to be doing. It was only Llewellyn who insisted the reference was to Pell's conversation. He would bore from within.

A fraught half-hour later he sidled into the familiar office and, with intermittently twitching fingers, plugged in his bootleg kettle. For some reason the office was equipped with two-pin, 2½-amp sockets of a variety thought hopelessly passé in the 1950s, but scientific replacement of touchy fuses with reliable copper bars had seen to it that the kettle worked. Tappen's tongue dangled dryly as boiling water met leaves of finest Earl Grey tea in the 250cc Pyrex beaker he'd swiped from the plutonium laboratory (and, of course, washed).

Knock. It was Llewellyn, looking perturbed. "Sure you didn't stow my stuff in your cupboard, Roy? Asked after the string bag;

they'd never heard of it. Or any, like contents either. If you've been pulling my leg ..."

Tappen sighed, and stretched. He'd never before appreciated the deep philosophical truth of the ancient saying "Misery loves company." Luxuriously he said: "Sit down, Joe, and have some tea; and let me tell you a story."

Six

In the dismal beforemath of Tuesday morning's NPIWP meeting – the concentrated essence of dentists' waiting rooms, with a tinge of what condemned men might have felt before the drop – Tappen was brooding on deadlines.

Joe Llewellyn had taken the glad news moderately well, merely staggering theatrically forward to clutch Tappen's throat, with cries of "I told you so. I knew it all the time. What's the canteen like these days in the Tower of London?" With foxy furtiveness they'd sifted through laboratory after dusty laboratory to locate the 334 section's dummy weapon core (same size, same colour, handy for checking measurements or impressing high-level visitors whose surprise and delight at being allowed to cradle this fat little baby would sometimes turn their fingers to jelly ... Legend had it that one dropped and cracked core had had to be quietly disposed of by decontamination squads, along with the undersecretary who'd been holding it). This dummy "pit" was returned, in the usual flurry of paperwork countersigned in triplicate, to the care of a now increasingly impatient r/a materials store. Which was fine for about ten days, after which time the thing would turn into a pumpkin – cut open by bored technicians to reveal whether some test or other had or hadn't reduced its explosive might to that of an Alka-Seltzer.

"Don't suppose they'd believe we were testing this death ray that makes plute disappear from inside warheads," Llewellyn had predicted glumly. Tappen was inclined to agree; but replied, "Look, I have this plan ..."

Lizzie's deadline had been more nebulous. "I told you so; I knew it all the time," she'd said unfairly and untruthfully. "Either that object goes or ... you do. Go and live with it in a hotel

46

somewhere. Love Me Love My Bomb is *not* going to be the motto of this household. Darling."

About fifteen other stretched and broken deadlines hovered dismally in the air of the Building 334 committee room, an airless chamber plainly designed to test trained astronauts to destruction in an atmosphere of asphyxiation, claustrophobia, overheating and mindless tedium. The Nuclear Public-Image Working Party was about to begin its 375th meeting, and excuses for its failure to utterly transform public opinion were shortly to be paraded for the 374th time. Twelve sets of minutes, still warm and static-charged from the photocopier, were dealt round the table by Tappen like menus at a cheap restaurant.

Staverton, black-haired, bearlike and overweight, sat down heavily and began to rustle papers. His glorious title was Superintendent of Nuclear Operations (SNO), lording it over Fortmayne and thus Tappen, but subservient to the exalted and rarely glimpsed Chief of Research/Applied Physics (CPRA). Ash fell from his noxious cigar as he took the minutes at a run. "Chairman: my turn this week. Apologies for absence: Tamlyn, Bergeron, Farmer. Minutes of last meeting: all agreed? Excellent. Item one, Promoting Cuddly Image for NUTC –"

The others were still pulling up chairs and fumbling for their own papers. Llewellyn, Tappen, Fortmayne and Pell representing the pure and unworldly aims of Science; the Superintendent of Public Information, the Press Officer and a brace of high-echelon Security men, covering the worlds of Politics and Literature; and at the far end of the table, a clot of bewildered and invariably silent engineers whose look of resentful boredom seemed (to Tappen) a fair representation of the General Public.

"Excuse me," said the wizened SPI, Crane, from within the dense clouds surrounding his pipe-lighting manoeuvre. "There was an item in the minutes about smoking ..."

Staverton flipped pages, ran a finger down the text and recited: "'In accordance with NUTC fire safety policy it was decided that at future meetings, smoking will not be permitted while working papers are on the table.'"

"That makes sense," said the more anthropoid of the two

Security men as he lit his fourth cigarette from his third.

"Safety regulations begin at home," Staverton murmured. "So shall we get these working papers off the table and conduct the meeting from memory? Or perhaps this particular item could be shelved for discussion – eh?"

He was looking hard at Tappen, who in his secretarial way was writing everything down, and who nodded guiltily. He said: "I thought it would tie in with Item Four, the Nuclear Weapons Are Safe Weapons approach. See, we could contrast the thousands of people dying each year of lung cancer caused by smoking, with the far smaller number killed annually by nuclear weapons."

"Saw this article, in *New Scientist* it was, about passive smoking," said Llewellyn helpfully. He, Tappen and Fortmayne were now the only committee members not puffing away, though Pell's silage cigarettes hardly counted. "Means you're too sensible and healthy to smoke yourself, but you get stuck in buses, pubs, railway compartments. People breathe fumes at you so you get cancer just the same."

The Security man lit a fifth cigarette from his fourth.

"We must stick to the agenda, gentlemen," Staverton said rapidly. "Item One: promoting cuddly image for NUTC. Anything new from the Press Office on Winnie-the-Warhead and the soft-toy approach?"

"Excuse me," said Crane again. "I believe Appendix A needs a little clarification."

Everyone turned to Appendix A in the minutes, except Tappen, who knew perfectly well that there wasn't one. But there was. What had the typists done now? Belatedly he took a look, and realized that last week he'd pulled more pages of draft minutes out of the desk drawer than he'd put in. They'd even followed the layout. A hideous curse on Pell and his broadsheets.

"MAKE ROBINSON HEATH A NUCLEAR-FREE ZONE!" Staverton was reading with relish. "BURN THE WARMONGERS OF NUTC! MARCH IN THE NAME OF PEACE ON THE ATOM BASE MADMEN! KILL THEM BEFORE THEY KILL YOU! Ah, Mr Secretary, could this be another decision of the previous meeting which has slipped my mind?"

Pell had become elaborately interested in his fingernails. Llewellyn began to quiver reprehensibly.

"A mistake," said Tappen as firmly as he could despite a sensation of falling backwards into bottomless quicksand. "A mistake by the typists. It's quite simple."

"All our typists are Positively Vetted," snapped the Security man who was able to talk. It sounded, Tappen thought, like a final solution to the typist population explosion.

"It's an example," he said desperately. "It exemplifies the poor image which our establishment has achieved in certain sections of the outside world, and represents the considered statement of those forces which our committee is striving to combat. It was included in these minutes for informational purposes, but ..." He wondered how long his surge of Ministerial prose could keep going and whether anyone had noticed he only talked this way *in extremis*. "But unfortunately the typists seem to have mislaid the covering note explaining the reason for its inclusion."

"Very ingenious," said a deadpan Fortmayne, looking hard at Tappen and then at Pell. "You're saying that we need to come to grips with this kind of nonsensical thinking, that we on this committee don't really appreciate how *irrational* antinuclear thought can be ..."

Pell appeared to be grinding his teeth, while gazing at an imaginary horizon somewhere far beyond Staverton's left shoulder.

"That would come under Item Five," Staverton said tediously. "Item One ..."

Time went by, with infinite slowness and on tiptoe. The ashtrays filled and overflowed. Tappen began to think of his lungs as parched flaps of something resembling smoky bacon. Smoky bacon crisps. Dutifully he wrote down the droningly expressed Thoughts of Chairman Staverton: one of the first lessons in Secretarymanship was that you need only record the Chairman's drivel as he'd invariably insist on having the last word. (Once when Staverton had had throat trouble he'd got away with an entire set of minutes saying "The Chairman agreed. The Chairman disagreed. The Chairman thought both proposals had much to recommend them ..." etc.) The Chairman *would* always be a he, since by some fluke the committee featured no women; no doubt the same fluke which affected every other Ministry of Defence (An Equal Opportunity Employer) committee Tappen had known.

Months went by, years went by, the glaciers of the next ice age rumbled southward, the Sun cooled, the heat death of the universe began to loom, and it still wasn't lunchtime. Item Eight: the Press Officer again tabled his dislike of the emotionally loaded term "plutonium", and the scientists were again invited to look into the possibility of substituting another element in warheads. Item Nine: owing to budget cuts it was agreed that during next week's Royal Visit the Queen would not after all be invited to open the new weapon assembly building by pressing a button to launch a small model Trident missile which would travel fifty yards and devastate a cardboard simulation of the Kremlin. Otherwise the 113-page Draft Plan of Operations and Staff Etiquette Guide (representing most of NPIWP's last six months' activity in defence of the British way of life) would apply throughout the visitation.

Any Other Business: as Staverton pronounced these potent words there was a sense of relaxation and uplift, as of a condemned man in the electric chair whose ears prick up at the arrival of a panting messenger with news of a power cut. Lunch ...

"There is just one small thing," Tappen said, feeling like a second messenger arriving hot on the heels of the first with news of a standby generator.

"Oh God," said Llewellyn in an undertone, face greenish from the deadly fumes of the hell-chamber. Tappen glanced at him severely: "Oh yes," said Llewellyn with false enthusiasm as he remembered.

Trying to summon up the ironclad sincerity of the Mormon missionaries whom each week Lizzie drove from the door with cries of "There is no God! Religion is the crutch of the weak and ignorant!" Tappen spoke. "One of the greatest problems with public image is that the public – incredible though it may seem – don't think too highly of MoD security and safety precautions." Suddenly he knew what it was to be a godlike universe-manipulator in an SF novel: "Of course it was to illustrate this point that I included the P – the propaganda flyer as an appendix. Look in the smaller print, two-thirds of the way down: *These maniacs juggle all day with frightful atomic forces with which personkind was not meant to meddle – a moment's slip with a test-tube could destroy us all in accidental nuclear holocaust!"*

"Ah?" said the Press Officer, activated as though by a hidden PLAY button. "What it's necessary for the general public to realize is that living near NUTC is in fact *much safer* than elsewhere. Firstly, NUTC has stringent safety precautions to ensure that no nuclear accident can happen here: can you say as much for Birmingham or London? Secondly, many cancer deaths are caused by natural background radiation from the soil etcetera: the lead screening and concrete barriers used to safeguard NUTC experiments actually *seal in* this natural background and reduce the hazards to less than those of living elsewhere ..." Abruptly he seemed to recall that he wasn't now enlightening the general public, and subsided, covering embarrassment with the smokescreen of another cigarette.

"We dealt with that under Item Five," Staverton said automatically.

"Anyway," said Tappen. "It seems to me that a good way of counteracting some of these absolutely irrational fears would be to organize a demonstration or exercise, sort of like army manoeuvres, to show how foolproof our gate security is."

"What a marvellous, wonderful idea," Llewellyn said on cue, so warmly that it sounded like deep sarcasm.

"I don't quite understand what you're saying," put in a suspicious Fortmayne.

"Well, imagine, just pulling an idea out of the hat at random you know, imagine some of us playing the part of terrorist infiltrators trying to steal the guts of a nuke. It would be like a wargame, scientists versus gate security, smuggling out r/a material – though of course they'd fail, and the publicity point is that not even the people on the inside can break NUTC security."

"Damn right," said Security, mysteriously moved to speech. "I had a mate in the SAS who went on games like that. One time they had to infiltrate a farm on a given day: the army moved in a week before with ten tons of radar, barbed wire, you name it, and made that farm bloody impregnable. Come Tuesday and suddenly there were two SAS blokes with itchy trigger fingers holding up the command centre in the farmhouse kitchen: 'Oh', they said, 'We've been hiding out ten days in the dungheap while you built the defences.' Fucking brilliant."

Tappen realized rather quickly that it was time to change the subject, but Fortmayne was there first. "You're saying we play silly buggers with live pits. What did you have planned for the outside chance when someone *does* get one out, Roy?"

"A dummy, of course. I remember we've got one somewhere, a harmless lookalike with a harmless r/a source inside to make it a fair mock-up of the real article. And the beauty of it is that if a loophole in security shows up, we plug it there and then. It's only when you see the water coming through that you know where to put your finger in the dyke."

"No lesbian jokes, please," said Staverton absently, and then coughed to distract attention from this lapse in masterful chairmanship. "I don't know that I'm a hundred per cent in favour of this suggestion. We should think it over carefully."

"Oh, but it's a really wonderful, marvellous, brilliant idea," said loyal Llewellyn.

"It needs to be tried fairly quickly," Tappen added with his fingers tensely crossed under the table. "Because it would be unfair if the rumour got round and gate security were alerted, don't you think? Real terrorists wouldn't ring up beforehand to say they were going to pinch a warhead and be sure to keep an eye out for them ... Even the IRA doesn't fight to claim credit for next week's forthcoming outrage."

Ponderous wheels could be heard turning within Security's head; his expression of extreme cunning made it plain that even if the exercise was scheduled fifteen minutes hence, the grapevine would somehow have alerted every NUTC gate policeman with time to spare. "Absolute security," he said. "Secret operation. Of course."

"You're saying," said Fortmayne in his favourite conversational gambit, "that you can spare time to piss around with exercises when we're past deadline on the Polaris/Chevaline revaluation, the

Trident update, the test reactor design, the Royal Visit demonstration stand, the ..."

"I don't think that really falls within the scope of this meeting," murmured Staverton. His eye strayed round the table, to halt at smirking Security. "I'm sure our gate staff will be well prepared for any such exercise ... but I'm not sure that we really need such contrived publicity. Let's hold over the decision, and end the meeting here. Next Tuesday, then –"

He rose, an awful and appalling sight, since Dr Alastair Staverton (SNO) consisted largely of paunch with a vestigial physicist somewhere behind. Chairs squeaked on the hard floor and there were almost audible noises of salivation now the whistle of freedom had blown ... lunch was lunch, even in the NUTC canteen – or the Microbiological Research Establishment, as some had called it since the closure of Porton Down.

"I'll talk to you later," said Fortmayne to Tappen, acridly. Fortmayne's speciality was the production of instant objections to every proposal: this, despite the well-informed brilliance of each objection, was thought to be why Staverton was a Superintendent and Fortmayne wasn't.

As they stampeded from the choking room into the corridor, Tappen caught the eye of the articulate representative of Security. A faint smirk was still visible about his lips, and one could detect the odour of grapevine twining through his thoughts. Tappen matched him smirk for smirk: if only the exercise went into action, he thought happily, no amount of forewarned preparation by gate security would be proof against their lad's own favourite SAS trick of having pierced the defences long before they were set up.

Seven

The walls of Tappen's cubbyhole were painted in the most popular of the standard Civil Service shades, known as Congealed Pus. As much as possible of the wall area was covered with blackboards, whiteboards, graphs, nuclide charts, yellowed scraps of paper headed *Things Which Must Be Done Today Or I Will Be Fired*, and the inevitable computer-printed Snoopy calendar. ("Sorry, no nuclear criticality simulation runs this week," the computer centre would announce at the beginning of each year. "We're all tied up printing the Snoopy calendars.") Hidden behind the door from casual visitors was a draft Daily Timetable some years old, which Tappen kept meaning to take down:

0830 Office. Fall into desk chair. Moan. Paracetamol.

0945 Feel better. Unlock safe, filing cabinet, desk drawers, storage cupboard, paperclip boxes. Arrange TOP SECRET documents and paperclips tastefully on desk. Just time to put them away in safe, filing cabinet etc. before

1000 Coffee room. Listen respectfully as senior scientific staff conduct high-level discussion of sex, football, the decline of the West, the awfulness of the TUC and the vileness of the coffee.

1045 Retire to bog with improving magazines, New Scientist, Playboy, etc.

1100 "Committee meeting" – official codename for long-term project to test resistance to cancerous fumes of younger scientists' lungs. (Beagles too expensive these days, animal rights lobby too stroppy.)

1200 Lunch. Seniors discuss sex, the decline of football, the vileness of the TUC and the awfulness of the food. Intensive study of salmonella cultures being incubated in sausages etc. for airdrop over

USSR in next war.

1400 Various tasks.
 (a) Valuable research. Read New Scientist again.
 (b) Administrative efficiency. Ring engineers, ask for a fact or measurement. Swoon in amazement if they can answer. Fall dead with heart attack if answer is either prompt or correct.
 (c) Application of scientific method. Ring Computing and ask why last week's jobs haven't yet been run. Not considered tactful to mention last month's.
 (d) Defence studies. Inspect warheads, tapping each with small hammer. Ting. Ting. Ting. "Lots of lovely megatons there," says aged Hereditary Custodian of the Queen's Nasties. Ting. Ting. Plunk. Another flaw in Britain's Independent Deterrent system is detected and expunged.

1500 Tea. Seniors expound on the decline of sex, the awful ness of football, the appalling remoteness of five-thirty.

1600 Slump in office, exhausted by shattering exertions of day. Practice wrist action hurling darts into HM door. Answer phone, losing 1 point for each fact, measurement or admission about project status revealed in answer to questions. Up to 10 pts per original excuse for noncompletion of last year's projects. Not tactful if questioner mentions the year before.

1630 Think about going home, until
1730 Go Home.

Once upon a time this had seemed mildly funny, and to newcomers it still did; old hands passed it over as mere truism. He had entered the "slump" phase now, pondering with half a brain cell over a passing crossword clue ("Mucous plug by which the rectum of a polar bear is blocked during hibernation." Six letters starting with T. Bloody hell), and wondering on which side Staverton's malicious mind would come unbalanced.

After the meeting, Dr S. would surely be reasoning, the chances of sneaking even a dummy past the gates would rival those of smuggling the maximum-security block out of Parkhurst. By comparison, camels would leap in herds through needles' eyes with lithe and lissom grace. A successful, meaning an unsuccessful, smuggle would kindle glory for the committee and therefore Staverton, but had the crippling disadvantage that a share of glory went to Security. Impasse.

But, reasoned Tappen, whoever tried and failed to sneak one of those through the fence would look vaguely silly – would be the straight man standing all gormless and eggy-faced while Staverton and Security basked in applause. All that was needed was to make Staverton sufficiently irritated with scientist X or Y or Z – or, more plausibly, L or T – and the exercise would be on, with that very scapegoat booked for the officially sanctioned faceful of egg.

(Could it really be possible, even in a crossword, to express, in seven letters beginning with S, the concept "Loathsome venereal disease producing fungal growths resembling a raspberry"? Not the sort of thing you found in the Rubber Bible, the Chemical Rubber Company Handbook of Chemistry and Physics ...)

For one reason and another, the feckless Llewellyn seemed the best person to incur the overweight wrath of Staverton and become an official smuggler. He was quite likely to do this by accident, as when he'd swapped round the fuses to restore power to his illicitly imported toaster without the bother of calling a union electrician, and the blown fuse had wound up in the Criticality Alarm circuit, provoking widespread panic at the failure, while the NUTC electricians blacked the whole 334 area for weeks after.

Tappen merely needed to persuade Llewellyn to be annoying once again: Alka-Seltzer or laxatives in the tea-urn, a buttered floor outside Staverton's sumptuous office, exploding cigars at the next NPIWP meeting, the possibilities were endless. It was just a matter of going next door and in a few brilliantly articulated phrases persuading the chosen sucker (a word not to be used amid said phrases) to stick his neck out. Llewellyn. Definitely.

The phone rang.

"Double-six-four-three Tappen."

"This is Alastair Staverton," said a silky voice. "Roy, have you by any chance cast your eyes over today's *Redbury Chronicle*, especially page five?"

"Not till I get home," Tappen said cautiously. "Even then I only look at page three, ha ha."

"Ha, ha. SCIENTISTS ON TWELVE PINTS A DAY."

For a long, piercing moment Tappen thought of hurling the phone again into the bin and fleeing gibbering into the sunset, never again to be seen by mortal man save as a gaunt figure haunting the marshes around Bogley and rending the night air with shrieks of demonic laughter. He shook his head, took a breath so deep that his toes felt the draught, and said "Are they?"

"'Atom base men must drink pint after pint of beer to flush deadly neutron particles from their bodies,'" quoted the remorseless Staverton. "'These are the secret facts revealed by informants "Roy" and "Joe". Employees of local atom centre NUTC, Joe and Roy dare not give their full names for fear of prosecution. A horrifying situation in what we call a free country. For eight hours a day atom men are bombarded with deadly radio waves. A doctor refused to comment ...' Need I go on?"

"Did you want me to add it as an appendix to the NPIWP minutes?" said Tappen, wondering why it made him feel measurably better to screw his eyes tight shut. Perhaps a bucket of sand would help even more.

"Did I –! Yes, Yes. Include it by all means. You might care to add that the Press Officer rang to make a statement, and heard descriptions of these hoaxers. Rough descriptions, to be sure, but the names are significant enough. Wouldn't you agree?"

"I was ... wondering about the ... coincidence." Actually he was wondering how you went about signing up for Supplementary Benefit.

"The impression *I* received was that the one called Joe was merely an irresponsible young idiot, while the one called Roy was not only the ringleader but old enough to know better. H'm. However ... that isn't what I was calling about."

"It isn't?" Tappen tried hard though with little success not to sound as though just informed of a medium-sized Pools win.

"No. Noooo ... I thought you'd appreciate knowing that after consideration I and SPI believe the demonstration exercise is worthwhile enough to be tried, at least on a small scale. You might slip that into the minutes, just before the appendix in which you will no doubt quote long extracts about our nuclear policy from the pages of *Pravda*. And of course you yourself are the *logical* choice for what one might call the inside job ..."

"Thanks," said Tappen with a gulp. Had it sounded too sincere? Not sincere enough?

"I should plan it out with Michael Fortmayne and make your move quickly – in time for the next NPIWP meeting, eh? Excuse me if I cut this fascinating conversation short, but I must make another phone call, to Security –"

Tappen was left staring with raised eyebrows at his crossword. "What the best laid plans of mice and men aft gang," he muttered at last. "Five letters starting with A."

Joe Llewellyn didn't know how lucky he was.

Later, on his way to the main gate and the bus, Tappen was less than amazed when Alf Rossiter, in the full glory of his MoD Police uniform, caught his eyes and emitted an ostentatious wink. Followed, of course, and in case he had any lingering doubts of grapevine efficiency, by an embarrassingly detailed inspection of his briefcase, pockets, and other likely places for concealing weaponry such as between his thighs.

Eight

At the midpoint between bus stop and home, he cringed to see a white car pulling out from precisely outside the Tappen residence's gate, a white car topped like some elaborate ice-cream with the red sign MOD POLICE and a blue light poised to flash terrifyingly. There seemed to be a sniggering note in the engine noise as it accelerated up the road and away. As he walked the last few dozen yards, Tappen felt that the hunt was baying on his trail, that every tree, car or shadow could now conceal lurking watchers, terrible and inexorable as bloodhounds or VAT inspectors.

"Don't overreact," he told himself sternly while somehow lacking the moral fibre to stride manfully up the centre of the pavement. He hugged the comforting but prickly hedge, another phantasmagoric slide-show playing in his head: The watchers. The siege. Terse sentences into walkie-talkies. A man with a peaked cap and megaphone. *We know what you've got in there.* Himself at the bedroom window. *A free pardon and safe conduct abroad, or I light the blue touch-paper!* Suddenly SAS men emerge from their long concealment in the kitchen pedal-bin ...

Eventually he went up the path as though it were a plank jutting over shark-infested sea, and Lizzie opened the door as he reached it.

"Hello, darling," she said with her head tilted a little to one side. "We've had a visitor."

"About the pit?"

"The what?"

Tappen was eager to avoid the point for a few seconds longer. "The pit. The thing in the attic. They call it that at work, or the chaps who like the American jargon do: you know, pit, what the Yanks call the stone in a peach, same with the weapon core inside all that explosive that touches it off. Um, I read a book once saying it's all US prudery, because stones used to mean balls as well. They call cocks roosters, and depending on context they call stones pits or rocks or fourteen-poundses, and ..."

"What you probably need is a cup of tea," Lizzie said. He closed the door behind him and followed submissively to the kitchen, still prattling his hasty whitewash over any possible silence:

"Really I don't see why people here have to imitate the way the bloody Americans talk, their pits and nukes and CB jargon – I hated those handbooks of how to talk American CB in five easy lessons, the whole point of the thing was a sort of spontaneous private language that grew out of CB chat, it was so bloody *silly* when our homegrown CB loonies did bad imitations of US slang when they could have been inventing their own. You should hear Mike Fortmayne driving down the M4 rabbiting on in this fake American accent about breakers and smokies and foxy ladies, and every so often sounding a shade embarrassed when he has to put in a bit of English ..."

"Hobby horse," said Lizzie definitively, slamming the kettle onto the hotplate with the decisive energy which every so often cracked and fused the electric ring. "You can do that recitation in your sleep, sweetie; in fact you sometimes do ... I said We've Had A Visitor. Are they threatening to promote you? Again?"

"God, no. On present form they might reassign me as assistant target in the proving grounds, but ... What visitor?"

"One of your dear playmates from Security. He looked like an ex-policeman, face like a potato, a potato someone's been playing squash with. He was sitting on the doorstep when I came home; he showed me bits of paper and muttered about PV, and went into all those rude questions, just like the last time they were persuading themselves not to do anything unwise like promote you."

"Bugger," said Tappen with feeling. Positive Vetting, the irregular check on one's credentials, purity and preferred positions in bed. "That's bloody Staverton, he's got it in for me because of, er, something I said to someone. And the security exercise is a great excuse ..."

"What's that?"

Tappen cheered up slightly. "That is my infallible master plan to – well, when a PV's on the walls have ears and probably bloodhound noses, but I should definitely be able to tidy out the attic soon."

"Make more sense if you did something about your computer junk in the back bedroom ... Oh, I see." She studied the tea cosy as though for hidden microphones. "Potato-face – perhaps that's unfair, he had a beetroot nose and a couple of cauliflower ears as well, not to mention aspen fingers – The MoD man didn't ask anything about attics, love. Or holes in the ground. Or fruit: no, I'm wrong there. Just like every time before, he came up with that question."

"'Might Mr Tappen be a homosexual?'" he quoted wearily.

Lizzie's face lit up in a grin. They didn't need to say anything. Both remembered the joyous moment of Tappen's first PV shortly before his acceptance into the arms of Robinson Heath. They'd been living in one room of a bedsitter, *in Sin*, as Lizzie observed with relish. She'd kept tactfully behind the scenes while Tappen was interrogated – "Are you now or have you ever been?" – by a thug whose scarred face reminded him not so much of vegetables as of a British Rail map. "So you say you didn't belong to any political clubs at university? Most people do, you know. Are you sure? No good saying later how you *forgot* you'd joined the Workers' Revolutionary Party, mate... Any of your friends involved in organizations under Communist influence? How about their families, then?" Tappen had confessed to knowing someone who had once voted Labour, and was told not to make things harder for himself.

The high spot had come next morning. Unannounced, the thug returned to ask a few "overlooked" questions. "Mr Tappen, I have to ask you this and I hope it'll cause you no offence: Are you a poofter? I mean, a homosexual?"

"No," he'd said in all sincerity, feeling uneasily decadent as he shivered in his dressing-gown, pointedly blocking the bedsitter's doorway and not asking the visitor inside, where a partially dressed Lizzie was turning unseemly puce and stuffing handfuls of pillow in her mouth to smother shrieks of hilarity.

"Have you ever been?" continued the MoD man with narrowed eyes, while Tappen resisted a growing urge to fling wide the door, and with each draughty second out there in the hallway his dressing-gown seemed more padded and gaudy-lapelled and precisely what Oscar Wilde would have fancied. Ah, those romantic memories.

"I thought being one of those was all right these days," said Lizzie over the sudden mating call of the kettle.

"Defence is a different country, they do things differently there. Quotation. Nearly... Darling, being gay is a security risk: thus spake Zarathustra."

"Yes, but if you can *come out* (do you think those fatuous society girls in London still call it coming out when they put up the Rich Husband Wanted signs, these days?) ... if you can flaunt it and the Marquess of Whatsit can't bundle you off to Reading Gaol, where's the risk? Oh rats, I forgot the tea." She found it and spooned in Darjeeling leaves which floated like buoyant insects on the clear water in the pot.

"If I can just vault quickly over a hobby horse, love, it's like this. Imagine the MoD decided that if you like vodka you're an unemployable security risk – after all, look where the stuff was invented. An enormous hulk with letters like MoDP and GBH after his name comes and looms over you and says *Are you now or have you ever been a vodka-lover?* If you say yes you're suddenly unemployed. If you say no but you like the odd vodka and tonic really, you get your MoD post but a terrible burden lies on your wicked conscience, and now sly little men from the Soviet Embassy can tap your shoulder and say *Psst! Hand over the inside leg measurements of the Minister of Defence or we'll rush your boss this photograph of you in intimate companionship with a bottle of Vladivar!* And there you are. The baddies have a hold over you and you're a security risk. Thus it is that anything the clowns in Whitehall decide is a security risk automatically turns into one. Q.E.D."

"Hobby horse ... oh, I suppose I encouraged you that time. Why don't you become a university lecturer, dear? Here you are. Pretend the black bits on top are radioactive contamination or something else you're used to."

"Thanks." He leant and kissed her cheek, spilling tea from the mug as his hand momentarily shook; the mention of r/a had sent thoughts buzzing up like disturbed bluebottles, towards the loft and the thing that was throbbing there like a painful, swollen boil which if squeezed ... What an awful mind I've got, he interrupted himself inwardly.

Vaguely reaching for comfort, he put his arm round Lizzie's shoulders. This would be the cue for her to pass acid remarks about spilling tea on the floor; but she seemed to sense the weight of complication that made his shoulders sag, and nestled against him as they stood in the too-small kitchen, and tea from both their mugs spattered on the floor. "Love you," Tappen was saying automatically, indistinctly, nose and mouth tickled by her warm hair, as the doorbell rang.

"They're *watching* us," she said breathlessly. "There's going to be another wretched thug out there and he's going to say thanks, our teapot camera shows you're not gay, now will you fill in this schedule of questions on your practices in bed, prepared by the Committee for the Investigation of UnMarywhitehouseian Activities –"

Tappen had already splashed through puddles of tea to the dim hallway; a diminuendo muttering followed him to the door, "Are you now reading or have you ever read the *Kama Sutra*? Are you now trying or have you ever ..."

He opened the door and screwed up his eyes. A tall and sinister figure stood silhouetted against the red dazzle of sunset. "Oh, er, I see you're home," said the voice of Roger Pell.

"No detectors. Absolutely no r/a detectors. The doctor's found Lizzie's allergic to them. Makes her come out in huge boils all over her, well, all over." Pausing, Tappen wondered whether the relief at finding it was only Pell could be showing in his voice.

"Pardon? The detector? It's funny you should mention that because I'm almost sure there's a hot spot on your roof. Suppose, say, a contaminated bird, just hypothetically you know, had dropped its droppings. That would explain so much ... pity I've not got a long ladder."

"It gives a whole new meaning to the word fallout. Come and have a cup of tea. The Turds of Doom. It's Roger, dear," he added, turning and bumping into Lizzie.

"Boils," she said darkly.

"Ah, I came to say I'd had a visitor. I arrived home a little early, er, on business, and this enormous fellow dropped in, with a face like an ex-wrestler or something ..."

"A potato," said Tappen, ushering him into the sitting-room and deftly shoving a heap of irreparable socks and tights off the sofa and under the coffee-table.

"Possibly; a mashed potato, if so. Of course I was, ah, slightly nervous since the Security people take such a dim view of perfectly legitimate opinions. I mean, nobody persecutes tax inspectors if they suggest the tax system is, well, inequitable, and it's the same thing. So after that little pamphlet turned up in the minutes – er, a *masterstroke* of propaganda of course, Roy, but just a trifle tactless, wouldn't you say? – after that it was all rather worrying. Only instead ..."

"He asked you if I spent too much time in office hours writing sonnets to Joe Llewellyn."

"No, no, he wanted to know if you liked Russian novelists, and he asked whether you had many foreign visitors; of course I did tell him about those Mormons, and also that you rather discouraged them on the whole."

"I suppose that's right," said Lizzie as she reappeared with a visitor's ration of tea, no mug but a standard cup and saucer: "The tactful way Roy shouts, 'Piss off, we're atheists' could be discouraging to some people."

"Not enough for the Mormons," said Tappen.

"And then he asked – you know, I do think this might have had sort of PV overtones now I come to think about it – he asked whether you were fond of gay bars. Of course I set him straight, er, I said yes, you like your pint but only in moderation, and the Goat and Compass down the road is as gay a place as any since they redecorated, and so on."

Tappen's eyes met Lizzie's. "Thanks a load," he said.

"I was wondering whether all this might be a cover-up, you

know, they ask about you but they're really watching me. I did feel quite worried. Do you think I've, er, got anything to worry about, Roy?"

"No," said Tappen slowly and with hard-fought calm. "Not yet."

Nine

"I mean," he said to the darkened ceiling, "you can't expect me to sleep. This evening I've had a grievous shock to my manhood. Terrible self-doubts are preying on parts of me that deserve tender loving care. I know you're not asleep."

"Oh yes I am," said Lizzie's muffled voice.

"Nuclear devastation hangs over my head. The spectre of unemployment and worse is beginning to fasten a bony, clutching hand on my goolies. Every day at Robinson Heath is starting to feel like thirty years on Devil's Island ..." He wriggled a caressing and diplomatic hand into the other half of the bed; it was firmly intercepted at the frontier and conveyed to the attention of small, sharp teeth. "Ouch."

"I'm asleep. I told you. Anyway, you never asked me whether I'd been having an awful time at work as well." There was a small sniff.

"My dearest, did you have a nice day at work?"

"Nothing special. The usual, routine West Indian lady who announced that one of her bunions was the new incarnation of the Lord, come to judge us all. We had to sing revivalist hymns to it for two hours before she'd put down the axe. In the end we sort of soothed her ... very tiring ..."

"You could sort of soothe me," he said hopefully.

"Nobody's going to take creepy Roger seriously about the Goat and Compass. Nobody with any brain. End of soothe ... I'm asleep."

"Funny about him," Tappen murmured, momentarily distracted. "When you changed the subject, thus saving me from assault charges, and asked him tactful things about his fall-out shelter, he went peculiar. Last year he wanted to show us round it every day; now he goes into jitters if you suggest another look. Maybe he's got it fitted up as a kinky retreat, all black leather and whips and fur. Speaking of which ..."

"No. I expect the wretched thing's leaking or falling apart ... spends his time hovering round it with his respirators and silly black boxes ... oh you selfish beast, I'm awake."

"And you feel nice – *ow*."

"I told you. Not until you've disarmed the attic. Unilaterally."

"Lysistrata," he complained. "You know I can't do anything about that till tomorrow at the earliest. Inspire me, darling, inspire me to greater things."

"Mmmmm," she said dreamily. "Tomorrow night at the earliest would be a lovely ... lovely time for ... that ..." Gently and sleepily her voice died away, like the high ideals of young scientific officers at Robinson Heath.

Tappen lay sleeplessly staring at the ceiling until he had to close his eyes against the round, luminescent, radioactive patch his completely unreasonable imagination kept nearly seeing there. A vague thought about the possibility and desirability of sheep-counting led into a detailed vision of endless security police vaulting athletically over the tall steel gates of Robinson Heath, intercepting with uncanny accuracy the procession of plutonium cores (with legs and grins like Mr Men) trying to hop across in the other direction....

Ten

Building 334 and its surroundings were the heart of NUTC, without a doubt, thought Tappen, and anyone from 334 and its surroundings would agree. Sprawling out about the central Admin block like suckling pigs in various stages of obesity, runthood or glanders were two dozen architectural errors, from the disintegrating shed with a string-secured door (where they kept the toxic chemical reagents) to the huge eyeless blockhouses of the test reactors (bordered with wide swathes of grass which every autumn sprouted toadstools, neatly arranged in fairy rings). Here was the famous wall you hurried past owing to neutron leakage from the accelerator, here was the brownish patch of grass where the lost uranium sample had oxidized, washed into the soil and betrayed its presence at last, here was the scrawled graffito on the endemic pipework, PLUTE LEVELS IN NUTC STAFF MAKE THEM UNFIT FOR HUMAN CONSUMPTION. After ten years Tappen viewed it all with a kind of nostalgia. "Nostalgia is masochism tempered with boredom," he murmured experimentally, and hoped it didn't sound like Oscar Wilde.

Almost definitely the heart of the 334 area was 334d, where a picked staff objected to nuclear policy decisions (Fortmayne), put off designing test experiments (Pell), nearly provided theoretical backing (Tappen), misprogrammed vast simulations (Llewellyn) and jerry-built the wrong apparatus (Munt and his tea-ravaged technicians). At the heart of 334d was the computer terminal room, or more properly cupboard, and here Tappen found Llewellyn hard at what looked like work. It was Wednesday morning.

"Shut that bloody door!" came the usual cry from Fortmayne's office as the hideous clatter of the teletype machine-gunned out into the corridor. As the computer staff too frequently pointed out,

68

when you've bought a super-duper Crayfish computer to handle all NUTC's data-processing, you can't expect HM Government to stump up for poncy new video terminals as well. Take what they used in 1955 and be glad of it.

Tappen shut the door behind him. There was precisely room for one person to stand and another to sit (anorexics preferred) in the White Hole of Calcutta, with its all-over acoustic tiling which sealed in both sound and stifling heat. Verboten to turn on the air-conditioning fan, whose lifelike Concorde impression disturbed the subtle mental processes of Fortmayne's daily crossword.

"Today's the day," Tappen bellowed over the hellish mechanical clatter. "I said TODAY'S THE DAY."

Llewellyn hit a control key to stop the remorseless printout, tore off and wadded up several furlongs of paper, and stuffed the result into the bin. "Think it's working now. Got it from one of the programmers in T section, he spent weeks adapting it to grotty old terminals like this. Really triff – look –"

He typed a line of command language. The teletype resumed its tatta-tatta-tatta-tatta, like a high-speed replay of bad disco music, or the military band accompaniment for a regiment on the run. It was printing clumps of asterisks, row after row after row, tatta-tatta-tatta-*ching* at the end of every line, the whole building up with painful slowness into a picture, ten columns of six little asterisk-clumps whose shape had a kind of familiarity. Several blank lines beneath the bottom of all this was a final shape built from stars, a small centred triangle, and below that:

TYPE L TO MOVE LEFT; R TO MOVE RIGHT, F TO FIRE MISILE.

With a triumphant flourish Llewellyn typed FL, and the chattering began anew. Tappen's eyes widened in realization as the fresh picture built up on a fresh yard of paper, the suddenly all too recognizable shapes above, the triangle at the bottom now shifted slightly left, a lonely asterisk above it to represent a missile on its soaring upward course ...

"Bet you this is the world's first Space Invaders game to run on a teletype," said Llewellyn with considerable pride.

"Science," Tappen said reverently, "is wonderful. Just how

many centuries does it take to finish a game?"

"Well, this wally from T said it was a good idea to come in early in the morning. Done better than him though, I've patched the program so you can stop any time and start next day or whenever, just where you left off. Play it right through even if it takes two weeks. Pretty brill, eh?"

"Slug Invaders," Tappen intoned, slightly limp from this revelation of wonders. "Glacier Invaders."

The teletype completed another picture. At this rate Llewellyn's first missile would very likely find its target by lunchtime. But instead of unleashing his deadly reflexes on the fire control, he turned his head to squint over one shoulder, up at Tappen.

"Today's the day for what?"

"Today, Operation Filing Cabinet goes into reverse ... which reminds me, come to think of it, you owe me an evening's piss-up. I won that bloody bet after all ..." He hadn't thought of this before, this bright spot on the order of learning that despite the ravages of leprosy and the Black Death the pimple on one's nose was clearing up nicely; all swallowed in the general stress since the cabinet had begun to disgorge free gifts like a jumbo cereal packet. Perhaps now the shock had subsided he'd solve his problems with cold merciless logic, which sounded good. Perhaps he was merely getting blasé about 200 potential kilotons of unpleasantness: less good.

"Got my end of it sussed," Llewellyn said smugly. "Let me just finish the game and I'll show you –"

"You are *not* finishing that bloody game!"

"Worry not, Roy. I'm ahead of you. Said I'd been improving the thing, didn't I? You look at this." More control keys. More clatter.

*** IN AUTOMATIC MODE *** (said the teletype.)

"Autopilot – no need for printout or key-pushing – plays through the game for you and –"

*** GAME OVER ***

YOU HAVE BEEN UTERLY DEFEATED, THE ALEINS HAVE OVERUN EARTH!!

YOUR SCORE WAS 262,939,415,000

TYPE R IF YOUD LIKE ANOTHER GAM

"I see your programming's going through a bad spell," said Tappen.

"Eh? No, you always lose, that's the way these games are, but *what* a score ... OK, let's get out of the Invaders software and I'll print out the machine-code listings."

He'd typed LIST SHELLGAME before Tappen stopped him: "No. Life is too short to read horrible machine code programs, ever. Pause, marshal your thoughts, such as they are, and tell me what you're talking about."

Within thirty seconds he was regretting that. Behind the gawky, innocuous front Llewellyn presented to the world, a frightful and grey-souled computer bore was always lurking ready to spring. Tappen's comprehension and consciousness kept hazing out as technicalities came at him like doses of Valium, "level 4 file security ... had to go down into assembler ... protection codes ... binary patch switches execution ... simulating the authorized file editor ... overwrite data byte by byte ... now the really interesting part is ..."

"Enough," said Tappen, reaching down to clamp his hand over Llewellyn's mouth. "Not here. Not now. Had we but world enough and time, This coyness, lady, were no crime."

The door opened as he was saying this, and the uniformed security man waited politely for the end of Tappen's quotation before saying, in a carefully neutral voice, "I had a few questions to ask Mr Roy Tappen; but I see you're busy. I'll call back later." He went. Suddenly Tappen was very conscious of the hot, sweaty aroma of this cosy hell-hole.

"Mmmmmf," quipped Llewellyn. Tappen took the hand from over his junior's mouth, and would have gnashed his teeth if it weren't for some dodgy fillings.

"I think we have just been found in a compromising situation," he noted. "Bugger it – no, *no*, I didn't mean that," he added with a nervous glance at the closed door. "As – I – was – saying. Tell me again what you've been up to, and this time with English subtitles."

"I told you, didn't I? It's the old shell game, that's why I called the program that. Fiddles plute storage records and serial numbers. Shell game – the bean's always under the shell you don't expect. Pit game – no matter what pit anyone else borrows for measurements, experiments, basketball, the records get shuffled and tweaked so they never find the bean. I mean they never end up with the dummy. Ace stuff, eh? Should be able to cover for weeks."

Tappen smiled wanly. "I'd pat you on the back, only the Morality Patrol would burst in with full equipment, from video cameras to Mary Whitehouse. And never mind the weeks. Lizzie – my conscience won't have it. Today, as I've been trying to hammer into you, is *der Tag*. Come to the office and I'll show you the sketch. One picture's worth fifty kilobytes of machine code."

"What's all that piss about compromises and Mary White-house?" said Llewellyn in the dingy brown and yellow corridor. His mind extricated itself only slowly from the tasty honeypot of programming.

Tappen told him. The resulting high-pitched giggles were, as Tappen sternly observed, probably just the thing to set evil-minded Security men thinking and wondering.

When the ritual preparations had been made – Llewellyn shining his trouser-seat on the edge of the desk and the tea poured out – Tappen unscrewed a side panel of the junked oscilloscope where he kept really important things like reserve supplies of Earl Grey, and extracted a roll of A3 paper.

"Now here's my plan," he said as he spread it on the desk. With fondness he gazed on the classical beauty of the design, sketched less than an hour before.

"It's a bloody catapult."

"Technically, as we weapons physicists should be expected to know, it's a ballista. Small portable model. The old Roman ones used stressed wooden bows, of course, or cords of gut, but I've substituted rubber tubing 'cause there's miles of it in Lab Three. Plenty of steel and aluminium scrap for the frame, and Ed Munt can probably knock this up easier than he could a mangonel or a trebuchet. Wouldn't you say?"

He was rather pleased with the layer of dusty erudition still clinging to his mind after ten minutes with NUTC's well-thumbed and outdated *Britannica*.

Llewellyn appeared to be counting very slowly from one to ten; or perhaps, being a computer buff, from 0 to 1. "Sod the mangel-wurzels," he said distinctly. "The whole problem is that you've *got* the thing out. What's all this for, to smuggle out a few more? Starting a collection?"

"We don't have to get a pit out but we do have to have been able to get one out ... if that's not too complicated for your tiny programmed mind. Imagine yourself back in school. 'What, dear boy, is the answer?' says your kindly teacher. 'Forty-two,' lisps the infant Joseph. 'Splendid,' the master says, 'and how, pray, did you arrive at this result?' 'Er um well, it says in the back of the book ...?' and an intercontinental ballistic piece of chalk hits you smartly on the nose."

"All right, all right. This is going to be your worked example." He brightened. "Your flowchart, sort of."

"Keep your poxy computers out of this," said Tappen. "Yes. They gape at the ballista, and they scratch their heads in wonderment at my awesome intellect, and then they go off and plug this hole in their security which we'll just have *proved* is big enough to launch Polaris through. Wonder how they'll cope."

"Make catapults taboo, same as cameras."

Tappen stared out of the window to where the high perimeter fence was just visible between Lab Five and the fissile fuel store. "How tall would that have to be to keep flying weaponry safely inside? Twenty feet, twenty-five, thirty: that's a lot of fence. This lark could leave next year's security budgets scrambled like Roger's politics ... How tragic."

"Eggs and omelettes. Creates jobs, boosts Britain, worth a CBE any day of the week." An expression of tortured concentration passed briefly over Llewellyn's face. "De fence of de nation," he said as though expecting applause.

A knock on the door, a precise quarter-second pause, the handle turning: that was a characteristic Fortmayne entrance, and Tappen's trained reflexes twitched in abortive effort to sweep some non-existent science fiction novel out of sight.

"Right," said Fortmayne, slapping both hands down onto the desk and leaning forward at Tappen. "I think we need to go over the details of this charade you're planning." His eyes looked like twin lasers improbably tuned to radiate grey light. Tappen wished he would put slightly less effort into being dynamic.

"It's all planned and ready to go," he said as firmly as he could, which felt not a lot firmer than an overripe raspberry or a governmental spending estimate. "I'm just about to take the sketches round to Ed Munt –"

Fortmayne took the sketch with a lordly air of *droit du seigneur*, held it at arm's length and contemplated it for a long while with awful impassivity. It was hard to tell whether he was hearing Tappen's mumbled explanations. The overall tableau was paralysingly like some Victorian father regarding a piece of vile scurrility confiscated from a wilful elder son, a page of Darwin, perhaps.

At length the dreaded words came. "I don't agree with what you're saying, Roy. I don't think this scheme has the right sort of credibility. It needs to be *foolproof*. You simply haven't thought it through."

"I, er, thought it would take them by surprise. An unexpected angle of attack; you know; they concentrate on the gates." Tappen was babbling, finding himself outflanked and vulnerable, caught off balance by this attack from an unexpected angle, this totally unfair supposition that his ballista should be required actually to *work*.

Fortmayne was ticking points off on his fingers with relish, the sketch waving and flapping and rustling with each movement of his hand. "Firstly, you can't test this contraption without alerting the MoDP. Secondly, it only needs a second's bad luck, a touch of mistiming, and you're spotted by one of the perimeter patrols. Thirdly and most important, this method is feasible for dummies but no one in their right mind would suggest it as a possibility for the real thing. Even an irresponsible lunatic traitor would hardly fire whole kilos of plute into the air and risk breakage and major contamination. Fourthly, Ed would take a week to build this and three to get it right. Fifthly, I have a better, much better, approach which I've sketched roughly here ..."

Tappen writhed, appalled as always by an off-the-cuff speech which could keep track of points as far as "fifthly", unable to counterattack with details of how his own brilliantly conceived mechanism evaded almost every awkwardness by the simple process of not needing actually to work.

"Well," he said irrefutably. But already fluttering under his nose was a vast sheet of draughtsman's paper covered with elaborate views and elevations which (as usual with a Fortmayne "rough sketch") looked as though it had occupied the efforts of NUTC's entire drawing office for about a week. He blinked. While his own wonder gadget resembled a mediaeval siege-engine, Fortmayne's was like the besieged castle itself. "We could build them both," he muttered, "have an ordeal by combat and use the winner."

"What's that you're saying?" said Fortmayne. Llewellyn was crowding to look, and it was he who eventually said, "Bit obvious, isn't it," with the fast-ripening smugness of one to whom it had only just become obvious.

It wasn't an ambitious castle. More of a blockhouse, small and cubical – very small – bricks enclosing a space big enough for, say, a football.

"The lead blocks are the lightest ones we have. Get them from the cupboard in the hot lab. They'll soak up x-rays and gammas. You should be able to tell me what the lining is ... ?"

"Wallpaper," Tappen offered.

A snort. "Cadmium shielding. Should help stop neutrons. Ask Ed for the scraps left over from the Army Jockstrap test series. And there you are. Any comments?"

"Certainly that lot ought to keep plute radiation from the gate detectors," Tappen mused. "Like smuggling out a piece of classified paper by hiding it unobtrusively in a steamer trunk. Perhaps I could slip it all into an inner pocket; or should I drag it behind me with an air of nonchalance and a small trolley? That's the only problem I can see."

Llewellyn giggled and choked over the beaker of tea he still held. The sound Fortmayne made was a sort of anti-giggle which cancelled any fallout of humour there might be in the air.

"None of your jokes," he said. "Use a car; if you get to it right now you can finish the whole thing this evening. Joseph, you should find our dummy pit in one of the Lab Two cupboards: check its r/a source is a fair imitation of the real thing, and bring it here. When you've quite finished your tea-drinking hour, Roy, you can see to the rest of the materials. There. In this place I have to do everything myself ..."

Though Tappen could imagine about fifty objections to Fortmayne's ideas, he relaxed as usual and let the Cult of Personality overmaster him. On the one hand it never did any good to argue with one's boss in this place; on the other, this new scheme looked quite capable of being perverted to appalling Tappenesque ends.

"I'll drop round later to see what you've achieved," Fortmayne said. "Oh, and I wanted to ask you – no, in a few minutes." One of the site messengers had come bumbling in with internal mail for Tappen; Fortmayne fled to see what had come for him and take instant, dynamic, sometimes even correct action. Tappen's postbag consisted of several thousand pages of staggeringly important technical reports, compressed by the miracles of modern science into a slim pack of microfiche, and thus not precisely readable until further wonders of modern science replaced the bulb in 334 area's only fiche viewer.

"Whose car we planning to use for this?" Llewellyn asked warily.

"Yours. You've got a nice enclosed boot, mine's a peekaboo tailgate. Also that heap of yours is so decrepit, three wheels in the grave, nobody will notice if the suspension is a foot or two down at the back."

"No way! Last night they did everything but vacuum out my belly-button for forensic dust analysis. Bust me quick as a flash."

"I wondered about that," said Tappen omnisciently. He hadn't. He thought for a moment and went on, "But I have this plan ..."

Knock-pause-rattle-squeak. Their lord and master was again among those present. "The Press Office passed *this* on for evaluation," he said, throwing a slim blue book onto the desk. Tappen and Llewellyn squinted. *An Experiment with Space*. It had a tantalizingly lucid blurb: "Internal vortex lifts 9-metre disc by space dynamics: angular velocities of 20000 to 40000 revs/min mean molecules moving at 11 km/s. YOUR PLANET NEEDS YOU to consider and investigate possibilities that may radically transform civilization. Like neutralizing gravity and debunking materialism."

"I suppose it's another crank book," Fortmayne said distantly. "Press Office always passes the buck this way when they're asked to comment."

"I know it's a crank book without opening it," Tappen said, pointing. "Foreword by the Earl of Clancarty. That tells it all."

"What I really wanted to say, though, was that I had a security chap round earlier. Didn't realize you were up for another PV. Asked some very odd questions, I must say. Er, Roy, are you fond of T.E. Lawrence?"

"No," said Tappen, who'd never got very far with *Seven Pillars of Wisdom*. Remembering the cult of Lawrence of Arabia and his dashing military reputation, he thought "all's fair in love and positive vetting," and corrected himself: "Yes, I mean." Then he remembered something else for which Lawrence was slightly famous, and hastily concluded, "No, of course not."

"Oh," said Fortmayne, seemingly more embarrassed than Tappen. "Never mind. I'll tell you what. We'll allow ourselves a drink in the Mushroom Cloud after work – a post-mortem on the smuggling racket, yes? And I'll witness that you have the booty with you."

"Great idea," said Tappen with false enthusiasm. Another cosmic scheme in ruins: not only doomed to an approach which might actually work, he now had to let it be seen to work.

Fortmayne looked at his watch and said, "Coffee time."

"Be with you in mere nanoseconds," said Tappen. And when the PSO had gone: "All right, Joe. I know. We really actually do have to smuggle the dummy out: after which it can be swapped, with deep and diabolical cunning, eh? All right. This is the latest master plan, and I hope you never mock your friend Roy's mighty brain again. Now's the time: I know he always leaves them on the desk ..." He went on for a minute or so, each sentence sounding feebler than the last.

Llewellyn sighed. "It's one of those smartarse ideas that work in books. Suppose we'll have to try it – but I *bet* you something cocks it up."

Of course he was all too right, though of course the state of play at the day's end managed not to resemble any of Tappen's horrible imaginings. It was as though, Cassandra-fashion, he'd made dismal predictions of fog and rain, only to be amazed by plagues of locusts, a continent-wrecking earthquake, and an invasion by the barbarian hordes of the Moral Majority.

Eleven

Because of his burden of guilty intrigue, Tappen felt he should make his behaviour as excessively and even offensively normal as could be contrived. It wasn't easy. Towards the end of the morning the messenger brought a photocopy from Library Services, the famous *Chronicle* piece headlined SCIENTISTS ON TWELVE PINTS A DAY, "sent at the personal request of Dr A. Staverton. For your information." Tappen at once wanted to go and be very rude to someone, but heroically restrained himself. Yet another Security man came by to enquire with sinister casualness about his putative familiarity with unlikely-sounding places like the Subway Club, the Leather Parlour and the Gaylord Tandoori Restaurant: with a mighty effort Tappen suppressed the jokes that sprang to his lips, and instead quite gratuitously shifted the desktop piles of computer printout to reveal the picture of Lizzie he'd kept there for years. (It was a bad moment when Security continued the conversation with, "Who's he?") Before that interview was over Llewellyn had popped in, radiated furtiveness at several hundred millirem, tapped the side of his nose with one finger, and said in deeply conspiratorial tones, "FT451".

"Pardon?" said Security, perhaps wondering if he should give a secret countersign. ("Elephants are seldom seen in Milton Keynes." "Ah, greetings, comrade!" and so forth.)

"Ah yes, that component number," said Tappen quite truthfully, peering at Llewellyn as sternly as he dared. "If we're to meet our experimental deadline you'd better run along and, ah, requisition one now. After all, it's the *key* to the whole apparatus, isn't it?"

His subordinate looked inexpressibly malign. "I thought you were going to –"

"Not now. On your way; it isn't far." And certainly it wasn't

79

more than a hundred yards to the Stores warehouse where people usually requisitioned parts; but Joe Llewellyn was going to be driving a mile and a half to Bogley Garage & Auto Services. There was a distinct I'll-get-you-for-this light in his eyes as he departed.

"These young fellows," Tappen said tolerantly, aligning himself with the partially mummified Security man (who must be thirty years older than Tappen) against the awful forces of rebellious youth embodied in Llewellyn (perhaps eight years younger). "Always looking for excuses, always trying to get out of work, always dropping in to ask silly questions and waste everyone's time ... Now where were we? Like a cup of tea?"

But it seemed that even Security men on the dreaded PV duty could take a hint. Tappen was left alone to reflect on the missed opportunity for subtle questioning: over the Oolong it would be so simple for an interlocutor to probe Tappen's liking for biscuits dipped in his tea, and thence move on to examine a whole series of possible affinities with Marcel Proust.

(Why, the acoustic tiling of the computer cupboard practically made it a cork-lined room. Um.)

Plunging into feverish work, he placed his feet on the desk and opened *An Experiment with Space*. It would be nice to construct a small flying saucer from the stunning theories contained, and nonchalantly float contraband over the fence.... Unfortunately the theory was simply that if things went round and round fast enough they would rise weightlessly into the air (as satellites went around the Earth very fast indeed and This Proved It). It corresponded to Tappen's experiences at some parties, admittedly. He calculated on the back of some old computer printout that if the book was right the NUTC cyclotron, in which particles went round and round at a fair fraction of the speed of light, should long ago have floated gently off over the Downs to alarm the peasantry and make the security forces put straws in their hair.

At this point Carol rang from 334's Admin office and disconcerted him by hoping sweetly that he'd recovered from his collywobbles of Monday morning. "And I do hope you'll feel up to coming to Ric Hailstone's little party today; the boy's getting married and we're having drinks in 334 Conference Room. Twelve noon. Oh yes, and Dr Staverton has an unexpected appointment this afternoon and would be so grateful if you could help show a party of VIPs around the showpiece areas. Two-thirty."

Tappen's free hand, which was drawing an increasingly gloomy sequence of skulls and gibbets on the blotter, tightened in annoyance. The pencil broke. He hated drinking foul sherry at lunchtime, he hated giving baffled visitors the Grand Tour, he had his suspicions about Staverton's appointment and he couldn't offhand remember who Ric Hailstone was.

"Of course," he said through his teeth. He was going to keep a low profile if it meant digging a grave and lying in it. Of course, Llewellyn would now be lumbered with all the master plan's donkey work, ho ho ...

"That's *mar*vellous. We'll see you soon. Bye-bye." Soon? Already it was quarter to twelve and as usual no actual work had got itself done: hastily Tappen sketched a rough plan for the complex nuclear-fireball demonstration model he was supposed to arrange for the coming NUTC exhibition. At the touch of a button *here* the precision airpump would smoothly and swiftly inflate the quite ordinary toy balloon *there*, while a halogen lamp controlled by intricate electronic dimmers would gradually glow brighter and brighter within the red balloon. The whole high-tech apparatus thus modelled the expanding fireball from a nuclear explosion, at the appropriate level of complexity for royal visitors.

Before noon he'd also scribbled a succinct ten-word report on the scientific merits of *An Experiment with Space*, torn it up, and substituted something a trifle more tactful. A good morning's work, he considered, for Robinson Heath.

Ric Hailstone proved to be a pasty-faced young fellow, as well he might be, as one of the Health Physics crew in 334h who had succulent tasks like boiling down quantities of scientifically gathered urine to search for such lumps of plutonium as NUTC staff might have passed unnoticed. His colleagues would have some specially pathological samples to examine after the present orgy: thirty or forty scientists and others packing the smoky conference room to densities found normally only at the centre of the Sun or a rush-hour Tube, forcing down quantities of sticky-sweet British sherry to mitigate the horror of their condition. For the hundredth time Tappen noted how the bottles were opened and glasses replenished, tacitly, by the only women present, Carol and a bulging lady called Chrissie whose main function was to guard the 334 photocopier from anyone who might dare to use it. Silently he raised a glass to the Ministry of Defence, an Equal Opportunity Employer.

"God, you looked pissed," said Llewellyn, materializing at his elbow.

"I was contemplating the strange pleasures of the multitude," Tappen said austerely. "Did you get it?"

"Yes. You owe me 40p. Here –"

"No, no, *you* look after it, Joe. (Have I got enough change? Yes, that's forty.) It just happens that dear old Al Staverton has co-opted me this afternoon because he's got a quote 'unexpected appointment' unquote ..."

"Oh yeah. Saw the golf clubs in his car."

"And the Bellman remarked, It is just as I feared, And solemnly tolled on his bell."

"Can do without the Shakespeare, thanks, Roy. Look. This means you're landing me in it."

It was a difficult moment, as Tappen had more or less been congratulating himself on landing Llewellyn in it. A bottle of sherry whose very label made him cringe came hovering close, and he was able to murmur something rapid and soothing to his junior before tossing a sickly "Thanks very much" to Carol. She favoured him with a smile. She was fond of a species of pale, heavy makeup which doubtless gave as much radiation protection as the average fallout shelter, and once in a while Tappen wondered what her round face might be like underneath. Then Carol had wriggled plumply on through the mob with her life-giving bottle, leaving a white dusting of powder where she passed, like a moth shedding wingscales. Tappen was left with Llewellyn eyeing him critically.

"I've just been reading this book," he said soothingly. "It predicts that if only the sherry turns my stomach fast enough and sets it spinning, it'll become weightless, and it certainly feels that way."

"Sort of gyroscope," said Llewellyn, momentarily distracted. "Internal stabilizers, even. You'll end up pissing with circular polarization – *you're changing the subject again.*"

By now the two were pressed close together in a corner of the room and Tappen was suffering lumbar puncture from an angular box where 334's overhead projector lived. "I'm *sorry*," he said, "I have to give the ruddy Grand Tour to some VIPs, and ten to one they'll be Americans and I'll have to listen to them telling each other how much bigger their facilities are and how every one of the six or seven projects I'm trying to cope with all alone has a team of thirty assigned to it at Livermore or somewhere ... makes you sick. All you have to do is a little fetching and carrying – and I'll give you a hand, till two-thirty."

"Can you guarantee to keep Mike Fortmayne off my back?"

"I – yes, why not? He usually does the grand tours, he likes it for some ungodly reason. In a previous incarnation he was a shepherd and still likes to guide his little flock. I'll entice him, that's what I'll do – Mike! *Mike!*"

Fortmayne had bobbed up only six feet away, trying to escape a tall bore from A section who'd reached the point of self-pitying monologue. ("And I said to my wife, I said, how much are you getting now with the 1¾% pay rise, and she said so-and-so, and I said bloody hell, and you know what, she's theoretically a grade lower in the Civil Service and she's getting more than me, of course, I said, that's because she's in a boom industry and I'm in the slums, I mean, here I am in defence and there she is helping pay out unemployment benefit, and so I said to her –") He turned towards Tappen, seemed to be sucked briefly under the crowd's surface-level, and emerged wriggling dextrously backwards into another of the projector cupboard's many sharp corners. His ensuing remarks were perhaps not covered by strategic arms limitation talks but should have been.

"You look shattered," said a sympathetic Tappen. "Overworked. What you need is a change of pace this afternoon."

"No." Fortmayne pushed back his mop of iron-grey hair and glowered with suspicion, imagining no doubt a nefarious plot to decoy him to the NUTC Library while Tappen and Llewellyn were left free to play Space Invaders all afternoon.

"Let me explain," said Tappen, feeling so persuasive and subtle that he quickly shook his head in case he was about to fall over. After a few minutes of golden rhetoric it was settled, objections gently dissolving in sherry: Fortmayne would lecture the VIPs while Tappen tagged along to observe the fine points of oratorical style for future use, leaving a practically clear coast for Llewellyn to wield the magic power of FT451.

"I'll want to see the screening arrangement all ready in your car boot before two-thirty," Fortmayne stipulated. Aha, Tappen managed not to say even under his breath, you have been manoeuvred into my trap....

Chrissie, secret mistress of xerography and famed for a physique like two camels fighting in a sack, came by with another bottle of Extra Sticky Sweet Cream British etcetera: "More sherry?" The conversation took a new turn, Tappen maintaining that to survive the afternoon you needed to swill enough of the potion to deaden the effects of what you'd already drunk, while Fortmayne insisted that more than two glasses would make him tiddly, and Llewellyn stayed verbally aloof during four quiet refills.

Twelve

"Two-fifteen," said Fortmayne and tapped his foot on the tarmac. Thin watery sunlight fell on him and Tappen, the latter thinking that he himself should be glowing in just that faint way after sweating to shift his quota of lead bricks. This was the far edge of 334 area, where a scatter of cars were parked against the ugly, corrugated wall of the fissile-fuel store. The juxtaposition had led to several bets being placed by the more morbid 334 staff. Which would happen first? Would brake failure or driver failure let a car smash into the wall and breach the radiation safety precautions, or would mishandled fuel go critical inside the store and cook some unsuspecting driver with hard rays? Tappen's money was on the first: he'd seen Llewellyn drive. (He hadn't at that time seen Llewellyn handle r/a material.)

Llewellyn was nowhere to be seen and the boot of his dung-coloured Ford (about which you could only say with certainty that it was newer than the Model T) was locked. Fortmayne snapped "Two-twenty," and Tappen began "He only went to fetch ... there he is."

Around the corner came Llewellyn, weaving athletically, head bent, dribbling something that wasn't a football. "And the Argentine centre forward goes for him, but no, the Welsh boy does a brilliant feint and dodge, his incredible ball control running rings around the stodgy opposition, and it looks like time for a lightning cross-pass, but no, no, he's pulling out the big one and IT'S A GOAL and there the ball is in the corner of the Argentine net, oh hello."

"Not quite in." Tappen put his foot on the dull metal sphere as it tried to roll under the car. A good thing Joe wasn't a cricket fan.

"Jesus Christ," murmured Fortmayne. "If the safety officer had seen that he would sprinkle you with holy water and make you write one thousand times, 'I will never ever again move even a dummy pit except on the proper r/a transport trolley.' Is that how you carry plute from lab to lab?"

"Of course not," said Llewellyn virtuously, luckily not going on to mention his fondness for string bags. He unlocked the Ford's boot. There revealed were Fortmayne's famous leaden fortifications: "I simply don't agree with your layout," the architect said predictably enough, making minute adjustments to the stacking of the bricks. Tappen picked up the bulky gamma and neutron detectors from the ground where he'd put them, and proved to his and Llewellyn's satisfaction, and much later to Fortmayne's, that the ostensibly harmless r/a source in the non-football was working, and that when it was tucked away behind lead and cadmium shielding it become almost "invisible" ... "Like the theoretical support group in 334k," he said cheerfully.

"What's that you're saying?" Fortmayne enquired.

"You know, the boys who're supposed to help with programming. I don't know what they *do*, but last year this notice went up on the board, RUPTURED? TRY OUR AMAZING THEORETICAL SUPPORT, INVISIBLE TO THE NAKED EYE!"

"One of your better efforts," Llewellyn said.

"I'd wondered who to thank for that," Fortmayne said coldly. "There was an official complaint from TS ..."

"Nearly two-thirty," Tappen told him with blinding speed. "We'd better dash round to 334 and greet your visitors, eh? Come on – you'll see all this again in the Mushroom Cloud car park after our brilliant success."

"I'll just suss out the meter readings one more time and lock up," said Llewellyn in the leaden voice of a Bogley Village Dramatic Society player reading a line from his shirt cuff.

"Take as long as you like," said Tappen with a wink as he turned to go. He was rewarded by the expression of Llewellyn's face, approximately the look a brilliant Welsh centre-forward might wear while deciding to flick his boot with deft sportsmanship into an opposing player's groin.

All moving like clockwork now, though possibly rusty clockwork, and clockwork which if it followed the general pattern of NUTC experiments would either not work at all or go *sproing* and whip off your face with five feet of unleashed mainspring.

"Good afternoon, gentlemen," said Fortmayne with hideous suavity as he wheeled into 334's entrance hall. "Welcome to the Nuclear Operations Division of Robinson Heath, and I'm sure you're all going to have a wonderful time ..." Tappen detected a fruity sherry-flavoured bonhomie in his tone.

"They're your responsibility now," said a Security policeman, stepping forward. "Sign here." With the air of masterful command which had made him a Principal Scientific Officer, Fortmayne stood aside to let Tappen receive the buck.

The five visitors were Services high-ups, thankfully out of uniform since the amount of brass involved would very likely have tripped every metal-detector in the restricted areas. They had weird titles like Comsolantair and Secnucinterzone. Probably Tappen misheard the ones that sounded like Cretinousoaf and Comintern. Not so bad as Americans, but then, not so good as the intermittent parties of carefully screened schoolkids (unclassified sections only), who could be relied on for the occasional almost intelligent question.

A short forced march, and: "This is the control room of the NUTC linear electron accelerator, the third most powerful in Europe ..." (And about the hundred and fiftieth in the world, Tappen brooded. Bloated plutocratic Americans.) "This chap in the white coat is called the *operator*, and as you'll see he's sitting at what in scientific parlance we generally refer to as the *control panel*. The big red light in the middle, or red warning light as we call it, indicates that the accelerator is *on* and that there are dangerous radiation levels in the actual accelerator lab, which is why that large concrete block has been cranked in front of the door *there* both to shield against r/a leakage and to prevent our walking into what scientists call an *ongoing rigor mortis situation* ..."

Even at this not very intellectually taxing level, the visitors were beginning to assume glassy-eyed and petrified expressions, like the African kings in that Rider Haggard book who were gradually converted to stalagmites by a constant drip of, perhaps, edifying conversation. Tappen's head was buzzing with sherry-flavoured fog, and he had a suspicion that Fortmayne had long since disengaged his brain from his mouth. It looked as though he shouldn't have persuaded his lord and master to take that extra glass or three.

"This is a far more interesting control room," Fortmayne lied, "as this is where we run the experimental laser installation which lives in the lab behind – ah, I see you've already noticed the concrete block. One day lasers of enormous power may be able to melt oncoming nuclear missiles and vaporize spy satellites, and already our experimental one is quite good at punching holes clean through not too thick pieces of cardboard; I'd demonstrate this but the laser control room operator, as we scientists call him, isn't available this afternoon."

Actually two of him were in the room: on the approximately annual occasions when the antique laser's awesome cardboard-perforating powers were called into play, Tappen or Fortmayne or Llewellyn had to put on a white coat and perform the intricate ritual of watching two meters and pressing the button.

Another identikit control room which might have operated anything from a BR ticket office to the Imperial Death Star. Fortmayne indicated a bank of inert indicators and lights: "From here we can sense every fluctuation in the working of the small but very important SLIMER, or Small Low-Intensity, er, eMission Experimental Reactor. At present it's doing some very important work for Army Supplies – excuse me, Bob –" He nodded to the lab-coated operator and consulted the clipboard hanging at the console's side – "Ah, yes. This is of direct interest to the lads in the field; we're performing massive irradiations of standard field rations to find whether the flavour is harmed by, say, neutron attack. Today's test sample is dehydrated SY-1 ration, and if it tastes all right we'll know that neutron-bombed servicemen will be able to enjoy one last tasty reconstituted strawberry yoghurt before the radiation poisoning gets to them. Roy here is our computer genius and theoretical whizkid, and did the simulations; he'll be glad to explain the neutron transport theory to you on our way to the next building ..."

So as they left SLIMER, Tappen (who'd been meaning to let slip that the M actually stood for Mediocre, punishing strawberry yoghurt being about the limit of SLIMER's capabilities) was forced into eloquent recitations of "Er, you see," and "Well, it's like this." It seemed to take hours.

Entering the blockhouse called 334b, one of the craggier and more intimidating of the sightseers finally asked a question.

"What exactly *is* a neutron?" he said.

Tappen resisted an inviting line of explanation which led up to how scientists on twelve pints of beer a day were all as pissed as neutrons. "It's an elementary particle with no charge ... like a Freepost letter."

A look of slow dissatisfaction began to spread over the craggy military features. Ahead like some dreadful conversational crevasse Tappen sensed what was to come. What were elementary particles? It's a generic term covering protons, neutrons, electrons and so on. Well, what are *they*? Er, elementary particles, actually, old chap; easier to explain the Nature of the Mind of God or how many angels could dance on a military pinhead.

He was saved by a flight of stairs they climbed in single file, to yet another control room, gleaming even more than its predecessors with high-tech white and chrome. A barely audible groan leaked from somewhere unspecific within the little knot of VIPs. Little did they realize that so far it was standard Fortmayne/ Staverton procedure to tour the glistening and deeply boring control rooms while avoiding the wonders of what they controlled. Visitors might be disillusioned by the appalling places where real experiments took place – where integrated circuits lay squashed like multi-legged insects on the grimy floor, festoons of wires ran up and down the walls like ivy or extended snaky feelers to trip you up, DANGER RADIATION signs hung at an angle on one strip of peeling sellotape, if they hadn't fallen to lie invisible among junked equipment in corners where spiders spun their webs ...

Luckily 334b was a showcase laboratory, containing the suavest, nicest to look at and most old-fashioned of all the NUTC reactors. A wall-sized window gazed out over a hall with the air of a primitive temple, where scurrying acolytes did worshipful things thirty feet below to propitiate the featureless central idol which towered over them all like the Heidelberg Tun or a similar alcoholic fantasy.

Fortmayne led the party through a steel door and out along white-painted catwalks to the thing's rim. Tappen brought up the rear and could hear him lecture: "SPERA ... swimming-pool experimental reactor assembly ... six megawatt nuclear reaction at the bottom ... no, no, quite safe, the water moderates the reactor and cools it *and* screens radiation ... you can spend up to ten minutes here ... take a good look down ... resist the opportunity for a refreshing plunge bath ..."

And very pretty it was, the warm blue water coming to within six inches of their feet, intricacies of gleaming steel tubing plunging into the depths as if probing for North Sea oil, and there near the bottom, pouring from and surrounding the squat bulk of the uranium core, a hellish blue glow of Cherenkov radiation that lit the water like some dazzling undersea effect in a James Bond film but far, far more expensive.

"Yes, yes, we could heat all of Robinson Heath with the power generated here ... no, we don't actually *do* that, we throw it all away as waste heat, this was built before the energy crisis was invented and it's too late to convert it now.... I don't agree with what you're saying, this is valuable basic research ... for example SPERA's slow neutrons are stopped more by light atoms – in water – than by heavy ones, so we can take exciting neutron radiographs like these of daffodils snapped through six inches of lead ..."

Fortmayne didn't mention, no doubt because VIPs would think it frivolous, that expenses were slightly defrayed by a deal with a Hatton Garden jeweller. At the bottom of one of those steel sample tubes, in a hailstorm of neutrons, there would usually be a little bag of diamonds: after a while the neutrons did unspeakable things to their atomic structure and they went yellow, which for mysterious reasons known only to jewellers made them more valuable. You had to be careful not to leave the stones too long, since even as novelty items the Hatton Garden experts said there was no market for black diamonds.

"If you dropped so much as a screwdriver or a tuppence down there we'd have to shut SPERA down in case it damaged the core

... If you fell in yourself? No, wouldn't shut down for that, not if you floated. Fish you out, scrub you off, that's all."

For some reason this seemed to disconcert the sightseers. Fortmayne looked at his watch and said, "Time presses, time presses, we've still more calls to make," and in single file they trooped back along the catwalk. Tappen felt a moment of nostalgia which metamorphosed into nameless dread. Ten years or so before, he as a new Scientific Officer had been shown the mysteries of Robinson Heath, control room after wonderful control room, and it was surprising how little had changed. Therefore ...

A minute outside in the weakening sun (which still hurt the eyes after too long in evenly lit temples of technocracy) and they reached the plutonium handling labs – extra security pass checks, everyone into white coats and floppy overshoes. DO NOT TOUCH ANYTHING WHATEVER YOU DO OR HORRIBLE THINGS WILL HAPPEN LIKE ALL OF YOU HAVING TO BE AMPUTATED. The plutonium innards of nuclear weaponry lay there for all to see, spread out in perspex-walled cabinets, as though at a cafeteria serve-yourself counter. However, as would probably improve the average motorway-services caff no end, these cabinets were firmly sealed. Fortmayne explained the merry English Roulette fun of fingering the stuff inside using long rubber gloves built into the boxes: you juggled bits of extreme unpleasantness (he demonstrated) and hoped the glove seals didn't chance to fail.

The five looked suitably intimidated, especially at Fortmayne's casual explanation that all you needed for a fatal criticality incident and radiation overdose was to let a few pieces of plutonium close enough together. "Nature then takes its course," carolled Fortmayne, holding two lumps at a just-safe distance in his gloved hands. The craggy visitor backed away so far as to bump into another glove-box, lurched forward in new alarm and might have gone into perpetual back-and-forth oscillation if Tappen hadn't crowded him against the others as he moved towards Fortmayne.

He whispered: "Er, Mike, I remember this tour. You finish by letting them fondle the dummy in Lab Two, don't you?"

"You're saying I'm stupid, aren't you, Roy? I know perfly, perfectly well where the dummy is – they can have a look at it right there and hear about the Manoeuvre while they're at it. Make a change."

"Then I'd better warn Joe Llewellyn to get his arse in gear and be ready to unlock his boot, hadn't I?" whispered Tappen, and hared off before he could be crushed by a reasonable, impossible reply such as "Why bother? We'll collect him on the way –"

After several near-collisions with trolleys carrying sinister cargo between the sprawling lines of Pu handling boxes, Tappen managed to find a telephone.

"... One-eight-two-eight. Redbury Municipal Abattoirs here."

"Joe. I don't suppose you've got round to shifting that stuff yet?" said Tappen hopefully.

"Bloody hell. Haven't got round to it, he says. Every last blasted lead block has been shifted from my boot as per R. Tappen's instructions. I'm sitting here groaning with arthritis and lead poisoning, and gout and you name it. Practically in shock. System crash. Be days before I can lift heavy teacups again."

"Ahhh. Joe. I have some good news and some bad news. The good news is that I'm buying you lots of drinks tonight, you lucky fellow. The bad news ... look, can you get it all back in *your* car boot in ten minutes. If I remember Mike Fortmayne's spiel on the Fat Man Effect, that's just about as long as you've got. Seriously. Jump to it *now*."

Llewellyn seemed to be having some difficulty in talking, as though the effort of humping assorted hardware had strained his vocal chords. Though fascinated by what sounded like the death rattle of a Pekinese with cleft palate, Tappen put the receiver tactfully down.

"... the Fat Man Effect," Fortmayne was saying with a great air of spontaneity. "You've never heard of it? As I was saying up on the diving-board (that's what we scientists call the SPERA catwalk), the hydrogen in the water around the core has a 'moderating' effect on the nuclear reaction. Take the water away and SPERA stops working. Now it seems that this American lab had a bare reactor, one with extra uranium so the water wasn't needed, and one day they took out some of the fuel rods by remote control and went in to inspect it, half a dozen of them. The amusing thing is that they were American scientists with these big potbellies, all water and fat full of hydrogen atoms, and lo and behold, as soon as they were all standing close around this little reactor core, it went critical and the radiation level started to go sky-high. Counters clicking; alarms ringing, I'm told no one had ever seen overweight Americans move so fast. The Fat Man Effect. What's that you're saying? Oh, I think they all survived, nearly."

The VIPs, and in particular the two modestly potbellied ones, edged yet further from the plutonium boxes.

"All ready ahead," he told Fortmayne.

"Roy, there was really no need; you're far too impetuous ... Gentlemen, I'm sure you'd love the opportunity for a *really close* look at the warhead core for the Polaris/Chevaline upgrade system. Just follow me."

Judging by the glances the plumper visitors exchanged, there was a vague lack of enthusiasm about getting *really close*. A hell of a world where even if you were quite conscientious about the jogging, the nuclear flab-detectors of modern science could at any moment arise and smite you.

The smallest and roundest of them all fell into step with Tappen at the rear of the procession, and unbent slightly. It occurred to Tappen that it must take lashings of concealed personality and drive to achieve the dizzy status of Jntsecmegdeth or equivalent while being not in the least imposing or craggy-faced.

"You know," said the unimposing one, "this world of science you people live in is so different. I suppose you see lumps of – plute, is that what you say? How charming – you see it every day. This was my first time, and there it was behind the glass, and it looks like a bit of old tarnished scrap metal, that's all. You'd expect it to glow purple or something."

Tappen forebore to mention the time he'd slipped luminous paint into Llewellyn's urine-sample bottle, to the horror of Health Physics staff when they boiled it down and happened to study the result in a shady room. The other was still talking:

"I suppose you scientists really appreciate what a nuclear explosion means," he said wistfully. "Some of you have even seen one. You have this detailed mental picture of the fireball all in technicolour, the circles of destruction spreading out, the smashed cities, the millions of fatalities, the fallout liquidating enemy personnel miles and miles away ..."

He licked his lips.

"No," said Tappen, who today felt hypersensitive and suspicious of PV traps in any shape or form. "We scientists mostly concentrate on our research. I mean, if Isaac Newton had spent his time thinking ahead to apple pie he mightn't have worked out the law of gravity and made the apple fall ..."

"Oh. I see." The VIP sounded at the same time mildly disappointed and mildly relieved. Tappen merely felt mildly unclean.

The rabbit-befouled tarmac paths between the huts and buildings of 334 complex were warm and yielding in the hazy sunlight; the air clung close, sticky and humid. But even in Death Valley or the Amazonian rain-forest, the gasping Llewellyn would have looked unusually overheated and sweaty. He glared at Tappen as with leisured indolence the party sauntered up to the dung-coloured Ford.

"Good heavens," Fortmayne said mildly. "If you still look like that two hours after a spot of fetching and carrying, you aren't well enough to be at work at all."

Llewellyn said something that sounded like "Nnnnng," and favoured Tappen with another malevolent look before turning to open the Ford's boot. Tappen rather thought that seconds before they came round the corner of the 334p fuel store, he'd heard that same boot slam shut. Such timing, such timing!

"If you would just lift off the upper layer of blocks, Joseph," said Fortmayne casually. Breathing hard and growing pinker and pinker, as if some internal safety valve were close to blowing, Llewellyn obeyed. Tappen suppressed a remark about the way sitting at computer terminals made you flabby and out of condition; he didn't leap forward to his colleague's aid since, as matters now stood, it seemed all too likely that should he come within range, one of the massive leaden bricks would semi-accidentally get dropped on his foot.

"Here you are," said Fortmayne expansively, as Llewellyn

reeled away exhibiting the symptoms of rickets and whooping-cough. "This is the heart of the whole weapon system, the aluminium-cased plutonium core, the pit as we call it, the central gadget which when properly triggered and collapsed makes what in the esoteric terminology of science we call a *very loud bang* ... No, no, this is perfectly safe," he added, just in time to prevent the VIPs scattering for the horizon. "It is in fact a dummy weighted and loaded with a harmless radioisotope source to accurately simulate the real thing." The audience relaxed somewhat, free from the threat of a Moderately Plump Man Effect or of Fortmayne's accidentally pulling some problematic trigger.

"Perfectly safe," said the showman, heaving the thing into the air and catching it. He swung it in a rugby pass to Tappen, who ostentatiously caught it one-handed and passed it to his small, plump interlocutor. Each of the VIPs hefted it dubiously and without pause handed it to the next: *What's the fastest game in the world?* Tappen remembered Munt asking in paroxysms of glee, almost as if he knew what paroxysms meant: *Pass-the-parcel in a Belfast pub, har har har!* The hugest and craggiest one gave it finally to the still panting Llewellyn, who with seeming scientific deliberation coughed and dropped it.

"Very interesting," said Small and Plump nervously, wiping his hands several times on his trousers.

"I'm most intrigued by your unusual launch vehicle," said Huge and Craggy, examining the decrepit Ford. "Is this a new sophisticated cruise missile design we haven't heard about?"

"You can put those blocks back now, Joseph, thank you very much ... No, gentlemen, this is all part of a little military manoeuvre we're planning. All very confidential, naturally ..." He went on to explain the great smuggling game, while Llewellyn, moving as though with one foot in the grave and the other stuck fast in quicksand, replaced the final blocks in Fortmayne's grand design – for the fourth time, calculated Tappen as he realized the heartbreaking need to tell Joe Llewellyn that the famous spheroid should be inside the shielding and by no means lying sad and neglected amid the endemic rabbit turds.

Llewellyn was too weakened even to snarl when Tappen picked

the thing up and made tiny, tactful hem-hem noises. With the slumped mournfulness of a maltreated dumb animal he began to lift out lead bricks once again.

"So much for that," Fortmayne was saying. "And now I'm sure you'd all like a cup of real British Civil Service tea."

"You've seen our nuclear strike capability, now taste what we can do with chemical warfare," Tappen explained. "I'll just stay and give Joe a hand."

"No, no, no," said Fortmayne airily. "You come along with us, Roy, I'd like you to tell our guests about your own project work. A few well-chosen remarks under the overall title *Mañana*. Joseph's nearly finished in any case."

Helplessly Tappen tagged along after the departing group, afraid he'd hear Llewellyn's limp body slump with a final, sickening thud to the ground. The donkey-work, alas, was some way off being finished, since now the whole lot would once again have to be shifted to ... oh dear. Before turning the corner around 334p he called back: "As many drinks as you like! See you later! This'll be the last time, I promise!"

He rounded the corner, slightly shaken. What he'd just seen in Llewellyn's eyes he'd always thought a figment of over-emotional thriller writers: a crazed red glare of bloodlust. Perhaps after all his labours they were merely bloodshot.

Unless they had the most unbelievably bad luck with gate security, this evening should see the end of the trouble. Tappen crossed his fingers and touched the wood of a passing window-sill. He wasn't superstitious, but he'd heard these things helped whether you were superstitious or not.

Thirteen

"Bad luck we should happen to pick on you," Alf Rossiter said with offhand solicitude, leaning on a patched area of the Volvo's wing which, Tappen hoped, might quite conceivably crumble beneath his weight and do him an injury.

"It almost looks like coincidence," said Tappen, pointedly staring at Llewellyn's car, which had been called off the road just ahead of Tappen's own. Both were almost invisible amid an antlike swarm of blue uniforms. Curious glances kept coming from the drivers of other cars which moved out through the northeast gate of Robinson Heath in an unhindered double line. What vile criminals had been pounced on by the NUTC's tirelessly efficient security force? KGB moles, perhaps, caught red-handed and red-politicked in the act of smuggling out the secret blueprints for constructing Margaret Thatcher?

"Tightening up, tightening up all the time," Rossiter said.

"Yes. Yes, I remember the old slack days of long ago, like last week, when you'd look into every fourth or fifth car. I bet all those people zooming past are really sweating now you've clamped down on them like this."

Rossiter winked again. "Sorry mate. Word gets around ... you're sitting doing your duty and you hear some smart bugger on the Science side is cooking up crafty plans to make you look a bit of a tit: you take some extra care, that's what you do. Nothing personal, now."

An undersized and pained-looking young security officer, the one Tappen had met at the gate on the day his troubles began, extricated himself from a spelaeological investigation of the Volvo's underside. "Nothing," he reported, blinking and blinking again. "Rust keeps falling in your eyes under there. Some people don't

97

look after their cars very well."

Tappen regretted the missed opportunity to tread on him. "It's a security precaution," he said, "against light-fingered lads who crawl under cars to steal valuable exhausts or differential gears. Can I just look through your pockets now? Fair do's, you looked through mine."

"I – I –" The pink young fellow displayed all the shock and outrage of royalty invited to take a turn at washing the dishes.

"Never mind, son," Rossiter soothed. "Go and take a butcher's under the other one. – You shouldn't say things like that to the lads, Roy. They've got their pride."

"So had I until I started working here."

Ahead the hue and cry was raised. Despite all his low cunning the notorious Joe Llewellyn had been found out. A double ring of blue uniforms surrounded the malefactor as a sergeant flayed him with stern words. A pencil, it seemed, had been found in Llewellyn's pocket, or rather a pencil-stub, but though a mere three inches long its markings proclaimed it the property of a jealous government. Shameless theft, wanton pilferage, premeditated larceny ...

Eventually Llewellyn was let off with a reprimand, and Tappen breathed again. The MoD Police retired in fairly good order, though not without injuries: the young one had burnt the tip of his nose on Llewellyn's pendulum-like exhaust pipe, another had sustained small cuts while probing a jagged hole in the bodywork for hidden cruise missiles, a third had acquired a bashfully blushing complexion after disappearing in clouds of steam when he followed a particularly enticing trail of clues to inside the radiator cap. ("Yes, it overheats rather quickly," Llewellyn had explained helpfully.)

"Should be feeling dead proud of yourself getting such a clean bill of health," said Rossiter not entirely happily. Tappen watched three large Transit vans hurtle through the gateway like InterCity expresses, closely followed by Fortmayne's lovingly tended Granada, and permitted himself a slow, mysterious smile. "No chance of slipping anything past you," he said with such false sincerity that Rossiter demanded a look inside his as yet unsearched wallet. The atmosphere was not improved by the sinister slip of paper Tappen had typed and placed there weeks before, for just such an occasion, only to forget its existence: *Trouble with unhygienic security police? Have them disposed of cleanly and efficiently by ZAPFUZZ, the vermin control experts who care. Call Redbury 314519 today!* Actually the number belonged to the local Scientologists. It had seemed a good idea at the time.

"Ha," Rossiter said distinctly; and, after an interval, "ha."

"Er, toodle-oo," Tappen said and got into his car. Ho for the wide open spaces, the pale synthetic beer of the Mushroom Cloud, and an approaching end to all the worries of a home nuclear stockpile –

Fortmayne had reached the Cloud's car-park first, of course, and Tappen parked as close as he plausibly could – also of course. An inert and shattered Llewellyn was extracting himself from his own vehicle as if from an iron lung.

"I should kill you," he said weakly as he caught up with Tappen at the pub door. "I should pull your head off and eat your heart and dance on your grave. Only I couldn't put the boot into a green-fly after today. A small greenfly."

"I'll get you a beer. I said I would."

"Don't suppose I'll be able to lift it. You see this piece of limp dangling spaghetti? It used to be an arm once. You see these ugly bruised sausage things like bits of Dr Moreau's rejects? Once I called them my fingers. You see –"

"Drink," said Tappen firmly, and led the way in.

Fortmayne was brooding over a riotous half-pint in one corner. "Did you succeed?"

"Oh yes, of course," Tappen said.

"I'm glad to hear that. I had the impression that I saw you being searched."

"Ah, we outsmarted them with scientific cunning. They were putty in our hands. We could have slipped out whole filing – the whole SPERA outfit if we'd tried."

"No doubt. You're saying the, ahem, is in your car now? I must see it for myself, of course, so I can vouch for that." He began to stand, but Tappen interjected, "Beer first," and made for the bar.

Soon they were congenially discussing the awfulness of security police, and Fortmayne's habitual sober responsibility was developing new cracks at the vision of the one with a neat round blister on the end of his nose.

"You look as though you want to go to the toilet, Joe," Tappen said hopefully.

"No, no, after you, your need is greater than mine," Llewellyn countered, glaring.

"Don't you owe me – thanks." Two flat pieces of metal passed from hand to hand, and Tappen slipped out before Fortmayne could start worrying about unspeakable assignations in the Gents or whatever else the PV interrogators might have put into his head.

The pieces of metal were standard car keys, one with code number FT451, curiously similar to one of the bunch Fortmayne had left as usual on his desk that morning. Whistling a casually innocent little tune which would have made a spring lamb or new-hatched chick instantly and deeply suspicious, he sauntered to the blood-red Granada and opened the boot. Poor old Joe, shifting this lot to and fro all afternoon to spare Fortmayne the awful truth that he'd been nominated as Trojan horse. Poor old Alf, assuming quite correctly that Fortmayne wouldn't be party to such childish manoeuvres, and not bothering to stop *him* ... It'll be the work of a moment sorting this out, now.

Ten minutes later his clothes felt like the interior of a sauna. He'd crushed a fingertip between two lead blocks. He'd nearly dropped the "football" twice. But all was safely stowed in the Llewellyn Ford, and it only remained to cover the spoils with a tastefully arranged lab coat, stashed in Fortmayne's boot for that very purpose, after which he could –

"You!"

As his heart tried to escape by hitting some internal ejector-seat button, Tappen wondered whether to run, to pretend to have a fit, to dive into the boot and pull it shut after him. He stood there.

"It was you, you were here last week, you hoaxed me. Let me tell you I'm not very happy about that," spluttered whatsisname – Green – from the *Redbury Chronicle*.

It could be worse.

"I'm really sorry," Tappen said a little unevenly. "I meant to tell you straight away so we could all have a laugh, but you dashed off so quickly."

"A likely story. Oh, all right, you needn't look like you're facing the firing squad. Guilty conscience, eh?"

"If you must know, I've just smuggled out a nuclear weapon from the site. You can touch it if you like."

"Ha flaming ha. Pull the other one, it rings Kent Treble Bob Major."

"All right, all right, read about it next week in the *News of the World* instead. Tell you one thing about the power of the mighty *Chronicle*: after you ran that story, the NUTC recruiting office was swamped. Even the horror of drinking twelve pints of beer a day can't deter our brave English lads."

"Bollocks," said Green, seeming slightly mollified. "Give me a real story someday, eh? Robinson Heath's the only place in this bloody awful county where you can hope for a whiff of news, and that Press Officer: gorblimey. His lips aren't just sealed, they're stitched together, superglued, spotwelded, must feed him through a tube up his nose."

Tappen grinned as he casually slammed the Ford's boot shut, leaving huge, wet, sweaty, casual handprints on it. "I'll give you a story," he confided. "Get this down in your shorthand book: my superior officer, Michael Fortmayne, PhD, PSO, likes two lumps of sugar in his tea! – No, seriously. That's *information gained in the performance of my official duties*, that is, official duties such as making him tea. And as such its divulgence is covered by the Official Secrets Act, and if they had a grudge against me they could throw the book at me for telling you that. Isn't British justice wonderful? And that, my friend, is why the Press Officer clears every syllable he says with three different MoD departments, otherwise he might end up ... well, whatever's the legal equivalent of receiving a retirement gift of concrete socks before being dropped gently outside the three-mile limit."

"Could work something up from that," Green said, scribbling in dextrous shorthand and then frowning as he apparently rewrote his notes the slow way just to make sure.

"Well, if you do, make bloody sure you don't rabbit on about your informant Roy. Call him Marmaduke or Theophilus ... Excuse me. Somewhere in there a pint mug is dying a horrible slow lingering death, poisoned by contact with Fairey's Bitter, and I must rush to its aid. 'Bye."

"Oh, goodbye. Would that be Marmaduke with a C or a K ...?"

In the bar Tappen found the others chatting on the perennially tedious subject of cars. Once he'd thought car bores the worst of all bores in creation, that being back in the palmy days before the awful emergence of the home-computer bore ... but the first words he heard from Fortmayne held him with weird fascination. "You're saying you have this road-holding trouble? My own car felt most peculiar on the way here, as though I was steering with a ton of lead in the back. Rear suspension looked down a bit, too, but surely –"

"Optical illusion," Llewellyn said confidently. "Noticed that kind of thing myself, after a hard afternoon's work. A pint of beer calms you down; bet that car feels much better when you get back on the road. – Hi Roy, what kept you? Must have been your longest pee in years, you should have saved it for Health Physics."

"Oh, it's the Fairey Liquid," Tappen said, still limp with exhaustion and relief. "One day I'll get the Nobel Prize for my work on the physics of time reversal – the secret's in this beer, the only one that makes you ill *before* it makes you drunk."

"Obviously you haven't been to America," Fortmayne said.

"Have another, both of you – since I'm standing up. Flush out the system the way it said in the *Chronic*."

"No thanks," said Fortmayne. "Yes," said Llewellyn. "Oh well, just one," said Fortmayne.

By and by they moved into the car park; Fortmayne studied the squat and slightly dishevelled heap of blocks in Llewellyn's boot, made offensive remarks about the ability of retarded three-year-olds to do a neater job with matchboxes, peered at the football-shaped thing inside, and half-turned to go.

"Wait one minute," he said. "This is your idea, Roy, and you should be the one to present the goods at the gate tomorrow morning. Let's just quickly shift this into the back of your car; we can do it in a moment."

Translation: the barely recovered Llewellyn and the still aching Tappen had the inestimable privilege of doing all the work, while Fortmayne displayed managerial skills such as observing, "Look out, you'll drop it on his foot," with such uncanny timing that he reached the last word at precisely the same instant that the lead block under discussion met Tappen's foot.

As Tappen drove home, though, the dull pain of each pressure on the clutch, and the uneasy sensation of steering with a ton of lead in the back, were blotted out by general ecstasy – by the thought that, tomorrow, it would all be over. He could hardly wait to tell Lizzie ...

"The way I see it," said Lizzie unfeelingly, "is that tonight we have two of the things. Darling. It's enough to give me two head-aches." And she retreated to a corner of the bed so remote as to seem accessible only via long-distance telephone.

Fourteen

Tappen didn't often dream, or forgot most of what he dreamt: just the odd remembered image with all the searing emotional relevance of a stainless steel platypus. But on bad nights he'd drift half-asleep and suffer half-dreams scripted and directed by half-wits, circling in slow motion around some gigantically boring and futile half-truth, leaving him in the morning with half a headache. It was like that in the small hours of Thursday morning: he hazily knew the first of his problems was gently irradiating a cardboard box in the loft, while the second sat for sentimental reasons in the lowest drawer of the filing cabinet, itself a source of added frustration since he'd noticed the identical article in Bogley Surplus Stores for only £30, but the two things were so much *alike* and suppose he got them *mixed up*, which of course he couldn't have since he'd carefully not brought the live one down from the loft just in case, but suppose he'd absent-mindedly *changed them round* ready for the morning, which would have been quite a logical thing to do, in which case he should change them back in case he forgot he'd changed them round, except suppose he changed them back and then remembered changing them round but not changing them back, or vice versa, and now he couldn't remember how many times they'd been changed or confused or unconfused even hypothetically, let alone out there in the horrible cold real world, he'd have to work it out with pencil and paper now, that was the only solution, or program it on his tatty home computer, which would mean getting up, and if he got up could he later be sure he hadn't mucked round with the pit and the dummy ...?

At about this point he'd find himself staring hot-eyed and wholly awake at the dark ceiling, his bladder feeling approximately the size and shape of the Graf Zeppelin, only if he went to the loo he'd wake Lizzie, and somehow he'd force himself back under into the half-world and it would all start again, the pit and the dummy and his bladder and Roger Pell's head all looking so alike, so round, so featureless, so easily confused.

By breakfast time his head felt like the thing in the attic at some nebulous future date, just after being compressed by high explosive to golfball size and just before blossoming out into a cubic mile of flame. His breakfast coffee soused his mouth in foul aftertaste without the usual intermediate step of having a taste; his breakfast egg outstared him coldly, cowing him as jungle beasts are supposed to be cowed by the human eye. Of malice aforethought Lizzie casually referred to the acquaintance who for every meal liked Weetabix crumbled over boiled potatoes, and Tappen stumbled from the kitchen in rout.

The loft, the string bag, the tailgate space of the Volvo. Tappen handled the weapon core very gingerly indeed; it was something dull, mundane, quotidian at Robinson Heath but all too alarming at home, like the difference between a hungry tiger in Whipsnade and a hungry tiger lurking under one's bed. For many long minutes it seemed staggeringly improbable that he could ever drive safely to work with *that* load. A moment's carelessness, the caprice of metal fatigue, a burst tyre, a brief stroke, coronary or epileptic fit, a falling mass of jagged frozen turds ejected from the toilets of a jumbo jet far off in the stratosphere: anything could happen, and that was without considering the gibbering lunacies of other road-users. He was still considering them, in a cold sweat, as his reflexes steered him safely and obliviously into the visitors' car park outside the main gate of NUTC.

On foot, but keeping a cautious eye on the Volvo for fear of its being towed away or scooped up by some passing UFO, he moved to the glass enclosure where very important visitors were rudely delayed to remind them they were only mortal. The duty office at the counter agreed to take a message.

"So that's it, eh?" said Sergeant Alf Rossiter ten minutes later, staring into the back of the car. "Can't say I've ever seen one of them before, mate. Can't say I'm too pleased to see one now."

Tappen recognized the tone and almost expected to hear him

go on: *"Course I'm not exactly on form, Roy me boy. Buggered up my wrist, gardening."* At squash, Rossiter wasn't a particularly good loser – or winner.

"I'd have thought they'd show you photos in glorious technicolour," Tappen suggested. "Things To Look For In Suspicious Characters' Y-Fronts."

"Not on your nelly. No clearance for the likes of me. So. So you slipped chummie here right under our noses yesterday, did you now?"

"That's it," Tappen said nervously, and launched into a short and polysyllabic lecture on radiation screening, lead blocks, cadmium shields, lunchtime, and the peculiar brilliance of R. Tappen. Fleetingly he hoped he wasn't this insufferable when he won at squash.

The speech over, Rossiter pulled out a grey plastic transceiver. "232 Rossiter calling Police One, 232 Rossiter calling Police One ... Charlie, you need to turn up the spotters, give 'em all you've got ... Yeah, I know, but one of those sodding eggheads has come up with something ..." (He stepped back to appraise Tappen's car.) "And Charlie, we need a footnote to SOP, the lads on the gates want to keep an eye out for cars a bit low on the old rear suspension ... You've got it. 232 Rossiter signing off ... sod that, I'll report in half an hour ... 232 Rossiter signing *off.*"

"Very efficient. Instant loophole-plugging. You should have been a plumber, or a little Dutch boy."

But Rossiter appeared to be thinking, an effort of which Tappen didn't normally suspect him. "Do me a favour, Roy, and come along o'me to the gate – no, in the old banger, I'll just pace you with the red flag, right?"

Warily Tappen let the Volvo creep forward in first gear: Rossiter walked backwards just ahead of him, making come-on gestures, and the temptation was great to give the accelerator one hard accidental push. *Wheeeeeeeeeeeeeeeeeeee!* Instead his reflexes hit the brake, as the siren ran small red-hot needles into his eardrums, and ahead the automatic barrier crashed down but unfortunately missed Rossiter.

"Pull away, Roy, nice and easy – off to the side – that's it, and now we'll have a little heart-to-heart."

"I suppose that's 'turning up the spotters'? The r/a detection system?" Tappen asked warily.

"Mmm. Too many false alarms when we turned them right up high, but *you* had to be a clever prat and prove we need 'em set that way. Got you that time, though, eh? Cadbury's shielding and all?"

"Oh yes, great stuff. Nobody'll dare wear a luminous watch after this. Turn it off now for half a minute, Alf, it's time I rushed to my desk and saved the nation from the Soviet menace."

Rossiter stood there unmoving, leaning on the Volvo's roof, his face looming close and unsavoury at the driver's window. "Not ... just ... yet, chummie. I been thinking, Roy, thinking about clever buggers' tricks and why Mr Roy Tappen has got the jitters now when all the awkward smuggling's over."

"Come off it, Alf, I'm just worrying about an appointment I'm going to miss if you keep nattering any longer."

"Now, word came to my shell-like ears," Rossiter said as though Tappen hadn't spoken, "that some bright ideas got talked about at a certain meeting. About SAS men and laying groundwork sort of in advance, if you see what I mean."

"Surely your clearance wouldn't let you hear such things," Tappen said rather desperately.

"Clearance? I should need clearance for a little innocent chat about a meeting at – let's say the MoD Police Club? Fancy that. Like I was saying, I got to thinking about advance work, and why me old mate Roy should be sweating in his car this fine morning. I thought, suppose Roy decided to fiddle the odds and set up a game he couldn't lose? Suppose he never had to take a nasty out of NUTC at all because he tossed off this mock-up I dunno where, some workshop outside, maybe? A dummy NUTC never got to see, with a pinched lab r/a source, could be. I mean, I thought, that would sort of explain why Roy and his mate were clean when the boys gave them the once-over yesterday, only suddenly today he's back with the goods. You follow me, Roy my lad?"

"Effortlessly," said Tappen. "Honestly, Alf, I admire the way you project your low, scheming mental processes onto innocents like me. Have you finished now?"

It was all too apparent that Rossiter hadn't finished. In the slow, grinding advance of his mental workings there was something of that fascination one might feel at the sight of mating hippopotami or the inexorable forward surge of the Vatnajökull glacier.

"So suppose I make a little bet with you, Roy, with maybe a pint of lager on the side. Suppose we take that dummy down to the machine shop and have them cut it open, just in a friendly way, and they'll be referees – say whether it's one of theirs or whether it's the home-made job my nasty mind thinks. Fair's fair. What d'you say to that, Roy?" He was smiling a horribly unanswerable smile, and the wisp of moustache looked more Hitleresque than ever.

Tappen's head filled with white flashes of shock, as though a mad herd of press photographers was stampeding inside. All he had to do was say Yes and nobody would ever again mention Three Mile Island: the classic nuclear cock-up would be the Tappen Incident, an entire machine shop horribly contaminated with neat plutonium, estimated death roll now 57 not including the vile perpetrator Tappen who flushed himself down a nearby toilet in guilt and shame ...

"Fair enough," he said at last, conscious that all the blood in his body seemed to be taking cover under his socks. "I'll have to ask permission first, of course: even the dummies aren't cheap. You see that."

"Phone's in the Glasshouse," said a slightly disappointed-looking Rossiter, indicating the VIP quarantine pen where Tappen had met him several war-torn millennia ago, or fifteen minutes by the soulless, lying clocks.

"No no no no. I – I've got that appointment, at home, let in the plumber. Must dash; I'll call 334 Inventory Control from there and get their say-so. See you?"

Rossiter was probably saying something in response to this farrago, but already Tappen had thrown the Volvo into reverse for a swift about-turn. In the rear mirror he thought he saw lips working like worms under the loathed moustache; then he was through the gate and burning up the miles between NUTC and Redbury, lurching and weaving to avoid the deadly stream of hot lead from Rossiter's machine-gun tower – get a grip on your imagination, Tappen. By now he was regarding the latest version of his Master Plan with the same revulsion inspired by a technical report five times drafted, five times corrected and disimproved by Staverton's too-eager hand, and now clinging greasily to the desk like old chip wrappers ... It was too shopworn, too maddeningly familiar.

The easy answer was the good old Trojan Horse routine, he decided, fighting back the image of an enormous wooden Polaris left enticingly outside NUTC for the curious gate police to drag within. The dummy from the filing cabinet at home would be perched in Fortmayne's leaden commode at the back of the car, the real thing stowed unobtrusively under the seat. All the while he was driving with a random alternation of panicky haste and deadly caution, howling on two wheels round dangerous corners and a few seconds later slowing to a guilty crawl for stretches of empty road wide enough for jumbo jet takeoffs.

What could possibly go wrong? With murmurs of "Nothing up my sleeve," he'd offer Alf Rossiter a lift to the machine shop, allowing him to keep an eye on the dummy every inch of the way; the alarms would have to be turned off to let them through, and in would go the important contraband at the same time. For a moment he imagined Rossiter unreasonably refusing to accept the lift and demanding that they both *walk* to E (for Engineering) section, perhaps handcuffed together: but, he reminded himself, the things that went wrong were always those you hadn't thought of before, so *that* problem surely wouldn't come up now. It stood to reason, just like Tappen's unshakable conviction that he could conjure cloudbursts at will by walking on a grey afternoon without his umbrella.

Though at this stage he was almost equally convinced that he could produce far huger difficulties and disasters merely by breathing or allowing his heart to beat ...

By the time he pulled up outside 33 Rutland Gardens he was imagining more and more esoteric snags. Suppose the house had been burgled and the dummy dropped on the Corporation tip where Alf Rossiter would find it when he went to dispose of ten gross of empty gin bottles from the MoDP tea-hut? Suppose, for that matter, that a real policeman took an interest in his car? "Excuse me, sir, but I think your back tyres could do with some more air." TAPPEN (damp-browed, ashen-faced): "Oh ha ha, nothing to worry about, just some heavy stuff in the back." POLICEMAN (keen nostrils scenting the whiff of guilt and fear): "Really, sir? Mind if I just take a look?"

Tappen got out of the car, checked the locks, checked them again in case he'd missed one the first time, mopped his forehead with a handkerchief in which half an hour ago, he remembered too late, he'd copiously blown his nose; and went irritably into the house. He needed coffee.

Ten minutes later, gulps of oversugared brew were twingeing his fillings, scalding his throat, overstimulating his nerves and generally doing him much-needed harm. His feet were idly rolling the thing from the filing cabinet to and fro across the living-room floor; with his free hand, a sudden impulse, he was twirling the telephone dial. Might as well warn Carol about the mysterious absence of Tappen in 334d so far this morning. Besides, it meant another few minutes' delay before yet another queasy journey through the bumpy lanes to Bogley.

"... Carol? It's Roy here, Roy Tappen ... No I have not got a hangover, I can only afford one a month on my salary. No, I'm tied up in some Security complications, nothing I can talk about on the phone. I should be free by about ten-thirty. Tell Mike Fortmayne and Joe Llewellyn, could you?" That was enough to calm his conscience; but Carol remembered that Llewellyn urgently wanted a word with Tappen.

"Can't be that urgent," he said, drinking more coffee and absently trying to lift the heavy metal sphere between his feet as he sat by the phone. Hands occupied with coffee-mug and handset, the suppressed urge to doodle was transferred to his toes. "Oh, all right, I might as well hold his hand if he's got troubles. Can you transfer the call?"

Carol could. There were the usual beeps and silences and

random snatches of conversation classified "burn before listening to". Meanwhile Tappen found he could by power of foot alone lift the not-quite-a-football more than eighteen inches off the ground before it slipped and thudded massively to the carpet. He tried again.

"Joe? Joe, it's Roy here. What's the trouble?"

Llewellyn's voice sounded a little odd. "You're offsite, aren't you? Not come in yet?"

"That's right. I called Carol and she said you were running round in little circles wiggling your fingers and going wugga-wugga-wugga. More computer trouble?"

"You ... You could say that. Little bug in the machine code. Roy, you remember that dud computer program we were talking about in the Mushroom Cloud last night? With all the *dummy variables*? That one?"

Use guarded language on the telephone, Tappen remembered approvingly. "The one I took home, you mean? I'm just coming back with it."

"Yeah, well, take good care of it. Just one of those little bugs, you know, but it looks like the dud version got sent somewhere else. You've got a *fully operational*, er, program printout there, if you see what I mean. Not a dummy at all. Like I said, a little mistake in the filing. Sorry about that. So be careful, eh? Are you there, Roy? Hello?"

The muscles of Tappen's legs had abruptly gone tense and cramped as his stomach deflated with the unspeakable realization of what his feet were cradling ten precarious inches from the floor. Very slowly and painfully he lowered them, and when at last the metal thing touched down on the carpet he pulled away from it as though it were a real-life peril like a cowpat or a too-friendly moulting dog, rather than a mere doomsday weapon.

So now, lucky man favoured above all others, he had two of the damned things. And this was the one Llewellyn had dribbled along the gravelly tarmac outside 334p, which Fortmayne had flung in a dextrous rugby pass, which VIP after VIP had fumbled with ineptly, which Llewellyn had then *dropped*, which Tappen himself had been exposing his delicate toes to, not to mention letting it fall again and again on a thinly carpeted floor ... He shut his eyes.

"Roy? Are you all right there?"

"No," Tappen croaked, and slammed down the phone.

Fifteen

"It was just one of those simple little errors really," Llewellyn said nervously, sitting as usual on the edge of Tappen's desk but swinging his legs with abnormal jerkiness.

"It's probably treason," Tappen said to the unfinished NPIWP draft minutes before him.

"Bit of a joke really. One buggered-up instruction in machine code, and the record-shuffling worked the other way round. See what I mean?"

"There's something special they do to you for treason."

"Like this: instead of twiddling to make sure anyone with a requisition would get a real nasty not the dummy, the program coughed up the dummy, first request that came. Could have happened to anyone."

"I think it's still the death penalty," said Tappen.

"So there were only real ones left when I tried to pull out the dummy, and the dummy's on its way to Nevada. For one of our underground tests."

"Perhaps you get a choice of the rope or the firing squad."

"Yanks are going to have another giggle at British workmanship and that. Half a million or whatever it is for the privilege of going bang in a big hole in Nevada, enough instruments and recorders to give you action replays of every World Cup match, all the proving-ground staff holding their breath a mile from ground zero, and: phut. Can't help laughing."

"Probably the same penalty for accessories before, during and after the fact. We must get round to choosing our last meal some time."

"'Course it's the sort of tiny program error that could happen to anyone," Llewellyn said for perhaps the fiftieth time. "Most people

113

wouldn't even have spotted it, but I thought of it on the bus this morning ... You aren't listening, are you?"

"On the evidence of your Snail Invaders game *you* might get off on a plea of diminished responsibility. Diminished wits ... Of course I'm listening. Each syllable has a golden resonance when I think it may be the last I hear as a free man. I'm listening with all three of my brain cells that aren't either contemplating the roseate future or admiring the programming skills that nearly had a gaggle of engineers tearing into Pandora's Box (if you'll excuse the education) with cold chisels and electric drills. Urrrgh." He shuddered.

"Well, they didn't," Llewellyn said with loathsome pragmatism. "What did you tell Alf Rossiter in the end?"

"I haven't told him anything yet; give me a chance to recover from my morning trauma, will you? This is the general line in the minutes." He picked up a scribbled draft and read: "Item Ten (new subheading): Penetration Manoeuvre."

"Jesus. Sounds like a seduction manual."

"Yes. Dear old Chairman Staverton likes to make jokes like that, I picked the title to give him the chance. Might put him in a better mood for a few nanoseconds. 'A dummy weapon core was successfully transported outward through NUTC security defences, as a result of which the sensitivity of the gate radiation detectors was increased and security improved – the object of the exercise. It was simultaneously established that terrorists and other members of the public would be unable to smuggle nuclear warheads into the establishment without triggering the detection system. Unfortunately it was impossible to comply with a request from MoDP that the dummy in question be subjected to destructive examination to confirm (*insert suitable officialese for 'Tappen didn't cheat the way Rossiter's low mind thinks'*), since while offsite it was regrettably stolen from a briefly unattended vehicle ...'"

Llewellyn whistled. "Sounds like horse-laughs from the Security side and bollockings from Scientific. And you haven't mentioned Roger Pell's balls-up."

"Oh God, what's *he* done? Managed to get caught on the way in with 500 anti-nuke flyers in his surgical corset?"

"No, he did the same as you. Same as Mike Fortmayne, I mean, heh-heh. Furtively creeping out ... Leadlined suitcase thing with a pit inside: they felt his collar at lunchtime and I hear Alf Rossiter was so smug you could smell it from here. Would've told you before, only you kept going on about black caps and nine feet of rope."

Tappen's eyebrows oscillated gently. "Of course they'd turned up the detectors by lunchtime, thanks to me. Score one-all, with our goal disputed by the Security team ... What the devil was Roger up to, getting in on the game?"

"Team spirit," Llewellyn suggested. "He knew us two were marked and getting tackled all the time. Whether we had the ball or not. So he decided to join in and do a sneaky run for goal."

"You watch too much football," Tappen diagnosed, a little unfairly. "But I wonder ..."

Knock. Another withered Security man; somewhere they must keep an endless supply of them in dusty sacks. Stationery Stock Checking. About how much rough drafting paper did Mr Tappen keep on hand in his desk? Oh. Was he aware that a stock of not more than seventeen blank sheets was recommended by the Stationery Wastage Control Committee? Was he aware that the minute paper with Civil Service crests, on which he was drafting his NPIWP minutes, was intended for final fair copies only and that drafts should be restricted to the appropriate lower-quality stationery? (The stuff alluded to failed to resemble toilet paper only in being less sturdy and durable.) How did he come to be in possession of an entire pad of expensive graph paper when last month's internal circular had clearly laid down that such materiel was only to be dispensed one sheet at a time, as required, by the local Admin Office? Meanwhile, that bond paper with the CONFIDENTIAL heading should be treated as confidential and kept securely locked away, even though it hadn't yet been written on. And whose responsibility was the vacant office next door?

Reluctantly Tappen followed into Hacker's old room with all its discouraging memories of filing cabinets: his tormentor forced open the rusted drawers of the unloved cabinet with the grinning face outlined in dents on its left-hand side, and disclosed an Aladdin's cave of TOP SECRET headed paper, polar-coordinate and isometric graph pads, bygone rubber stamps saying things like FOR THE ATTENTION OF THE STAR CHAMBER ONLY (or perhaps Tappen's eyes deceived him) ... With promises that something would be done about all this, he left in a shower of tut-tuts like hail on a tin roof.

"I was dreading what he might say if he inspected the toilet," Tappen said to Llewellyn at last.

"One sheet at a time on signature in triplicate from Admin Office."

"Use both sides of the paper. Replacements will only be issued on receipted return of used sheets, which must be treated as confidential waste ... don't keep changing the subject, I was talking about Pell. If he's got a dummy (and where did he get hold of one?) we need it to keep your shell-game going and maybe to diddle Alf Rossiter if we can sneak it out. Right?"

"What do you mean we, white man?" Llewellyn quoted.

Half an hour of scientific research, which as Tappen observed was what they were being paid to do in 334d all day, established the not very interesting fact that Pell had rushed home after lunch. Tappen theorized that the sudden sirens and barriers had given him such a nervous shock that he needed a soothing afternoon of hobbies like digging geothermal central heating pipes or converting the turds of passing cats into methane for his kitchen stove. Llewellyn was more inclined to think Pell, once his car was soiled by the grubby touch of gate security, had felt a burning need to go home and wash it.

Dropping into Fortmayne's office, which had the appalling cleanliness and order of an operating theatre and much the same level of good cheer, Tappen delivered a heavily censored and slant-ed account of the smuggling manoeuvre's success/failure, falling back on the truth for several small details and leading gently up to the mythical theft of a mythical dummy pit from a car which itself sounded rather mythical, so unconvincing did Tappen find his own first attempt at full-length fiction.

"You WHAT?" Fortmayne began tactfully, and continued according to the old Hollywood precept "start with an earthquake and build up to a climax". Aftershocks were still rumbling between

Tappen's ears ("gross negligence ... promotion prospects ... court of inquiry ...") when he made his escape to be alone with the edifying thought of what Fortmayne might have said if he'd known what had really been smuggled out, twice.

The afternoon passed in a blur, Tappen making the tea and Llewellyn providing the sympathy, while next door in Hacker's former office there were hideous noises of furniture-removal as overalled men – tipped off no doubt by Stationery Stock Control – stripped the room bare and placed the booty in their blue-grey Transit van by a process which sounded like caber-tossing.

"Bugger. Wanted some of that paper for myself," Llewellyn complained.

"About as much use to you as a pocket calculator to Neanderthal man. Writing paper, when your fingers have withered to little stubs good for nothing but prodding teletype keys? Surprised you can hold a pen at all for that Picasso doodle you call a signature."

Llewellyn only grinned. "Like the man said, my fingers are willing but my thumbs are opposed."

"I don't wish to know that ... and if I write one more word on the Trident Ice Lolly nuclear-familiarization scheme I think I'm going to be ill." Tappen wrenched open the desk drawer and brushed the NPIWP draft sheets into it with a sweeping, dramatic gesture; then he doubled up in his chair to pick up the ones which with the agility of seasoned meths-drinkers had headed straight for the floor. "If we tiptoed past Mike Fortmayne's door I could give you a lift and we'd miss the lemming-rush at the gate."

"By about twenty minutes," Llewellyn said cheerfully.

"When I get home I'll be doing some overtime thinking about the problem of reducing nuclear stockpiles. If the Soviets decommission a hundred SS-20s and the Americans scrap the Pershing missile, I'm prepared to disarm 33 Rutland Gardens totally ... when I can work out how."

"Convert them to peaceful uses, swords and ploughshares (whatever a ploughshare actually is – how many of them make a plough I wonder?). Like, um, how long to November the Fifth?"

By now they were out in the open, avoiding the direct line of fire from high-ranking windows and heading for that parking space behind 334p. "A Guy Fawkes nuke would be good practice for Roger P.," Tappen mused. "You know he's got a nuclear shelter in the back garden?"

"Cleverly disguised wine-cellar, more like. Read somewhere local councils daren't refuse planning permission for shelters, not when they've got bigger and better ones of their own so they can nip straight out after the bang and reassess rateable values first thing ... So if you want an underground swimming pool, a squash court, a helicopter pad or whatever in your back garden, call it a shelter when you put in for permission and you've got it."

"I think Roger goes there to practise secret and despicable vices," Tappen said. "I think he hates that decaying-potatoes tobacco stuff he puts in his pipe, but he's ashamed to smoke the real thing where anyone could see or smell, and he lurks in there feeling socially irresponsible."

"Since you've got no bloody idea what he does in there I don't see why you can't splurge a bit more with the famous Tappen imagination. You know. Sensuous love-nest lined with swansdown, government surplus. Range of steel and leather gadgetry of curious interest to connoisseurs. The door's locked, Roy."

Tappen got into the blue Volvo and leant across to admit Llewellyn. "I was indulging in informed speculation," he said primly. "A couple of times I've *seen* puffs of smoke from a sort of ventilator pipe sticking out of Roger's gooseberries. I have not, on the other hand, noticed a leakage of swansdown, black leather fragments, sensuous perfumes or erotic bondage devices. Speaking of which, fasten that seatbelt."

"Never, you fiend," said Llewellyn, fastening it. There was something about the cold, fishlike eyes of positive-vetting interviewers, and their eagerness to probe one's secret practices, which seemed to encourage this kind of conversation.

The car ambled towards the gate, with one of the ubiquitous blue-grey Transit vans in front to discourage Tappen's famous demonstration of how fast you could go on private NUTC roads with no legal limit. Which was just as well, since ahead of the van the usual sirens and barriers did their party trick, now as irritatingly familiar as green traffic lights' habit of turning red at the least convenient moment. Had Tappen been calmer and less jumpy he mightn't have floored the brake pedal with such speed, and instead could have discovered a solution to the interesting theoretical problem of whether a whole Volvo could be got inside a Ford Transit. Then the van was waved through and Alf Rossiter's merry men turned their attention to the Volvo, Tappen and Llewellyn with the same enthusiasm as the gendarmes of Poe's "Purloined Letter" who subdivided an entire hotel into one-millimetre squares which were individually examined through microscopes.

"Have to make sure you've nowt in the way of valuables some light-fingered lad might nick," Rossiter said insufferably.

"Actually we had several complete warheads hidden aboard that van driven by our accomplice," Tappen said merrily, feeling like a whited sepulchre with all manner of foul language seething within.

"False alarm, false alarm, that was one of our lads," said Rossiter rapidly, closing the subject as the van sped out of sight and into Bogley. "Stolen from your car, oh that was rich, they'll be standing me pints all night when I tell 'em in the police club. You know I'm moving to Redbury when I find a place? Big Alf is watching – you need me to look after you, chum. And then your mate Pell; laugh, we thought we'd die ..."

"Hysteria indicates an unstable personality," Tappen said to Llewellyn in a stage whisper, but nothing could stop the voluble outpouring of Rossiter's epigrammatic wit and wisdom until at last the searchers retreated with their trophy of a paperclip which might well be Civil Service property.

Half an hour later Tappen was restraining himself from saying the same thing to Lizzie, who that evening couldn't share Rossiter's robust humour about the whole affair. Roy Tappen was a miserable worm. Roy Tappen was an incompetent failure. Roy Tappen didn't *care* whether his wife had a nervous breakdown on account of worrying about Soviet pre-emptive strikes on 33 Rutland Gardens. Roy Tappen was a wretched crawling thing who probably *liked* the idea of having nuclear balls as a phallic symbol or something in his despicable filing cabinet. Roy Tappen had no thought for the likelihood of his *family* (pronounced with an emphasis which conjured up several mythical children and a brace of live-in grannies) suffering ignominy or radiation sickness or cancer or atomic piles. Roy Tappen ... really those two words summed it all up, as it was only in her rare outbreaks of this mood that Lizzie squared her shoulders, looked at him through narrowed eyes and by way of ultimate insult called him Roy Tappen.

With the deep sincere conviction of a party political broadcast Tappen explained that all would be well, that he had a plan, that no, he hadn't actually sussed out the fine details yet but the broad outlines, well, he was still working on the broad outlines of the really brilliant general concept which hadn't quite yet taken final form

It was at about this stage of his charismatic reassurances, there in the musty living room, that Lizzie picked up the phone and booked a room in the Redbury Station Hotel. A single room.

"No, I can walk, thanks very much," she said.

"When you've got rid of those *objects* ..." she said.

"You should have thought about the Barclaycard spending limit *before* you decided to become a nuclear power," she said.

When the door had slammed and Tappen was left standing dazed, the worst thing of all seemed somehow to be that the Station Hotel kept the foulest beer in town. Deserted, for a place that dealt in Fairey Liquid? It was too much.

Sixteen

"Er ... hello," said Pell, peering round the edge of his front door like an aged spinster sizing up the gasman's potential for sex mania.

"Evening," Tappen said. "Since Lizzie's left me and my career lies in ruins, I want to end it all; thought I'd take you up on that standing invitation. The home-made wine, you know." It was the first excuse that had come to mind. He'd fortified himself heavily with Alka-Seltzer washed down with half a pint of salad oil which Llewellyn had once recommended as forming a protective lining in the stomach. He should have remembered oil's propensity for rising to the surface. Tappen's surface appeared to be somewhere in the region of his Adam's apple, and to be moving higher minute by minute.

"Er, em ... er," invited Pell, opening the door a little wider. For the first time in months, Tappen stepped in. The place was more like a filmic mad scientist's den than ever.

35 Rutland Gardens had started life as a mirror image of 33, but then Pell had happened to it. Mysterious holes had been knocked in walls, inexplicable pipes and cables threaded their way along skirting-boards or crawled caterpillar-fashion up partitions only to vanish without trace into apertures ranging in size from mouseholes to sheep-holes. As Tappen followed Pell into what in other houses might have been a sitting-room, the dim yellow lighting slowly waxed and waned, presumably in pace with the evening breeze and the lazily turning vertical-axis windmill which dominated the back garden and drove a home-made generator. (When there was no wind Pell would fall back on foul tallow candles tracing their ancestry to the previous month's pork chops; or, ultimate humiliation, he'd be forced to turn on the mains and

glower at the bright, clean, unwelcome lights of civilization.) There was a moist warmth as of compost heaps and the smell that goes with them; the one might be stored heat from the solar panels, the other was probably the biomass methane-converter in the kitchen, which Pell had constructed with vast ingenuity and several old dustbins.

"You'd like some of my, erm, whisky," Pell stated incorrectly, and left Tappen to wonder whether the rusting central heating system was in fact a disguised still. That might or mightn't explain the radiation meter perched on a crowded coffee-table, aiming like a pointer-dog at the grimy radiator and tangle of piping where Tappen's house could only boast a fireplace. Smeary plastic sheets obscured the windows (Tappen supposed these were low-cost double glazing), and large but random areas of wall were insulated with thick white polystyrene tiles, each with an elegant decorative motif of black fingerprints.

"I'm working towards the house of the future," Pell had once said.

"I think you'll find this, mmm, interesting," he said now, returning with a sinister-looking bottle and two tumblers of murky fluid. Tappen didn't doubt it.

"Cheers," he said, taking a minuscule sip ... seemingly one of those appalling whisky-and-wine concoctions people used to bring to parties and which were always found untouched next morning (they stayed untouched, too, until used as admission ticket to some other bring-a-bottle affair ... like Watneys Party Sevens). "Roger, I wanted to have a little word with you about your world-famous adventures at lunchtime."

"Er ... pardon?"

"You know. Jolly Roger, Scourge of the South Seas, celebrated smuggler, bane of the customs officers, yo-ho-ho. I was wondering just why, when Joe and I had this sort of official smuggling licence, you set up shop as a privateer."

"Tell me, Roy, what *do* you think of the whisky?"

"Oh, it's remarkable. Amazing how you achieve that fascinating cloudy effect. But about lunchtime?"

"It's, um, almost utterly legal," Pell said jerkily, demonstrating enthusiasm by knocking back the opaque fluid and refilling his glass. "The whisky. What you do is, er, this, you ferment up a tasteless white wine, from potatoes or something of the sort, with a good high-yield yeast to take it to, ah, thirty-something proof, and you add this *whisky essence* to give it the proper flavour, and there you are. It's, well, a clever psychological trick: your mind's prepared for whisky and doesn't notice this isn't so strong."

"*My* mind was prepared for methanol, furfural, ether and formaldehyde," Tappen muttered. "And I swear I can taste them all even now."

"Well, erm, that just goes to show ... Now of course vapour distillation's illegal, but there's somewhere, Northern Europe I think, where they bury a big barrel of local wine through the winter, and it slowly freezes from the outside in, and the alcohol gets concentrated in the middle. Freeze distillation. So I modified the whatsit, thermostat on the freezer, and, well, here we are."

He refilled the glasses defiantly.

Tappen took another sip and hoped the salad oil's magical protection was functioning. "Frankly, it doesn't seem the sort of deadly firewater you might expect. Now about your lunchtime smuggling?"

"Mmm, it's a step forward, at least. Freezer coils haven't been a hundred per cent effective since I borrowed them for my experimental heat pump."

"The one that dropped the temperature of our bedroom thirty degrees and warmed your place at our expense?"

"You should have better insulation, like me, and anyway, I was only toying idly with the, er, concept. Now I had a really interesting new idea for fuel cells, Roy, and I think you'd appreciate it; I'll show you the drawings if you just –"

"No," said Tappen. "Sit there, look me fully and frankly in the eye, offer me no tours of your generator shed or underground shelter, and tell me why you were smuggling pits."

Pell shied, afflicted with sudden nervousness. "I'm busy with, um, repairs to the shelter, Roy, some rather complicated work, it's off limits these days if you don't mind ... Did I tell you the detectors say there's a double-strength hotspot somewhere high up in your place? Most peculiar. Anomalous, even."

It was Tappen's turn to be evasive, not wanting even to think about the objects carefully segregated in the top and bottom drawers of the filing cabinet and partly shielded with Fortmayne's lead blocks for fear that together they might go critical and melt their way through the floor or worse. After all, hadn't that uranium bed in central Africa gone critical and become a natural reactor millions of years ago? Yesterday Africa, today the spare bedroom of 33 Rutland Gardens, tomorrow the world.

"A propaganda, er, coup," Pell said at last, with a pleased look of bright-eyed inventiveness. "I wanted to, as it were, discredit any publicity from this peculiar manoeuvre of yours – sorry, but you know how things are. Er, pictures and so on, showing how easy it was to borrow nuclear fuel from a lax place like Robinson Heath. Pity it wasn't so easy after all. It would have been good boring from within, that. Yes, yes, that was my plan," he concluded almost convincingly. "Have a refill, do."

"Interesting stuff," said Tappen without deceit. "After the first few pints you could get quite addicted. Roger, I have an ulterior motive of deep and evil cunning: the good old *dummy* core we keep around the 334 labs has gone missing, could be in Nevada for all we can trace it, and we need one for, for the Royal Visit. Always gives royalty a feeling of power when you let them hold the Egg in their own two hands; Princess Something nearly had orgasms, stood there muttering 'Half a league, half a league, half a league onward.' Never mind that. You've a dummy tucked away in Robinson Heath and we'd like to borrow it."

"Ah, a refill, let me top you up ..." And with slightly unsteady hands Pell topped up the glasses too soon and too hastily: his own overflowed in a two-inch puddle on the coffee-table. The wood under the puddle turned black and began to give off smoke.

"Jesus," breathed Tappen, and looked at his glass with respect. "Conc. sulphuric acid? Nitroglycerine? Polystrippa?"

"It shouldn't do that ... Oh, yes, well, the freeze distillation wasn't quite perfect, but you know, I liberated a little, mmm, absolute alcohol from Lab Three."

"Doesn't taste strong," Tappen said, rapidly draining his

tumbler and wishing it didn't taste at all. He choked. Something had bitten him on the inside of his throat, most unsporting.

"Have a refill, do have another refill, er, let me tempt you."

"All right ... Roger. The dummy. Let me take the bull between the teeth. I came to ask you about the dummy."

Pell took another strengthening gulp in readiness for the extraction. "Well, er, the fact of it is, Roy, it wasn't, as it were, what you might call an actual, not to put too fine a point on it, dummy ..."

"You mean ... But that's fucking criminal irresponsibility," said Tappen, inexplicably cheered. All at once he didn't feel as lonely as before. At great length and with great relish he delivered to Pell a watered version of Lizzie's lecture to himself, pausing intermittently to lubricate his throat.

"It would have been, mmm, *hypocritical* to deceive my associates with a mere lump of dead metal," Pell said primly. "That's a matter of, ah, principle."

Tappen grinned. Almost he wanted to shake Pell's hand and offer him half his worldly goods, or at least half the contents of a certain filing cabinet. Almost he could sympathize with Pell, who seemingly never quite gained the trust of groups like CND thanks to his unfortunate vocation and general weirdness. And very definitely he was envious of the older man for having tried and luckily failed, as opposed to being a doomed Jonah who despite never trying had succeeded, twice.

"I'm afraid it's all my fault," he said. "Hey, this stuff begins to grow on you after a bit, doesn't it? Like athlete's foot fungus. I'm afraid they detected my turn-ups. Turned the detectives up. The detectors."

"Mmm," said Pell fluently.

Why was the air in the dim front room quivering and humming with a gentle aroma of something not quite whisky?

"Should have tried it before," said Tappen, overcome with sudden sadness.

"Oh, I did. *Urrum.* I thought of, er, doing it, I mean I –" Pell shook his head firmly, tilted the bottle and spilt a great deal more of the arcane fluid. The carpet proved itself to be a modern synthetic fibre, by dissolving without trace wherever the droplets hit.

"Could have done it lots of times, lots and lots and lots and lots ..." mused Tappen, sinking ever deeper into existential mournfulness at the human condition.

"Easily," Pell confirmed, and violently shook his head again. "It's getting, erm, a bit late now, Roy. Look, nearly nine o'clock. Long way home."

Tappen found himself gifted with a strange new ability to shimmer from place to place without apparently moving his legs. Plainly the author of *An Experiment with Space* was right after all: lubricated by Pell and now set spinning freely inside his skull, Tappen's brain was transcending the tiresome laws of gravity. Because his mouth couldn't quite match the dizzying speed of his brain, his promises of countless weapon cores for the asking seemed lost on Pell, who said boring things like, "No no no, Roy, don't tread *there*, thatsh my mushroom culture tray, damn it ... mind that cable now ... not tha' pipe, itsh, erm, wobbly, I mean leaky, I mean too hot to touch ..." But Tappen had already grabbed hold of it to swing himself onto a new glide path, levitating towards the front door (the pipe was firm as several rocks and comfortably warm, and Tappen felt vaguely annoyed with Pell for deceiving him).

"Nighty-night," he called as he volplaned out along the driveway; Pell slurred some suitable goodnight greeting from behind, in tones of medium-strength relief, and with a warm feeling of moral and physical superiority Tappen explained to himself that the old loony was a bit the worse for wear after that euthanasia potion of his. What luck it was that Roy Tappen had a strong head. How strange it was that the oddly numerous street lights were gently waxing and waning as though controlled by Pell's erratic windmill-power.

As he closed number 35's wrought-iron gate and reached for that of number 33 close by, Tappen inhaled a huge draught of cool, invigorating night air. The effect was fascinating, as though his inner glow had been the embers of a fire which he'd now encouraged with a cool, invigorating bucket of petrol. Aircraft grade.

When the internal flash and long, rumbling blast had died slightly down, he found himself staring at three inches' range into the frost-cracked concrete of his own front path. Undeterred, the path stared coldly back.

Affairs became complicated after this, in the unreal orange glare of the sodium lamps: he told the forget-me-nots how he'd guessed what little game Pell was really up to, but a rather offensive rosebed took issue with his words, and when he tried to teach it the error of its ways the three holly-bushes (planted to deter vandals and drunks) most unfairly joined in, to leave Tappen outnumbered and ignominiously defeated ...

As Pell had remarked, it was a long way home.

Seventeen

Because it was the third Friday of the month there was a ritual observance for Tappen when he reached his office, and because he felt the way he felt it was twice as necessary today. With scratched and still painful hands (he must tell Lizzie that her policy with regard to roses and hollies was entirely misguided and wrong) he inserted his Type IV MoD-Issue Noise-Protector Earplugs, available only to machine-shop workers and special cases. A special case was someone who bought the supplies officer a pint at the appropriate moment. The plugs failed to block the noises echoing inside his head which felt like that vast acreage of Nevada converted to Swiss cheese by underground testing: they were trying out devices of at least ten megatons' unfriendliness apiece, somewhere in the tortured recesses of Tappen's brain, and the seismic shocks travelled huge distances to wake sympathetic pain in unimaginably remote places such as his toes.

Nor could the plugs quite block the monthly test of the NUTC Criticality Alarm, which shrilled and warbled in a manner designed to coagulate the blood and so terrify you that you stood weak-kneed and unable to sprint away from the flood of radiation the alarm might or mightn't be signalling. Tappen reached for his ever-friendly paracetamol. *Whee-eee-eee-eee-eee-eee-eee-eee-eee-eee-eee* ... If you wanted to sabotage some NUTC reactor and cause frightful outbreaks of radiation, you should be sure to do it at nine in the morning of the third Friday of the month, when everyone would sit tight with fingers, cotton-wool or earplugs blocking the intolerable warnings of danger.

Because it was the third Friday of the month, there was another grim little ceremony to be carried out, which scientists called the telling of the lies. A photocopied form of almost supernatural grottiness and illegibility materialized on every desk, demanding to be filled in with detailed accounts of exactly how each segment, to the nearest tenth of an hour, of each of the last 20 or 25 working days had been spent in the furtherance of Britain's nuclear independence. All Tappen's time was supposed to go on Projects 40 (weapon design) and 41 (weapon effects simulation): naturally neither had subheadings for such vital NUTC work as coddling VIPs, being NPIWP secretary, listening to Fortmayne on why defence research policy was misguided and wrong in every joint, hinge and detail, staring out through the window thinking vaguely of sex, or picking one's nose.

His natural rebelliousness did lead him to add an extra subhead, "Answering Offensive PV Questions From Filthy-Minded Security Man: 2.4 hours." It would make no difference in the long run when Carol prepared the 334 manpower summary, with the rude comments omitted and all figures adjusted to uncanny agreement with the official order of priorities sent down on tablets of stone from Admin Central. Even so, it was impolitic to mention all the Tappen-hours spent devising and misapplying vast schemes for smuggling r/a in and out of NUTC: the number of tenths-of-an-hour thus employed looked not so much a time allocation, more a Space Invaders score.

And where on the form did you note the 0.5 hours devoted to filling in the form, the 0.1 hours of deciding which category the 0.5 hours should be concealed in, the 0.1 hours of crossing out and rewriting the form to account for the previous 0.1 hours of cosmic decision-making ...? As in a collaboration between Kafka and Borges, if you were conscientious about filling in the form the effort would expand to fill the rest of your life. Like Parkinson's law, or his disease.

Fortunately Tappen wasn't conscientious. He scribbled down his creative improvements on mere lifeless facts, and drifted off into another fantasy sparked by a letter in the staff-association magazine. Some far-flung member with a hyphen in his name was protesting against the vile left-wing ideology, the knee-jerk pinko mindlessness, the appalling Marxist subversion, of a previous issue's comment to the effect that foxhunting might not be entirely a good thing. Another bit of Olde Englysshe tradition was here being threatened by the nihilist, leftist, etc. Already Tappen had rushed in a reply agreeing whole-heartedly with this courageous stance, demanding that the Middle Ages be not allowed to die, and calling for a revival of other merrie pastimes like bear-baiting, cock-fighting, witch-burning and the popular spectacle of public hangings. He could hardly wait to learn whether the hunt-lover was or wasn't so irretrievably hyphenated as to take this seriously.

Now there was a local hunt nearby, the Mormal Down crowd who rampaged periodically over those parts of Robinson Heath (the heath) not covered by Robinson Heath (the establishment). Their spokesmen thundered about the need to exterminate wicked, sheep-killing, rabies-carrying and – for all Tappen knew – cattle-rustling and dope-peddling foxes, by the tried and tested means of Merrie England. In between times, whenever the triumphant pro-gramme of protecting society from the demon fox was getting a bit too successful, the altruistic hunters of Mormal Down would import a fresh batch of foxes from special breeding farms which catered for this social need. Thus the balance of ecology was maintained.

Just as lawns breed dandelions and familiarity breeds con-tempt, so every hunt spontaneously generates a hardy breed of hunt saboteurs: and of course Roger Pell was one. He told his tales of sabotage with all the pride and glory of an MFH fingering his cherished memories at the Hunt Ball. It sounded such thrilling fun, annoying the stuffed shirts of three counties, spoiling their enjoyment and being able to feel virtuous about it too. Unblocking earths, laying trails of aniseed, spraying hounds with Anti-Mate by way of distraction, counterfeiting the sound of the horn, hurling thunderflashes and smoke grenades! Only a strange premonition of being trampled by large red-faced men on larger horses had deterred Tappen from going along to join in the sport and later telling friends, "The hunters *enjoy* being sabotaged really, it's more of a challenge for them, noble beasts that they are, you'd almost think they were intelligent from the spirited way they play their part in the day's excitement ..."

Then suppose, Tappen thought, that the thrills and adventure of a merry day's traditional sabotage could be varied to the advantage of R. Tappen? Suppose ... he felt he heard the unimaginably distant bells of adventure ringing, possibly thanks to the desk telephone and the earplugs he'd forgotten to remove.

In touched-up picture postcards the grey sea and grey sand of reality become searing electric blue and radioactive mustard: the new imagined scene sprang into his mind with that same unreal brilliance. The hunt in full cry, the sound of his horn, tootle-tootle-*toot*. Tempting trails of aniseed lead to a seeming find in Ghoul's Covert, a straggling thicket not a quarter of a mile from the south fence of Robinson Heath. Noises like "View halloo!" and "Tally ho!" and "Thar she blows!" echo over the grotty grassland. (Tappen was unsure of the exact terminology. Did fewmets and jesses enter into it these days?) The questing beast goes streaking off in a desperate run for the unhallowed sanctuary of NUTC, pursued by hounds in full cry and a great gallop of horsemen in their scarlet jackets which you had to call either pinks or pansies ... It could be done with a buried power-winch, a lot of nylon rope and a stuffed fox: these were mere engineering details and Tappen dismissed them with a physicist's lordly contempt.

The wild excitement of the hunt! The unstoppable momentum of fifty crazed hounds and God knew how many hundredweight of horseflesh, hurtling inexorably onward, tootle-tootle-*toooooot* and the baying of hounds and the pounding of hooves ... For a moment the thrilling image overcame Tappen and he found himself humming not quite under his breath,

Yes, I ken Roger Pell, and Ruby too,
  Ranter and Ringwood, Bellman and True,
From a find to a check, from a check to a view,
  From a view through the fence in the morning!

And the fence would have been subtly weakened, perhaps by a little deft work with wire-cutters or an accidental spillage of nitric acid, and the whole plunging fury of the hunt would burst through the spot to which the aniseed and electric fox had led them, and in the enormous confusion as hounds ran amok and decimated the fat, protected rabbits of NUTC, who would notice a figure swiftly slipping from the supporters' or saboteurs' Land-Rovers and through the breach?

Once inside he was Roy Tappen, senior scientific officer, with a site pass and a right to be there, and if he happened to be carrying a couple of, er, pieces of experimental equipment in a suitcase, well, dedication, overtime, stuff like that. Nobody would believe him, probably, but it would merely be assumed he was still playing the smuggling game, outward bound; indeed, he need only loiter suspiciously near the hole in the fence's mesh, with a suitable expression of grossly exaggerated innocence, and kindly Security men would escort him inside with firm hands.

All he needed, then, was to infiltrate the saboteurs via Pell, persuade them of the supreme embarrassment the Hunt would feel on being decoyed into the classified precincts of NUTC, bury a high-speed electric winch without being noticed, acquire a stuffed fox ... the window of one Redbury antique shop contained an immense stuffed otter with a peevish expression curiously like Fortmayne's: that would do at a pinch, otherwise Llewellyn might have to practice high-speed crawling in a fur rug.

Minor details, all these.

"Well well well, Roy my boy," he imagined Rossiter saying, "what's all this then? On the fiddle again so soon? Naughty, naughty." While Tappen hid a smile of triumph behind an expression of surly disappointment concealed by an attempted rueful grin (he'd have to practice that in a mirror), Rossiter opened the case to nod sagely over the two dull aluminium footballs wedged into opposite corners with lead blocks between them. Despite Tappen's attempts to keep his imagination on the right course, things began to go awry, as in slow motion Rossiter took the spheres and held them together in his arms, jocularity fading into puzzlement: "Ee, the buggers are *hot*," and the scream as they turned dull red in the heat of supercriticality, so naturally the agonized Rossiter dropped them but not before Tappen had seen his fingers turn blue with the hellish glow of Cherenkov radiation, and knew that those close by were now the walking dead, overdosed with x-rays, gamma rays, neutrons, from a neutron bomb in miniature, and half an hour hence the vomiting would start, and the distant bells and sirens of the criticality alarms could be heard....

"What an imagination I've got," said Tappen aloud, mopping his forehead with an expensive sterile tissue for laboratory use only. The flat sound of the words in his own ears, deadened as though by the frightful side-effects of balaclava addiction, reminded him of the earplugs: he popped them out and found the nightmare alarm bells had been the telephone, which as he reached for it stopped ringing and regarded him with dumb insolence.

Before he'd finished filling in a machine-shop requisition for more dummy weapon cores, which in unclassified memos had to go under the subtle pseudonym of D-181 Easter eggs, the phone rang again. A bored voice instructed him to attend a security indoctrination course in ten days' time. Tappen sighed: another tweak from Staverton, or perhaps a gentle reminder from the PV crew who hunted with such dedication for the love that dares not speak its name. Were they still putting two and two together about Tappen's strange supposed longings, as last night amid the ruins of the front garden he'd performed the same feat of arithmetic with regard to things Pell had said? He knew he thought he'd known something, but the memory was foggy: concentrating on it was rather like tightening the screw of a large invisible vice clamped round his head. He groaned again. It had been something preposterous and utterly Pellish.

In addition he'd had some devious thought about Transit vans, another notion which lurked like an elusive earthworm beneath the ravaged surface of his mind. Was Pell's central heating system made entirely from bits of purloined MoD Transit vans? Tappen shook his head and wished he hadn't.

"Hello," boomed Llewellyn's voice as he burst far too violently into the office. "You all right? Looking a mite pale and interesting ..."

"Yes, fine," said Tappen.

"How's the latest Tappen Master Plan? All sussed now?"

"Yes, fine," said Tappen.

"Hey, really? Tell us all."

"Yes, fine," said Tappen.

"... Roy, your fly is undone and you're exposing yourself. Hideous gross blatant indecency. Police would shoot on sight. Wasp just flew in there too."

"Yes, fine ... pardon?" With an effort Tappen pulled himself together, or parts of himself. "I think I've got a touch of 'flu this morning."

"Looks more like rigor mortis to me. Anyway. I'm nipping into Bogley lunchtime; fancy a jar, get the red corpuscles moving again?"

Tappen merely shuddered. The door closed gently but not gently enough. All this and now an NUTC course to look forward to. He'd been three times on the shunned computer course, which rounded up frequent computer users – i.e., people who knew all about it – and ruthlessly subjected them to a week of thuddingly elementary tuition in obsolete computer languages like FORTRAN. The security course was for anyone who annoyed Security, and consisted of staggeringly tedious lectures which after a while, if you annoyed Security as often as was a right-thinking man's duty, you came to know by heart. A Clean Desk Is A Secure Desk. Loose Lips Sink Spaceships. Change Your Combinations Every Week. Tell Nothing To Your Wife, She Could Be A KGB Agent. Accept No Lifts From Strange Men In Fur Hats. Avoid Using Top Secret Documents In Paperchases. A Body-Search A Day Keeps Suspicion Away. Please Inform Your Friendly Security Officer Before Emigrating To Albania ... and similar paste gems of wisdom, ad infinitum, ad nauseam. And then, familiar scene by scene and frame by frame, there was the Security Indoctrination Film: which at this point gave Tappen half an idea.

Knock. Knock. A weak, hesitant and diffident knock; feeling for the moment that he was a connoisseur of small noises like the terrible, insistent ticking of his watch and beating of his heart, Tappen admired Pell's ability to convey the entire force of his personality by two taps on a door. There was even a hint of stammer.

"Erm," said Pell as he came into view. "You weren't, er, at coffee, and Joseph said you looked to be in dire need of, ah, hair of the dog. It happens I keep an emergency flask of my whisky for, mmm, adulterating MoD coffee when it tastes too dreadful. So, as I suppose it's all my fault --" Awkwardly he set a plastic bottle on the desk, uncannily like a half-litre urine sample bottle, three-quarters full.

The only thing that prevented Tappen from expostulations about 'flu, a touch of food-poisoning, or wet-weather twinges in his old vasectomy scar, was that Pell himself didn't look too healthy, and himself exuded a faint, familiar aroma of ersatz whisky.

"Thanks," said Tappen with an effort.

"Oh, don't mention it," mumbled Pell with what sounded like the same effort.

Alone again, Tappen regarded the plastic bottle, found the sight too much, and hid it in a drawer. The slightly rancid flavour of that firewater was still hovering between his throat and sinus, indelible, where no amount of gargling could shift it. What had he been thinking? The security film. Borrowed from the Air Force, it traced the downfall of a youthful scientist who incautiously visited some London strip-show, there to be tempted with naughty caresses and champagne. After which, he was given an absolutely terrific time on the house.

These lavishly produced scenes were so erotically compelling as to leave the strong impression that unendurable pleasure indefinitely prolonged lay in wait for any classified researcher, be he ever so ugly, who cared to wander in low places. It was generally believed that countless red-blooded scientists had, immediately on seeing the film, gone hopefully combing Soho while clutching large envelopes labelled TOP SECRET in ostentatious scarlet.

Later portions of the film, wherein our hero was blackmailed with extensively revealing snapshots of himself exploring the untamed interior of the stripper of his choice, failed to stick so firmly in the mind. And since the blackmail threat of the vile unnamed foreign intelligence (with a predilection for fur hats) was to show the nice holiday snaps to the hero's wife, the overall message appeared to be *Do What Thou Wilt Shall Be The Whole Of The Law* provided you aren't married.

To his horror Tappen found himself thinking it might be beneficial to wander Soho and fall into the toils of aliens who could be persuaded to blackmail him into pinching two interesting souvenirs of NUTC (no more, no less). Good grief. Unless he was still faintly off-sober, his subcutaneous mind must be more traitorous or more randy than he'd known.

He tried and failed to visualize himself in a false beard and astrakhan hat, persuading Britain's counterespionage network (which he knew from books and TV was based in Cambridge Circus) that he was an incipient double-agent requiring only vast sums of money to arrange return of the lethal devices smuggled out in a daring and hitherto undetected midnight commando raid on NUTC. *No.*

In similar high-powered defence research the day went by. It was late afternoon, during his fifth queasy visit to the toilets, when he unbleared enough to spot his name on one of the shelfload of plastic bottles balanced tastefully and shakily over where you stood up to be a gentleman. Health Physics Wants You. By then he'd expended all his powers, and his bottle was to be filled in a single heroic day. He meditated briefly, fetched Pell's pint of poteen from his desk, and presently returned the empty plastic bottle to its mildly alarmed owner, with effusive and quite sincere thanks. That was about the one fluid he hadn't so far hoaxed Health Physics with; he wondered if after their analysis, they'd deduce this Tappen to be ever so slightly alcoholic.

Now feeling almost half alive again, he ought to dream up some more sensible scheme than the delirium of earlier in the day. Soon, before Lizzie decided to ask their solicitor about legal definitions of intolerable mental cruelty. Soon, before accumulated stress gave him high blood pressure, heart attacks, and ingrowing toenails. He twiddled his thumbs with deep concentration and in this intellectual position was discovered by Fortmayne, who entered faster than the speed of sound and arrived at Tappen's desk before the knock.

"Bloody hell, you gave me a heart attack," said Tappen as he adjusted his posture to that of the dedicated researcher. The words combined with memories of old *New Scientist* articles, hit critical mass and erupted in a fireball of brilliance which left Tappen once again dazzled by his own intellect.

"I don't agree with what you're saying," Fortmayne was already saying. "CPRA wants to know why we're eight weeks behind on the Niblick feasibility study –" Tappen hadn't even thought about that for approximately five and a half weeks. Niblick was a prototype all-British cruise missile which could be transported round the country by cyclists, its lightweight launcher being cunningly disguised as (the name was a dead giveaway) a golf bag.

"It went to the typists eight and a half weeks ago," Tappen said with only three weeks' worth of falsehood. "Ask them. Mike, there's something I think I ought to mention to the Royal Visit Committee; it came to me just now."

"You are *not* manning the 334d exhibition stand when the Queen comes round, and neither am I. Al Staverton loves a lord, rank hath its privileges, and he's bought a new suit for the occasion – so kindly forget it."

Mentally Tappen awarded him an Olympic bronze for long-distance conclusion jumping. "No, no. It just happens that I read a Sunday magazine article a few years ago, about Prince Philip being fitted with a heart pacemaker, the very latest model."

"I have absolutely no interest in royalty's health problems," said Fortmayne, who at erratic intervals was conscientiously socialist.

"Nor me. I simply had this vision of pomp and ceremony, the cheering crowds lining the entrance to Robinson Heath, the royal Rolls sweeping majestically past the visitors' car park to where the smiling reception committee awaits, so eager for their royal hand-shakes you'd think they wanted to be touched for the King's Evil ..."

"Spare us the lyric poetry, please."

"But at the penultimate moment before the entrance, when excitement is at its height, a rude interruption! Barriers crashing down and sirens wailing. Hideous insult to royalty's prerogatives. Loud crunching sounds if the chauffeur fails to stop in time. Subsequently, a dozen security police and the Assistant Director are shot for lese-majesty, and all because the Prince Consort has this wonderful pacemaker with a ... nuclear battery."

Fortmayne's eyes assumed the dimensions of TV screens; he swallowed eight and a half times before vanishing with never a word about r/a studies on Niblick's micro-jet engine, codenamed

Putter for the noise it made. Tappen leant back and reckoned he could depend on his very own PSO to think things through and arrange an all-day shutdown of the bloody awful detection system, for fear that royalty might run amok and stray too whimsically near a fence or gate. And – he could rely on politics-playing Fortmayne for this too – all without the suspect name of Tappen being mentioned.

Voices gabbled in the corridor, Fortmayne's hectoring, schoolteacherly tones drowning out opposition as usual. A minute later Llewellyn came in, saying, "Bloody hell, heard the latest? Mike's had a brainwave about Prince Philip and the gate detectors. Going bananas out there, he is."

"I know."

"Amazing how he thinks of these things. Me, I never knew Phil the Greek had atomic pacemakers built in."

"Neither did I," said Tappen comfortably.

Llewellyn hitched his skinny buttocks onto the other side of the desk and glared. "What a shitty day. All your fault. Like to guess what I've been juggling with all sodding afternoon?"

"Juggling. Er, skittles? Flaming torches? Coffee club accounts?"

"Getting warm. Plute inventory again: Inspection & Measurement wanted four countem four pits on the trot, and as you know there's this sort of shortage. Had to go all official on them, say 'one at a time only', and check the same one out and in again four times. *Talk* about shell games. Only my triff computer-fiddling stands between you and when you sit in solemn silence in a dull, dark dock, in a pestilential prison with a life-long lock, awaiting the sensation of a short, sharp shock –"

"From a cheap and chippy chopper on a big black block," Tappen recited. "All right. Your singing voice is NATO's deadliest secret weapon. Spare my aged eardrums."

"Came to offer you a lift home," Llewellyn said with elaborate casualness as Tappen plugged the kettle in. "Remember how I said I was going into Bogley lunchtime? Funny thing: you'd think I'd run a mile, I mean 1.60934 kilometres of course, to avoid a file cabinet these days, but after your famous burglary the idea sort of stuck. With lots of stuff on display, I looked into Bogley Surplus

Stores, and ..." Like an angler twiddling his baited line, he let the sentence dangle fascinatingly.

"And?"

"Like you to see for yourself. What'll the trained scientific mind conclude?"

"If this is a cretinous ploy to rub my nose in the fact that they're flogging off filing cabinets for 50p stock clearance price, I can do without it, Joe."

"Nothing like that. Would I lie to you?"

Half an hour later they were squeezing like potholers between Bogley Surplus Stores' long dim rows of second-hand office junk. Sharp smells of rust and corroded aluminium pervaded the place, calling up memories of Pell's home; a mouse scurried underfoot, calling up memories of Tappen's.

"There," said Llewellyn with the expansive gesture of one who has just produced ten pigeons, a bowl of goldfish and a voluptuous female assistant from the recesses of his shirt pocket. There, recently resprayed in tasteful dried-blood colour (you could still smell the paint), was a battered filing cabinet like any other. As Tappen inspected it, he saw with a thrill of recognition that the left-hand side was patterned with dents, outlining a well-remembered grinning face.

Eighteen

"Hello? Hello? Will you please put me through to Mrs Elizabeth Tappen?"

"I'm here. Roy, that's the first time in *years* I've heard your special voice for talking to switchboards and the proletariat."

"Oh. Hello, love. Er, what d'you mean, special voice?"

"Sort of effete, darling, and languidly e-nun-ci-at-ed for simple minds. Speaking of which, I was thinking of you only a moment ago."

"Absence makes the heart grow fonder, and all that."

"Out of sight, out of mind, Roy: and all that. There's this article in today's *Chronic*, though, that seems to have your fingerprints plastered all over it. I read it and proudly thought 'My man!' Would you like a recitation?"

"If you think I can take it without the support of alcohol."

"ATOM BASE 'SECURITY' WITCH-HUNT! (The harpy screech is supposed to indicate inch-high capitals, love, and the dying-gerbil squeak was for inverted commas. Well, you try saying headlines down the phone.) A lump of sugar led to persecution for an atom scientist, reporters were told this week. Marmaduke Theophilus –"

"I can't believe it. It's all a horrid dream. I'll wake up soon."

"Yes, Roy, it was when I reached that bit your name sprang to mind. I wonder why. Marmaduke Theophilus, as he asked to be identified, told how he was being hounded from his job at Robinson Heath. 'I told friends my boss took a lump of sugar in his tea,' he said, ashen-faced and tight-lipped. 'Now they tell me I could be imprisoned for life under the Official Secrets Act.' The *Chronicle* asks – well, it asks a lot of things, and I'll spare you the stuff about Senator Mary McCarthy."

"I am innocent, I am absolutely bloody innocent! I suppose the byline is Steven Green?"

"Aha, your guilty knowledge betrays you, darling. Yes. There's a tiny SG at the end."

"Stands for Specific Gravity, meaning some reporters are pretty dense. – Lizzie. Please. When are you going to come home again? I can't cope on my own."

"Can I get you the number of a reliable daily woman?"

"Oh, it's not *that* – well it is that a bit, but if I can learn to operate the NUTC pulsed reactor I should be able to master the washing machine one day. Hell: you know I'm sort of fond of you, and as a minor secondary matter it happens that being Separated From One's Wife is deeply bad medicine when Nuts security are poking and prying in the dirty laundry."

"Well, have you or haven't you got rid of –"

"*Public telephone line*, Lizzie, for God's sake."

"As I was going to say before I was so rudely underestimated: have you thrown out those two undesirable friends of yours, or are they still pigging it in the spare room?"

"I'm trying hard to get rid of them, love, but they haven't anywhere to go just yet – I'm working on two possibilities right now, though. Next week some time."

"Then next week is when I'll come back. In the old, old words, you're going to have to choose between those two roly-poly fellows and your own wife. Sounds sort of perverse, doesn't it? And I give you fair warning, Roy: I don't think I can stand it much longer, you working in that place. There must be something safer and better paid ... emptying dustbins, for example."

"Yes, well, that's like telling this wasted prisoner chained to the wall in a dungeon that he ought to go jogging more often for the sake of his health. I'm *stuck*, Lizzie, with those two chaps to support, for now. Afterwards: only today I saw a circular about transfer to tidal power research on the south coast, and I thought Great, but I need access to Nuts until – you know – and even then I'd have to talk Al Staverton and the Chief of Research into letting me transfer, and I'm not a teacher's pet in *that* department since the business in the canteen ..."

"What was the business in the canteen?"

"Oh, nothing."

"No, darling, *that* was the curious incident of the dog in the night-time. What was the business in the canteen?"

"Oh, it was the big plutonium scare, you know, some of the r/a workers supposed to be staggering and unable to walk thanks to the huge weight of plute contamination inside them. And, er, one day on every door of the canteen there appeared these neat typed notices saying, *In order to avoid assembling a critical mass, personnel are requested not to gather in groups of more than 5 and to stand at least 0. 6 metres apart (1.2 metres if wet).*"

"Hilarious, love, hilarious. You should sell it to Alan Coren. What happened?"

"Oh, about fifteen minutes later the notices got removed by stern-faced radiation workers using lead shields and remote handling tongs ... figuratively. Then CPRA decided the evil-doer ought to be ticked off for spreading alarm and despondency, and they made a security exercise of it, typescript comparisons, paper analysis, fingerprint checks and all. I'd have told you about it and given you a giggle, only the 334 coffee club betrayed me. One of our dear guardians dropped by to screen the toilet graffiti for subversive content, and he cadged a cup of coffee paid for by *our* syndicate, and some idiot – I think it was Roger Pell – asked him if he'd heard about Our Roy Tappen's famous gag. Later, chilly things were said to me."

"Poor Roy. You're a doomed man."

"So let me drag you down with me. Do you still want to see the Queen on Tuesday afternoon? Be bored by dull demonstrations, starved on half a cuppa and a wilting sandwich, alienated by five thousand Robinson Heathers at their bargain-basement garden party?"

"All right. All right, I'm an unreconstructed royalist. Some-times."

"If you can stand me on Tuesday, how about this evening? Let me come and sweep you away like young Lochinvar, for a pint of something drinkable. Always start the weekend with a healthy hangover."

"Oh, it's not you, Roy, you know that, it's the company you

keep. Do you dare leave those – people – in the house alone?"

"Can't stand them any more than you. If you decline my honourable invitation, I'll be practising solitary drinking at the Woodcock instead, and you know what they say about solitary drinking."

"They say it's cheaper. Or can two drink as cheaply as one?"

"The sensual presence of my exquisite wife will distract me from alcohol."

"*That* I have to see. I'll be waiting at hotel reception: but remember, I am not coming home until there's been a mass evacuation, right?"

"To hear is to obey, memsahib. Of course there are other alternatives."

"Before you suggest them, let me mention that I'm in a single room in a respectable hotel, and don't want to upset the manager's wife. After all, I may be staying here for a while, lover-boy."

"Lysistrata."

"If you're going to be like that, then Silas Marner to you."

"Who?"

"Silas Marner, darling. A fictional gentleman who got left holding the baby."

As he mumbled goodbye and hung up, Tappen sensed another frustrating weekend ahead.

Nineteen

"I have a theory about weekends," Tappen confided to Llewellyn as they glumly listened to the subterranean thumping of rabbits, making their contribution to the rabbit explosion beneath the hut's creaky floorboards. "My theory is that we only think we go home. What really happens is that Security gives us an injection, connects us up to computers that pump unconvincing memories of weekends into our brains, and then a few hours later they put us back at our desks. Increases productivity, saves on pay packets since we never *really* go home, keeps classified information safe ..."

"Science fiction," Llewellyn defined. "Not new either. In 1950 – something Philip K. Dick wrote – oh, I forget the title, but it was better than your version."

"My weekends aren't even convincing science fiction," Tappen said moodily. "With Roger Pell doing action preplays of World War III all over the back lawn."

"What does he use for bombs? Got a private stockpile like you?"

"Shut *up*, Joe. No, he imagines the mushroom clouds, and he trots up and down the garden path looking like a Martian in this ex-army respirator thing to keep out the imaginary fallout, and carries supplies to and from his home-made shelter ready for an imaginary wait till the radiation dies down and he can nip out and repopulate the world, with the help of an imaginary woman."

"God, you drivel on. Listening to you I know what they mean by a life sentence. Any thoughts about Bogley Surplus and their imaginary filing cabinets?"

Tappen was trying to twist a paperclip into a libellous profile of Alastair Staverton: his efforts fluctuated between Winston Churchill and Tyrannosaurus Rex. "I've been thinking," he said.

144

"You know about Plan A with the imaginary pacemaker; I hope I'll solve all our troubles tomorrow while the detectors are off. If anything goes wrong – and with my luck I wouldn't be surprised if I got abducted by UFOs on the way here – I have a sort of tentative Plan B, which is where you come in."

"In it up to here, I bet. First you explain, *then* I'll say no."

Tappen explained. Plan B depended on the school parties which would later be taken round the exhibition set up for the royals (minus classified bits), on the flawless incorruptibility of S. Green, reporter, on vast amounts of sheer luck, and on a chain of intellectual deductions even shakier than Sherlock Holmes's used to be.

Searching through Bogley Surplus Stores on Friday, Tappen and Llewellyn had been fascinated and intrigued to find many a familiar-seeming item of office equipment. They had exchanged significant glances on noticing bright file-marks on countless locks, just where one might expect an NUTC key-code stamped into the metal. They had practically danced a jig when it occurred to Tappen that certain antique and harmless radiation sources, stripped like everything else from Hacker's old office, would tend to explain the clangour of alarms as one suspicious Transit van left Robinson Heath on Thursday evening. And who, Tappen asked rhetorically, mysteriously refused to search that vehicle of crime? Aha.

Once you started thinking along these reprehensible lines, you might unpardonably wonder whether the stern rigour of MoDP searches wasn't like, say, the stern rigour of Victorian fathers who sacked the kitchen-maid for the unspeakable crime of having a boyfriend, and later that day enjoyed several ladies of easy virtue with a clear conscience. You might impiously ask how the vast pilferage from NUTC, which was supposed to partially justify the strict security and body searches, managed to stay vast in spite of the body searches and strict security. It was a vista of corruption beyond Tappen's wildest hopes.

Applying all his youthful optimism to Plan B, Llewellyn said finally: "It'll never work. Never in 24,000 years, which is the half-life of Pu-239, I swotted that up for the HSO promotion board."

"You didn't get promoted, though, did you?"

"OK, actually I swotted it up after the board asked me and I said 4.98 hours, which is *absolutely dead right* except that's plute 243."

"Well, while you're still a menial and an underling, you can set up your display stand in the marquee. That'll help you exercise your proven talent for carrying heavy loads, and relieve the strain on your intellect."

"What marquee?" said Llewellyn blankly.

"On the waste ground by A section. Perhaps the idea's that if the Queen should run amok suddenly she won't do any damage to expensive MoD buildings. No, I expect it's the school parties, better for them to set fire to an oversized tent than to SPERA or the AD's cocktail cabinet."

It was an article of faith in 334 area that the Assistant Director of NUTC habitually sprawled on an immense rotating circular bed, like Hugh Hefner's but more hedonistic, while a picked selection of the most nubile Admin typists hovered around in naughty poses and scanty outfits of red tape, massaging the sybaritic AD's naked thighs and plying him with exotic cocktails or champagne.

"What are *you* going to be doing?" Llewellyn asked suspiciously.

"Rotting my brain with this." Tappen gestured at the latest papers on his desk, rather as a lady of taste and breeding might gesture at a cold collation of partly decomposed rats. "It's the first draft proposals for the Nuclear Familiarization ad campaign. Vet it for scientific accuracy, they asked Staverton, who passed the buck to Mike Fortmayne, who – well, here it is."

"Polaris is good for you? Trident refreshes the parts that other nukes cannot reach? Cruise blazes 47% brighter than Brand X? You're never alone with a Chevaline? I mean, you can take a Chevaline anywhere?"

"No ... No, your natural good taste would prevent you from ever getting a job with the agency SPI hired."

"And all because ... the lady loves Pre-emptive Strikes!" Llewellyn declaimed.

"You're still outclassed. *Hi! I'm Winnie-the-Warhead, your cuddly friend who helps defend you! Me and my chum Ronnie Radar keep watch while you sleep. Having us around keeps the bogeymen at bay, because you know and they know we can be big trouble for trouble-makers!* I understand it's pitched at the median TV audience." He turned pages. "There's a whole slow campaign build-up here, with a soft toy tie-in and a special November the Fifth sequence ... CU KIDS WAVING SPARKLERS, HAVING FUN WITH BIG WINNIE-THE-WARHEAD MUPPET JOINING IN. VOICE OVER: *Winnie-the-Warhead knows fireworks are fun! You know it too. And that's what Winnie-the-Warhead's friends are, super-duper fireworks to scare off the Kremloids with their big, big bangs!* CRASH CUT TO STOCK FOOTAGE OF H-TEST (VIDEO FX IF AVAILABLE SHOTS NOT CUDDLY ENOUGH)."

"Kremloids ... totally fictional SF nasties, I suppose?"

"Absolutely. I can see you're ideal target-audience material. There's to be a special tie-in computer game called *Kremloid Blast*, with little Winnie-the-Warheads rising to zap these horrible, evil shapes that look just a bit like hammer and sickle designs ... videos of the Minister for Defence himself playing it, to show he's almost as human as the rest of us ..." He turned more pages. "It goes on. Like to hear the Green Crossbones Code for post-attack cleanup?"

"Fuck that. Me for the wide open spaces and the exhibition work. After that I can wash my hands; God knows how you're going to wash your brain."

"Well you should know: universal memory solvent, formula C_2H_5OH, available without prescription from licensed premises everywhere and suitable for oral administration ..." Tappen grew bored with this sentence and seized another of the photocopied sheets at random. "New Cruise with the neutron warhead. The elegant, slimline missile for real men, cool men, NATO men. New neutron filter design means 45% less harmful tar, I mean property damage."

But Llewellyn had fled before he could comment on the curious absence of a government health warning.

Left to himself, Tappen leafed idly through the masterwork of public relations planning. Parts of it reminded him of Wodehouse's clergyman spending long evenings trying to compose sermons which would practically make sense without being over the heads of his flock, and agonizing for hours on how to find a word of one syllable that meant Supralapsarianism. Difficult terms like "megadeath", "overkill" and "massive pre-emptive retaliation strike" were painstakingly rendered as, for example, "a good slap on the wrists". A throwaway line, to the effect that radiation destroyed bacteria and thus Winnie-the-Warhead would have potent disinfectant results and reduce disease, worried Tappen with its familiarity until he remembered he'd suggested it himself to the Press Officer, as a joke.

Meanwhile he was strangely untroubled by Security men bursting in, shouting "Up against the wall, punk!" or words to that effect, and demanding proof that his valuable Ministry-issue wastebasket, inventory number 5-271-009, hadn't been misappropriated or used for improper purposes. The lack of interruption began to worry him vaguely: you could suffer withdrawal symptoms if too many hours went by without your being asked to affirm in triplicate that you still possessed and cherished the HM letter-opener or sellotape-holder charged to your personal inventory. It took him a while to make the conscious connection: everything at Robinson Heath was askew, because it was R-Week.

Royalty Week. No far-ranging scheme of foreign sabotage by Kremloids could have paralysed NUTC so effectively as the royal visit it had manoeuvred for and demanded – as a pasty-faced kid might demand huge revolting confections of sticky chocolate, oozing goo, tooth-welding toffee and bright pink synthetic flavours, guaranteed to produce extreme unwellness on the, as it were, rebound. Security police were shining uniform buttons; scientists were turning their attention from science to simple explanations in easy language suited to royals and schoolchildren; typists had stopped typing to arrange nice flowers all over the Admin offices or construct model corgis from Blu-Tack; maintenance men were no doubt gold-plating the taps and pipes of selected loos, and substituting silken-soft toilet rolls for the shiny, scratchy Civil Service issue laughably stamped NOT FOR RESALE and known as glasspaper or Proctologist's Revenge.

Still unnaturally undisturbed, Tappen finished the Nuclear Familiarization draft and allowed himself a luxurious shudder before scribbling a cover note. "Has its good moments, but not so funny as *Protect and Survive*." He tore it up and wrote, "A profound and deeply disturbing social document which is a searing indictment of the society we live in today." He tore *that* up and decided he needed fresh air, a healthful walk to the exhibition marquee where he could spend an exhilarating half hour telling Llewellyn how his setting-up of the 334d display stand showed the acumen of a lobotomized sloth.

Some of the laws of nature remained operational even during R-Week, though, as Tappen learnt on his way out when the office door opened without warning and hit him on the nose. "Mail," creaked the tortoise-like NUTC messenger, oblivious to the spectacle of human suffering before him, and deposited a folded paper in the IN tray. "Morning," he added with lavish politesse as he withdrew, still tactfully ignoring the rude manner in which Tappen held his nose and spluttered.

Though the paper seemed to throb and pulsate with electrifying boredom, being only a printed NUTC circular, Tappen paused to take a look.

TO ALL STAFF
28 June
SECURITY PROCEDURES: ROYAL VISIT 29 JUNE
    For reasons of security all private traffic in and out of NUTC gates will be prohibited throughout 29 June. Staff travelling to work in their own cars should utilize the Visitors' Car Park or the overflow area set up in the NUTC Sports Club grounds.
    P.T.St.J. Hanratty, Assistant Director

In his mind's eye Tappen saw Plan A dive groundwards in a trail of smoke and flame. Obviously the detectors *were* going to be off all day Tuesday in deference to the assumed tendency of royal consorts to shower passers-by incontinently with radiation. Equally obviously, Tappen's Volvo wouldn't be sneaking in with the hoped arsenal. Momentarily he thought of hiding things in the royal boot (which needed a squad of SAS commandos, not one bumbling civil servant) or asking Lizzie to simulate pregnancy, twice (oh, but wives and guests at the "garden party" weren't allowed within the NUTC gates; all the thrilling inaction would be happening on the temporarily requisitioned sports grounds).

Tappen made a hideous face at the circular, picked up the phone, and dialled a number. "Hello ... *Redbury Chronicle*? I wonder if I could speak to your famous and talented reporter Mr Green?"

The trouble was, Plan B had looked totally brilliant and subtle so long as there was no risk of actually having to carry it out, but now ...

Twenty

During the afternoon of the Royal Visit, NUTC staff and their guests will be expected to proceed from place to place in dignified and orderly fashion, displaying a proper attitude of enthusiasm for the honour being paid, to our Establishment. Staff and guests will take particular care not to push to the front of the crowd, remain at the back, turn their backs upon the Royal Pavilion, converse in loud voices, lapse into unenthusiastic silence, or attempt to visit the temporary conveniences should a queue have formed. Transistor radios, cameras, cassette and video recorders, megaphones, firearms, banners, unsuitable clothing, children, pets, canned drinks, open-toed sandals (with or without socks), political literature, vegetable produce (fresh or otherwise) and musical instruments are strictly forbidden for the duration of the Garden Party. In view of the possibility that HM the Queen and/or other members of the Royal Entourage may converse with those present, staff and guests are asked to refrain prior to the event from consuming onions, leeks, garlic, beer, spirits, salami, curry, kippers, cheese-and-onion crisps, taramasalata or those highly flavoured cheeses listed in Schedule E of the Appendix ...

The official instructions did not exactly forbid umbrellas, but there had been a between-the-lines implication that such intricate engines were not only likely to harbour airguns or assassin's swords, but were also effete, hedonistic and unBritish. Nobody had brought an umbrella. The sky was pale and malign, not so much the colour of lead as of slightly corroded aluminium, and a thin drizzle fell on the dutifully enthusiastic, orderly and dignified royalists of NUTC. It was that misty ersatz rain, more fluid and penetrating than any honest water could be, soaking through "showerproof" clothes with the efficiency of Soviet infiltrators.

"Half-past two," said Tappen with false joy. "Only a couple of hours to go. Aren't you enjoying every thrilling moment, you desperate royalist, you? Only think, lesser folk without your drive and vaulting ambition are sitting indoors being dry and envying you."

Lizzie squinted as though down the sights of an Armalite rifle, and kicked him. "A thug turned up at the hotel last night to ask about people like you. I only wish I'd told him."

The whole NUTC sports ground had been sequestered for joyful celebration. To Tappen's right was a huddle of dingy tents which by and by would dispense a glorious golden bounty of tea and cakes. Twenty feet and several hundred people in front of him the roped-off no-go zone began, a sodden area the size of a football pitch and by a strange coincidence marked as a football pitch; on the far side loomed the Royal Pavilion, which those not in the know might have mistaken for a tent with one side missing, sheltering plush, upholstered chairs, two of them raised on boxes. The indoor furniture in this setting had a surreal look, like fur teacups, Magrittish airborne tubas or the NUTC Security Code. Tappen mumbled as much to Lizzie, and she mumbled something back which featured the word "pseud".

"They wanted to have a patriotic ER picked out in tiny simulated MIRV crater-clusters on the field," Tappen said encouragingly. "But that fell through because the football club complained. (Don't know why: after their fixtures it's as though the Golden Horde had raped, looted and pillaged every square inch, an n-bomb attack pales into puny insignificance.) Then there were plans for a huge mock-up of the new Weapon Assembly Building out here so HM could snip the red tape in full view of all these unclassified wretches like you."

Lizzie kicked him again, but more affectionately.

"Turned out that was the idea of the Security voting bloc on the planning committee. They get worried about people's names, that lot, you never find anyone called Patel or Singh on the NUTC payroll, no matter how British they are, and I swear they're not keen on names like Black or Brown because they sound sort of tinted, and Joe Llewellyn had a hard time getting cleared when we took him on, with Welsh flags and Plaid Cymru slogans flashing on and off in what Security people call their minds ..."

"How you do go on," said Lizzie, shaking her head dog-fashion and hurling a spray of droplets into Tappen's face.

"Did I hear my ears burn?" asked Llewellyn, materializing from the soggy crowd.

"Hello Joe ... So when they went rooting in the archives and found we planned to admit one former foreign national plus someone whose family had nefariously changed their name from Saxe-Coburg-Gotha, there was hell to pay –"

"Hi Lizzie. Tell me," Llewellyn said earnestly, "what's it like living with this guy when you've learnt the punchlines of both his jokes?"

Not really wanting to hear Lizzie answer this, Tappen swiftly said: "What's the news from the front, Joe?"

"Oh, she pushed the red button by mistake and started World War III. Bit more exciting than this, anyway."

Reluctance to trust royalty with the real controls of anything whatever had led to a cunning arrangement whereby HM the Queen was introduced to a special goldplated ceremonial control button, actually a brass bellpush purchased from Bogley DIY Centre. This theoretically activated the automated assembly line in the new building, but in reality sounded a small buzzer also purchased from Bogley DIY. Hearing the buzzer, a mere white-coated commoner secreted in the control room could then push the *real* button. Thus the integrity of Robinson Heath's workings was protected from vagaries of royal whim.

"Real joke is it's a sealed r/a area," Llewellyn said. "Nothing to see. 'Is anything going to happen? Should We be pressing harder?'" His impersonation was terrible.

Tappen nodded. "And the AD replies, 'It's happened, your Majesty. Didn't you see the movement of the assembly line through that tinted window behind the bars on the other side of the safety barrier beyond the lead radiation walls over there where I'm pointing?'"

"Listening to you," Lizzie said ominously, "I think of a pair of bad stand-up comedians trying to rally the passengers on the

Titanic. If you want shoptalk I'll recite you fifty case histories from the merry life of a social worker. If not, let's hear how you plan to smuggle two things like watermelons back in here. I would so much like to know, *darling*."

"*Ssh*," Tappen hissed. "The tentflaps have ears."

"Filing cabinet all sussed," said Llewellyn. "Old Tamlyn from Theoretical Support's on holiday, meaning he's moonlighting doing freelance game software. First thing tomorrow we *strike* and grab his cabinet for bait."

"And I've volunteered to take round a party of schoolkids from Mormal Down comprehensive. Mike Fortmayne was very ho-ho about it, and I had to swallow a lot of stuff about how I should report to the infirmary for medical check-up if I'd declined to the stage of volunteering for work: but it's fixed for the end of the afternoon. Not to mention a special pass for the *Chronic*'s densest reporter so he can see firsthand the acceptable face of the wicked atom base as its friendly, human scientists help educate the eager children who will be the scientists of tomorrow. Unquote."

"Buggered if I kiss any babies for him," Llewellyn intoned. "Timing's going to be hell. Bet you it doesn't work."

"The bleating of the kid excites the tiger: *Stalky & Co.* Have faith in your Uncle Roy, for he is a Great Man. – There you are, dear, all planned, even as you asked."

Lizzie squinted at him again. "Presumably that was *meant* to be over my head, darling. You watch it: remember, I did structural anthropology at Oxford, and I got a better degree than you, and –" In short order she disposed of Tappen's intellectual credentials, reducing him to quivering anthropoid jelly.

Out over the field and pavilion in their grey shimmer of rain, nothing continued to happen.

"Hear about the royal trip to Australia years and years ago?" said Llewellyn eventually, over the mutinous rumble of the moist hordes. "Seems she did the walkabout thing and met this guy, I mean cobber, a photographer. Said to him all brightly, 'I have a brother-in-law who's a photographer.' 'What a coincidence,' he says, a bit slurred, 'I've got this brother-in-law who's a queen.'"

"I don't believe a word of it," said Lizzie firmly. She consulted her watch. "Exactly how long does it take unskilled royalty to press a button?"

Tappen demonstrated the hollow groan he was getting so good at these days. "They make lots of speeches to her too, and then there's the tour of the official exhibition of wonderful NUTC achievements. The improved Gatling gun which can cut down rebellious natives by the score, radioactive caltrops to deal with enemy cavalry charges, a nuclear arsenal capable of knocking out anything Hitler could throw against us, lots of stuff like that."

"Modesty, modesty. Told her about your famous nuclear balloon?" Llewellyn said.

"Er, that's a highly technical simulation which is probably classified till the pips squeak, so I can't possibly reveal to you how a fireball is ingeniously simulated by a swelling balloon with a lightbulb inside. Nor dare I imagine HM's reactions when Staverton burbles, 'That burst of red light, your Majesty, represented a thermonuclear release on the order of 2 megatons, accompanied by a lethal emission of neutrons and hard radiation!' The Queen swoons, Prince Philip dives behind a nearby equerry with a characteristic 'Bloody hell!', and before Al Staverton and the AD can explain it's only a simulation they find themselves being prodded by Beefeaters' halberds in the Tower."

"Why did I marry a man who lives in a fantasy world?" Lizzie asked the dripping sky.

"Because you knew that one day my influence would admit you to the exotic pleasures of a low-budget royal garden party," Tappen suggested. "Look."

Figures had appeared in the distant pavilion, presumably royals and NUTC notables all the way up to the Director himself, who spent his days in Whitehall avoiding the awful reality of Robinson Heath but could be lured down by national emergencies or the equivalent. On the fringes of the group were highly-trained security guards doubtless eager to spot and gun down putative assassins. A murmur of excitement ran through the dank crowd, partly from royalist fervour and partly because flaps in the tents were being rolled up for the serving of tea.

Staff and guests will withdraw to obtain tea and cakes from the supply marquees in an orderly fashion, displaying reluctance at moving further from the Royal Pavilion and patriotic enthusiasm as they eagerly return. Each person present may request one (1) cup of tea with up to two (2) lumps of sugar, together with one (1) sticky cake or related confection. Refills and second helpings are most strongly discouraged. It is recommended that the sticky cake or related confection be balanced on the edge of one's saucer, which should be supported by the left hand while the right is employed to convey the teacup or cake to the mouth. Protocol requires that the little finger of the right hand not be extended whilst sipping tea, that the tea be sipped and not gulped (at least eighteen (18) sips are suggested for the emptying of a standard Civil Service cup), and that similarly the sticky cake or related confection be nibbled in decorous fashion (at least eight (8) nibbles of approximately equal size are recommended for the consumption of a standard issue sticky cake or related confection). Staff and their guests will refrain from emptying tea-dregs onto the grass or eating sugar lumps not required for sweetening tea. A note will be made of the name of any person requesting Russian tea ...

"Quickness of the hand deceives the eye," said Llewellyn, popping the third of his stock of small pink cakes into his mouth and diffusing an even spray of small pink crumbs. "Pity the rain dissolves the icing."

Tappen, who'd been feeling moderately daring for having swiped six sugarlumps, was vaguely resentful. Also he'd had an alarming premonition.

"... magnificent honour bestowed this day upon our world-famous research centre ... occasion of rejoicing and festivity ... step towards forging a lasting world peace through the organization of NATO ... new automated weapon assembly building which will be the envy of the civilized world ..." The Director's voice fought its way through a creaky PA system which reduced his doubtless magnificent speechmaking to an inhuman Dalek drone. Llewellyn went in search of further forbidden sticky cakes or related confections.

"I've been thinking, darling," said Lizzie as she dutifully took her thirty-third sip from a cup she'd normally have drained in four swallows. "Would it deflate your colossal male ego overmuch to let me into the secret of what you plan to *do* with a filing cabinet, a dim journalist and a class of mewling infants?"

"Luminous paint comes into it as well," said Tappen enigmatically. He contorted his features into what he fondly believed to be an evil leer, and laughed with what he hoped was the low, sinister laugh of a melodrama villain, Sir Jasper twirling his moustachios. "*Blackmail!*" he declaimed. "That's the secret, me dear."

"God help us all," said Lizzie, seeming to lose interest. One of her eyebrows rose significantly, though, despite its load of raindroplets: Tappen felt somebody close behind, and took the hint.

"... eternal vigilance is the price of democracy ... the tree of liberty must be watered with the blood of patriots ... strong arms will protect the peace ... extremism in the defence of liberty is no vice ... we will fight them on the beaches ... there is no alternative ..."

"Marmaduke," said a bitter voice in Tappen's ear. With a brief entrechat he turned, blinked to see the familiar face at an unexpected time, and hoped Lizzie's contralto hadn't carried too far as she spoke the magic words "Dim journalist."

"Tomorrow," he said. "I expected you tomorrow."

"Theophilus," said Green in the same wounded tone. "This morning the bloody Press Officer rang up and no-commented me half to death."

"I didn't say anyone *had* been sentenced to the death of a thousand cuts for revealing the secrets of sugar in NUTC tea, you loon: it was a hypothetical case."

"Have a heart. You show the sub a headline saying HYPOTHETICAL ATOM BASE HORROR, he asks you to make it a bit more punchy ... You think there'll be a story tomorrow?"

"Ninety per cent sure. Corruption, security breaches, a big exposure, the lot. You be there with your notebook poised to misreport each searing moment."

"It'd better be better than this bloody boring sideshow," said Green and sneezed.

With dangerous sweetness Lizzie said, "Roy, you must introduce me to the famous Mr Green. Isn't he the bold investigative journalist who exposed your habit of drinking twelve pints of beer a day?"

Green's expression was as unreadable as his journalism.

"... nor are the many talents of NUTC for warlike ends alone ... the spinoff of technological advance has made the quality of our lives what it is today ... swords and ploughshares ... to take an example at random from the field of medical science ..."

Tappen's terrible premonition returned with full force.

"... marvellous nuclear battery ... heard only this afternoon ... understand our royal guest Prince Philip is with us here today thanks to a heart pacemaker powered by such a ..."

At this juncture, the royal guest made a characteristic comment which was relayed by the PA system with awful clarity. A long, damp silence followed.

"Oh shit, oh shit, it's a scoop and I can't print it," moaned Green.

"... misapprehension ... ha ha ... all make mistakes ... ha ha ..." The Director seemed unable to rally his forces after the ghastly moment, and the speech concluded with this dying fall.

During the displays by Ministry of Defence security police, NUTC Machine Shop apprentices, the Plutonium Handling Division Barbershop Quartet, the Canteen Mystery Players, etc., staff and guests will pay close attention and preserve polite fortitude. Light applause will be given for a period of ten to fifteen seconds at the conclusion of each item: no whistles or catcalls will be permitted, and persons throwing crockery, tea dregs, paper aeroplanes (especially where constructed from portions of this document), sticky cakes or related confections onto the display area will be severely reprimanded. During the concluding National Anthem all present will naturally be expected to stand; since staff and guests (other than those granted a Royal Pavilion Seat Pass) will already be standing, it is desirable that attendees show due respect by standing up more prominently at this time, on tiptoe if required. Those seated in the Portakabin conveniences during the opening bars of the Anthem are permitted to use their own discretion ...

With strange paralysis Tappen watched a repellent horde of apprentices leaping one by one over a wooden horse with studied lack of grace. In the glazed expressions of the distant royals he imagined he could detect a longing to be under that horse and tunnelling to freedom.

"Darling, you look like one of those corpses in the ghost stories, the ones they find next morning in the haunted toilet with a look of dumb horror in their dead eyes, like an alarmed codfish."

Tappen told her: "It's the grapevine. The royal pacemaker went up the grapevine. Speak of the devil and he will hear about it ... oh bloody hell."

"What on earth ... oh. *Oh.* You mean that disaster just now wasn't *any* old disaster but a real Roy Tappen cataclysm engineered by my own dear husband?" Lizzie eyed him with her social worker's stare which could make gigantic wife-beaters drop to their knees and plead for mercy. Tappen almost welcomed the arrival of Fortmayne, which saved him from having to produce an ingenious, witty and completely self-justifying answer.

Fortmayne, though, wore the aggrieved look of a man who'd been on the receiving end of a snowball of recrimination swelling in viciousness on its downhill path from Director to AD to CPRA to Staverton to Fortmayne. He didn't say anything for a while, but Tappen had the illusion that the thin drizzle was evaporating into steam with a tiny continual hiss as it reached his boss's head.

"Just don't hold your breath for your next promotion," Fortmayne said at last. "Wait for the next blue moon. Wait for the melting of the polar ice-caps. Wait till the sun grows cold and one by one, without any fuss, the stars begin to go out. I predict you will see all these things before you see another promotion board at Robinson Heath, or get a cushy transfer either. Do I make myself clear?"

"Slip of the memory ... must have turned over two pages at once in *New Scientist* ... probably a typo, pacemaker where it should have been peacemaker ..." These and similarly inarguable and convincing excuses were drowned in precisely seven seconds of light applause, during which Fortmayne stalked away.

"I've always wanted you to leave Robinson Heath, my love," said Lizzie cosily.

"Yes but," Tappen said. "We have these two large round items of unfinished business, remember?"

On the field the MoD Police were demonstrating the feral savagery of their Alsatians. A plainly unwilling victim waved a menacing stick and the dog-handler gave curt commands supplemented by a furtive push: in seconds the innocent bystander was flat on the sodden grass, one arm gripped by large greenish fangs. Tappen mentioned to Lizzie that owing to overenthusiasm of past dogs in past displays, the guinea-pig's arm would be heavily swathed in protective bandages under his jacket, with last-minute novocaine injections in case the dog was too carried away with its painless restraint.

"Don't the Queen and Philip look excited?" he said to keep the subject drifting away from tender areas. "Probably never before in their cloistered lives have they been privileged to see an athletic display or a police-dog demo. How clever and considerate of NUTC to show them at last how the other half lives ..."

As three Alsatians belly-flopped in succession through a blazing hoop, one of them clearly decided to add its own special touch to the performance. It halted with its back pointedly towards royalty, shuddered, and deposited an immense, rank heap of steaming turds which the other two converged upon with the appreciative sniffs of wine connoisseurs. The dogs were hastily led away to prolonged and enthusiastic applause.

"Let me take you away from all this, love," said Tappen tenderly. "Let's go home."

"To the Station Hotel, cabbie," Lizzie corrected.

They crept away through the fine, steady drizzle to the special overflow car park; they were not alone. Not very many minutes later, driving back along the main road past the NUTC Sports Area but on the right side of the fence, Tappen and Lizzie thought they heard the premature strains of the National Anthem through the high wire mesh. They exercised discrimination about standing up.

Twenty One

"Do you sometimes get this *déjà vu* feeling," said Tappen as with Llewellyn he strained to slide the filing cabinet across the irregular floorboards. Theoretical Support, Building 334k, was another Terrapin hut not as well preserved as the Crystal Palace; their burden felt ready to plunge through the floor and convert the wildlife underneath to rabbit schnitzels.

"Let's have another look inside," Llewellyn said. *Déjà vu.* They'd removed several cubic feet of Tamlyn's useless printouts from the drawers. Suppose, though, they'd overlooked a lurking warhead of frightful destructive power? In these troubled times you never could tell. They looked again, found only a few suspicious rubber bands, and took a fresh grip on the obstinate metal.

Escaping Tamlyn's office was like threading a labyrinth: the computer paper was piled up to seven feet high, and for the sake of his nerves the fire safety inspector had long ago stopped inspecting. Tamlyn's great project for the defence of the nation was a computer program to conduct a complete probability analysis of the football pools, and every day or two, in or out of season, a wad of half a million sheets was delivered from Robinson Heath's computer centre to the security cupboard for classified printout in building 334. So even Tamlyn was useful in his way: thanks to his vast heaps of printout the cupboard door couldn't be closed, and everyone else was able to collect Top Secret program output without needing to remember a combination which in the interests of total security was changed every Tuesday.

"Mind the step," Tappen grunted as Llewellyn failed to mind the step. The filing cabinet lurched down the four steps outside 334k like a berserk warrior robot from a particularly low-budget episode of *Dr Who*, and treacherously rolled out its second-lowest drawer to threaten Llewellyn with kneecapping.

"I told you to mind the step."

"I'm not complaining," Llewellyn gasped as he kicked the drawer viciously back into place. "I never complain. Only the booze you owe my nerves since this time last week ... you'd need an IMF loan to buy it, I'd need spare kidneys to drink it."

Tappen heaved again, sparing just enough energy for a grunt intended to combine heartfelt commiseration, conciliatory soothing and the sentiment that one shouldn't waste one's breath in this weather. Just as Tuesday afternoon had naturally and inevitably shed fine continuous drizzle over countless best suits and garden-party frocks, so today the Tappen Theory of Cosmic Obstinacy demanded that this morning's shifting of filing cabinets would control the skies and drench Robinson Heath in the choking mugginess of a tropical rain forest whose inhabitants had all left their kettles aboil. Thin rivulets kept trickling down the insides of Tappen's legs, as though he'd had an unfortunate personal mishap.

At last the cabinet stood proud and lonely and erect in Hacker's bare office, like one of the statues of Easter Island; and Tappen and Llewellyn stood proud and erect as overdone asparagus on either side.

"The bleating of the kid excites the tiger," Tappen said again.

"Stop quoting fascist imperialists. Where's the paint? Any left over since your last Health Physics gag using *my* pissing-bottle?"

"Lots," said Tappen soothingly, producing the white bottle from his pocket. "I think a nice irregular splodge on the back to start with: oh yes, the aesthetic tonal balance there has definitely got a touch of Jackson Pollock. And *underneath* all the drawers in case it gets rubbed off the back. Do the label cards come out? Behind them, then ..." Using the practised techniques of the Robinson Heath r/a laboratories, he daubed the thick white luminous paint in all these places, with his forefinger.

The label cards slotted into holders on the front of each steel drawer read, from top to bottom, USE OTHER DRAWER, DO NOT OPEN THIS END, THE LABEL ON THE DRAWER BELOW IS TRUE and THE LABEL ON THE DRAWER ABOVE IS FALSE. Tappen had always known there was something about computer people.

"Tea," said Llewellyn. His tone of voice made it clear that this demand was but the first payment towards a twenty-year mortgage on Tappen's soul and beer money. A brief visit to the lavatories let Tappen fill the kettle and decontaminate his leprous finger; returning to his office, he found that as usual a snag had arisen.

"I have been waiting ten minutes for you," said the snag, otherwise known as Mike Fortmayne, and today very obviously Dr Michael Fortmayne, PSO, Immediate Superior of R. Tappen. "I see you haven't opened your mail. I would like to watch you open your mail, Roy. Do you hear what I'm saying?"

On a dim instinctive level Tappen felt overwhelmingly unkeen to open his mail. He poked cautiously at the aged wooden IN/OUT tray of a type probably favoured by Bob Cratchit, and Fortmayne watched him with grey eyes Tappen wished were safely behind a leaden radiation shield. Heaps of junk mail from outside NUTC, disintegrating re-re-re-readdressed envelopes from friendly fellow-scientists within, a horrid stapled slip of computer paper from Health Physics ... which left the ominously neat *white* envelope (scientists were only allowed manila) with a *typewritten* "R. Tappen, Bldg 334d" (scientists weren't trusted with advanced technology like typewriters) and a *sealed* flap (scientists were required to re-use envelopes fifty times at least and tucked-in flaps were the rule). He wrenched it open with the nervous energy normally reserved for dry-roast peanut packets, and unfolded the now torn contents.

Admin Central
30 June 9 am
Effective Monday 5 July, Mr R. Tappen (SSO, Superintendency of Nuclear Operations) will undergo security clearance downrating pending reevaluation. Until further notice Mr Tappen is assigned to clearance list 4F.
pp P.T.St.J. Hanratty, Assistant Director
(Distribution as per attached schedule)

List 4F was the security clearance equivalent of being set to swab out toilets and empty ashtrays. List 4F meant Tappen would no longer be allowed to read reports or minutes written by Tappen, run computer programs devised by Tappen, or do anything much bar sit at his desk staring out of the window for fear of letting his eyes fall on something mildly classified inside Tappen's office. It was the deepest of humiliations. It sounded great.

"I don't agree with what you're thinking," said Fortmayne with unfair perception. "While this nonsense continues – and I must say it seems a little extreme as a retaliation for yesterday, however indefensible your sense of humour was – while it lasts I expect you to do all you can from memory and working notes. Nothing is secret until it has SECRET stamped on it, right? You will bring me 'working papers' and I will classify them as I see fit. Oh, and before Monday you'll be expected to reset your security cupboard to a combination you don't know. Shouldn't be any trouble for someone of your talents." With a slight sniff Fortmayne departed.

"It couldn't have come at a better time," Tappen was saying to Llewellyn over steaming beakers of tea, ten minutes later. He still felt shakes and tremors within, as of an aspen overdose, but had always been the kind of idiot who grinned when clouted by the school bully and thus earned himself a further clout. "Firstly it gives me an incredibly convincing reason to call, say, Alf Rossiter and oh so casually drop the hint that lures him to his doom. Then, Mike Fortmayne rabbiting on about rubber stamps made me think –"

"Roy. I resign. Don't want to know. Look, you've got Lizzie to support you when they slip you their free offer of UB40 privileges. Me ... I think I'll just put in a few hours on the programming progress report, OK?"

Llewellyn was subject to these spasms of good behaviour, sometimes running to three or four days with a Pocket Gem Dictionary writing reports: he was a classic case of overdeveloped computeracy, and like millions with his unfortunate condition had trouble with most English words longer than IF or THEN or END.

Alone again, Tappen selected a xeroxed report from an unlocked drawer. *Nuclear Catastrophe Analysis* by Dr A. Staverton, unclassified, was so deeply boring that SNO staff swore by it as a means to achieve suspended animation and pass trancelike through the day to going-home time. Those whose eyes had stayed open beyond the first sentences reported it to be a fatuous application of trendy Catastrophe Theory to obscure and useless nuclear reactions, which had undoubtedly been rejected by everything from *Nature* down to *The Unexplained* before Staverton decided on the equivalent of vanity publishing by issuing the thing as an NUTC report – not, surprisingly, bound in limp mauve suede. Which only showed that even Stavertons are placed in this world for a purpose: the special qualities of *Nuclear Catastrophe Analysis* made it exactly what Tappen needed to build a better security man-trap and with luck stop them beating a path to his door.

He thrust out his jaw, tried to project stern and steely beams from his eyes, and marched to confront the implacable world of Security and Admin outside his office. The door opened as he reached it, and in came Pell, who stared at the apparition of Tappen defying the gods and recoiled. "Er ... I have another flyer," he said cautiously, and offered a dayglo orange sheet.

NUCLEAR POWER SHOULD BE FOR THE PEOPLE! WHAT DO THE WARMONGERS DO BEHIND THE CLOSED DOORS OF ROBINSON HEATH? WHAT ARE THEY HIDING FROM THE PEOPLE? ...

"You should know," Tappen said as he studied this with shaded eyes. "Nuclear power for the people doesn't sound very CND, does it?"

"No ..." For a moment Pell contrived to sound like the White Knight: "It's my own invention." He passed on, leaving Tappen momentarily paralysed by the injustice of who did and who didn't have their SECRET clearances snipped off while surrounded by a hollow square of security police. Would atoms-for-the-people mean something like the Tappen domestic scene, a nuke in every poor man's pot? He channelled a little of his frustration into slamming the office door behind him; small fragments of Terrapin ceiling tinkled and clattered around him, and several bulldog-clipped wads of announcements fell off the corridor notice-board. The first one Tappen picked up read "SAFETY AWARDS COMMITTEE. Handling safety improvement suggestion by Asst Machinist T. Scrope. The suggestion was approved for nationwide adoption and should save approximately £500,000 and up to eight major casualties per annum. A discretionary safety award to Mr Scrope has been recommended, to the amount of £15.00."

The next wad consisted of circulars about transfer vacancies which again and again were dangled before NUTC scientists' eyes like cups of water before parched wretches in the chambers of the Spanish Inquisition. Easier to get permission for a holiday in Red China than escape NUTC's toils by the transfer route. Top of the heap was a flyer describing SSO/physicist posts at the Tidal Power Research Establishment in sunny Milford-on-Sea: in a fit of petulance Tappen thrust this light-fingeredly into his pocket.

Minutes later he was saying, "Hello, Chrissie, love of my life, I want to beg the tiniest of favours which in your munificence you would be overjoyed to grant."

The startlingly convex guardian of the 334 photocopier pushed back her lank black hair and said, "Oh I'm *sorry* Roy, the machine isn't working, and even if it was we're out of paper and I'm supposed to be holding it for a priority job in any case, besides which you know I mustn't let you photocopy anything classified or anything that isn't NUTC work, sorry darling ..." For once Tappen declined the invitation to cuddly verbal wrestling (those who didn't understand her liking for this ritual combat could get the impression that Chrissie never let anyone use the copier at all).

"No, my gorgeous, don't tempt me with the forbidden pleasures of your erotic gadgetry. All I ask today is to use some of your delightful rubber stamps, here before your very eyes, absolutely no deception."

It was a sufficiently unlikely request that Chrissie hadn't prepared elaborate defences against it: "Oh, I suppose so," she said with mild subcutaneous disappointment, and Tappen set to work. It didn't take long to thump the blood-red stamps at top and bottom of every page, UTTER TOP SECRET/ATOMIC and UK EYES ONLY LIST 1AAA and (in smaller print) This Document Must Be Transferred Between Secure Offices Only Under Grade 01 Security Escort. By Fortmayne's advice and these potent modern ju-ju symbols, *Nuclear Catastrophe Analysis* was transformed from harmless soporific to red-hot document as safe to handle as a lump of plutonium, or even two lumps of plutonium.

Tappen blew a kiss to Chrissie, who showed signs of evolving reasons why he shouldn't be allowed to use the sacred red stamppad, and faded away in the direction of Hacker's former office, where the bleating of the kid would excite the tiger.

The Staverton report taped where it needed to be taped, Tappen examined his watch, gulped, and ran for the marquee on the waste ground by A section. How was it that people in books never found their boring daily jobs interfering with plans to trap the Asiatic masterspy, or expose the perpetrator of the blunt-instrument murder in the locked room? Hurrying through the moist, gravid air of Robinson Heath this morning wasn't so much like running as swimming ...

He reached the 334d fireball display on time, eleven o'clock, as he could tell from the twittering cascade of beeps up and down the rows of manned displays. In canteen, library, cinema, site bus or committee meeting you always knew the striking of the hour, because a repulsive cross-section of humanity had digital watches that went *eep-eep*. Soon the miracles of voice synthesis would make the bloody things go *cuckoo*.

The first VIP party had started at the far end and was receiving homeopathic doses of higher nuclear education with vacant eyes and doubtless uncomprehending ears. Tappen had a breathing space to take stock of this technological funfair, with its pervading smell of dank canvas, soggy grass, perspiring civil servant and moist electronics.

On his right a dispirited SO was ready to demonstrate NUTC's awesome lab-analysis computer power, a wrinkled old Apple whose flickering display screen issued pugnacious offers to take on all comers at noughts-and-crosses. On his left was a temptingly unattended setup with a button to push as in the Science Museum: furtively Tappen pushed it, and inside the glass case feeble smoke-puffs blew from twin nozzles at an Action Man soldier with red stars glued to his uniform. Hidden rods caused the doll to collapse in slow motion while a recorded voice enthused over the humane advantages of this new binary gas which harmlessly disabled the motor nerves to leave whole armies helpless. (Whether it harmlessly wore off again afterwards was not specified.) Opposite, a hastily Letrasetted panel from Inspection & Measurement gloated over the high standards of weapon workmanship: in the latest trial four weapon cores had had their vital statistics measured in a complicated and boring way using lasers. Wonder of wonders, the figures agreed with such uncanny exactitude you might imagine them to be four measurements of the same dull metal sphere ... Tappen allowed himself a restrained giggle.

Reaching the microcomputer, the knot of bored VIPs lit up in sudden appreciation of something they could understand, and happily ignored the attending Scientific Officer's attempt to be educational, in favour of a knockout noughts-and-crosses competition. It had been a long time since Tappen last saw grown men lose at this game.

"What's all this?" grunted a rotund and pink-glowing VIP in his mid-fifties, who emphasized his superior importance by striding ahead of the mob. Being dwarfed by a gigantic placard reading BRIGHTER THAN A THOUSAND SUNS: THE NUCLEAR FIREBALL, Tappen felt mildly redundant as he answered: "This is a simulation of the nuclear explosion itself. A nuclear explosion is what happens when a nuclear weapon explodes. This is caused by explosive surrounding the nuclear weapon core, which explodes --" (Tappen decided he'd have to improve the punchiness of this Fortmayne-devised script) "– and collapses the weapon core into supercriticality, causing the actual nuclear explosion." His deft fingers touched a hidden switch with perfect timing, and in slow motion the balloon inflated hissingly, bright light glowed within it, and the needles of simulated x-ray, gamma-ray, neutron, heatflash, blast and megadeath measuring instruments swung hard over to indicate something pretty exciting. In a final lingering fallout of verbiage, Tappen explained that this was only a simulation and that Robinson Heath and its environs were not in fact being razed by a fiery nuclear holocaust – a soothing postscript on which the Press Officer had insisted – and the pink man nodded sympathetically.

"Terrible waste of time for you boffins, all this, I imagine," he said.

"Oh, at least this way we get to meet people and remember how human faces look. I mean, being locked away from the public behind a five-mile security fence is nice for recluses but it can feel like solitary confinement sometimes. As for waste of time, it happens all the year round; you wouldn't *believe* ..." Tappen sifted through his memory for a safe, non-contentious, non-classified example. "Mere days ago I had to shelve the nuclear physics to evaluate some crank book called *An Experiment with Space*, spend hours reading this nonsense about, well, according to the author's theory the particle storage rings at CERN in Geneva should float away over the Alps because of how fast the things inside go round, ha ha."

A pink finger prodded his sternum. "I happen to know that the Swiss know all about this. CERN doesn't levitate because *they nailed it down.*"

"But ... But the book's a load of cobblers, and it's got a foreword by the loony Earl of Clancarty, the man who thinks UFOs should be called ASVs, Alien Space Vehicles, whether they've been identified or not."

The finger pushed harder, possibly seeking a nerve spot which would inflict cruel and unusual punishment. "Clancarty's a good man, did good work in the Lords UFO debate. What's your name and rank, young fellow?"

Tappen was painfully reminded that the scientific and political minds did not function in quite the same way. No doubt NUTC's disgraceful lack of touch with contemporary UFO science would shortly become the subject of a question in Parliament. The Minister for Defence would have to grovel and apologize for his scientists' stuffy, old-fashioned demand that theories should once in a while be supported by a little evidence ... He suppressed a tiny smile as he recited his personal details for the pink inquisitor.

The others clustered round, turning on his display that special look of engrossment which assembly-line workers reserve for the day's two hundredth exciting car chassis. Tappen exerted all his innate lack of charisma as he droned, "This is a simulation of the nuclear explosion itself. A nuclear explosion is what happens when

..."

Two hours later he made his enfeebled way to lunch, overcome by a nightmare feeling that all the VIPs were the same VIPs coming round again and again to torment him. His throat felt like a napalmed desert from saying the same things to apparently the same people. In the Robinson Heath canteen he leaned over the counter and hoarsely observed, "This is a simulation of the nuclear explosion itself," before regaining control and asking for sausage and chips.

The canteen was a hangar-like room which would have been light and airy if the oxygen in the air hadn't been replaced over the years with vaporized chip-fat, a layer of which also made the windows frosted and bleary as Tappen's eyes on the morning after. Eerie, glowing UV lights hung from the ceiling here and there, enticing the copious flies to their doom: small crackles continually sounded as bluebottles buzzed too close and were electrically zapped, subsequently falling with strange accuracy into luncheons far below. By chance, one of the people eating alone at the long Formica tables was Alf Rossiter, leafing with his free hand through a heap of Redbury estate agents' flyers. Tappen steered that way, glad to save the effort of trekking to his office for a phone call.

"Ah, be my guest Royo, I'll take the chance and let you sit, even if you are a dangerous security risk and that, ha ha."

"I want a word with you," said Tappen, spearing a sausage.

"Best thing I've heard for ages, Prince Philip and his atomic truss or whatever it was. Head of Apprentices is blessing you for it, you know, on account of you sort of took the heat off his athletics team. You hear 'bout that? Bloody awful performance because the little sods were playing silly buggers in the machine shop two or three hours before, and where d'you think the star performers were all afternoon? Back in the shop, if you please, pricks stuck to the big lathes with superglue. Seems the second team didn't like them doing a Lord Muck act about being good enough for Royal Command Performance ... Had to take 'em round to Medical with bits of lathe dangling out o' their trousers."

Tappen was spellbound; he shook his head to break the fascination. "I said, I want a word with you." His second sausage seemed to be held to the plate by a blob of congealed fat: he looked at it and was suddenly unhungry. "About ... Alf, I know your mates. It's like the fellow I used to know in the Customs – anything really juicy like Swedish mags gets passed around the office."

"Funny ideas you get." Rossiter was picking at a generic dish which depending on the canteen's whim might be curry, goulash, something bolognese or conceivably Lancashire hotpot.

"You know they're taking me off the 1A list on Monday. Just between the two of us, mind telling me why? If they're going to stick me to the Official Secrets Act with superglue, it would be nice to hear the reason."

"Ah, now, Roy, need-to-know, need-to-know! Couldn't let out a confidential thing like that to any old bloke I meet in the greasy spoon ... Three guesses."

"The Director and royals didn't like yesterday afternoon?"

"They did not, bless 'em. But no one grassed, it was all public school stuff, stiff upper wossname. Director covered for the AD and then took it out of him, same with CPRA, which it's all I knew till now. So it was you, eh, riding for a fall like usual, same as in the *Chronicle*?"

"That was going to be my second guess, actually." Tappen was annoyed: he'd hoped only a select few cognoscenti would have penetrated the secret identities of the Scientist On Twelve Pints A Day and/or Marmaduke Theophilus. Bugger, he thought.

"No way. One guess left, matey, time to extract the digit, eh?"

"Er ... could it be something to do with the plute inventory or that smuggling exercise that failed so brilliantly last week?"

"Plute inventory my arse ... Eh, what's that, then?" Sudden suspicion smoothed his face into a mask of policemanliness, and he seemed almost ready to intone, "'Ello, 'ello, 'ello, what's all this then?"

"Oh, there was a tiny glitch that had us worried in 334 for a day or two; all cleared up now, never was a Security problem anyway, all pure as the driven snow, much purer." By now Tappen had almost forgotten that this enquiry was to divert attention from the casual comment he meant to make while savouring his final chip. "What the hell's the reason, then? Did I fart in the wrong committee meeting? Did the genealogy squad find I'm descended from dangerous lefties like Wat Tyler? Did the thought-detectors at the gate reveal my secret longing for *soixante-neuf* with Mrs Thatcher?"

Rossiter leant back luxuriously, fingered a wad of succulent gristle from his mouth, inspected it at leisure and deposited it in a convenient ashtray. "Not for me to say, Roy my boy, not for me to say. But let me tell you a tale. Suppose, all hypo-thetical like, some silly pillock piled up trouble for himself. No names no packdrill. Suppose this wally pulled some legs about being sort of one of those, and suppose a bloke on PV duty found him feeling up an SO in the terminal room, the same SO he's talked about holding hands with on an open phone line, and suppose he starts acting guilty, shaky, talking through his arse about barmy smuggling projects like he wanted to distract us from summat else. And then a bit more of the old listening-in on phones, and it turns out his lady wife's buggered off because of blokes our pal's got in the house, and when one of our lads drops round for a friendly word with her in this hotel she goes all evasive-like, won't say why she left. Suppose all that."

Tappen's eyes had closed in anguished half-recollection of saying Llewellyn needed his hand held on one phone, and talking to Lizzie about "men in the house" on another. Oh sod it.

"Now some people like me might get the notion there was a big joke on the go, a big act by the kind of pillock who'd think it was funny to stick Chairman Mao's picture on his pass. Some people mightn't get the joke, though, Roy; could sort of start thinking about all those bent college guys (you was at Oxford, no? Well then). Spies and such. And when you go supposing all that, the next thing you think is, well, it flaming well looks like we've got to suppose someone's clearance rating gets chopped PDQ. Are you with me, Roy?"

Tappen felt he should laugh heartily, or rush guilty from the room, or leap across the table and plant a wet smacking kiss on Rossiter's cheek (ugh), or eat a last desperate sausage and simulate food poisoning.

"All that because Lizzie couldn't stand the noise of the plumbers putting in the new cistern," he said, waving a chip with a broad expansive gesture that sent a blob of tomato sauce outward in a deadly Exocet strike upon the front of the other's navy blue uniform. It made a soul-satisfying contrast.

"Funny she didn't mention it was just plumbers," said Rossiter, mopping.

"It was bad experience for her. One of them looked like a man who was horribly offensive to her once, a security man, and she wouldn't stay in the house with him. And," (Tappen said rapidly as Rossiter's mouth opened) "we'd paid half in advance so we couldn't change plumbers."

"Funny she couldn't nip home at night while they weren't around."

"You mean you've never heard of the 24-hour plumbing service? They work round the clock, take benzedrine to stay awake, I think: it's amazing what small firms will do to stay competitive these days. Pakistani, of course."

"Funny they never answered the door all the times our lads dropped round while you was out, eh, Roy?"

"I know, I know, they never answer the door for me either. I have to let myself in ... They're deaf. Talk to each other in sign language, you see; and they lipread. If I want them to open the door I have to push up the letterbox flap and let them lipread me through the hole. I suppose deafness is an occupational hazard of plumbing, you know, that agonizing squeak of pipe wrenches on rusty nuts and all the time a great Niagara noise of rushing water."

Tappen was so intoxicated with his inventive powers as to be quite ready to explain, should Rossiter query the lack of all-night lights in the bathroom, that in the interests of energy conservation the nightshift of his hypothetical plumbers was blind. Instead, Rossiter reached moodily over the table, raised Tappen's right hand in the air, and said: "I declare you the winner."

"Well, we were just supposing, as I remember it ..." He forced down the last chip and stared at the last bite of sausage rather than Rossiter's face, to which it bore many resemblances. "Oh, by the way, who do I ring to get a spare filing cabinet taken back to central stores? There's an extra one in 334d, the empty office: we want the room for a lab."

With what might be elaborate casualness, Rossiter said: "You're in luck there, mate. Got to have a word with those blokes right after nosh. 334d ... I'll see to it."

Tappen felt a strong urge to leap up and turn cartwheels all the way along the canteen aisle, uttering shrill war-whoops as he went. He said: "Oh, thanks."

Twenty Two

It was Children's Hour in the exhibition marquee. Large gaps showed in the rows of display stands, where too-sensitive items had been whipped out like too-sensitive teeth: the model Trident whose streamlining might be impressed on the photographic memories of midget spies disguised as fifth-formers, the missile samples they might shoplift and use for fireworks, the more risque items of glassware produced as a sideline by the chemical lab apprentices. Tappen was interested to see that after hasty amendment the Inspection & Measurement placard proudly claimed that four (items of unspecified equipment) as shown in the (photographs removed) had been measured by (a very interesting but classified method using lasers) with the impressive results given in the (table of figures censored), thus demonstrating (something). Also the nerve-gassed Action Man had been adapted into a warning to the young, about the perils of tobacco.

Another difference in the afternoon was the conversation. Why couldn't this lot imitate the decently double-glazed silence and expressions of their elders and worsers?

"This is a simulation of the nuclear explosion itself ..."

"No it isn't, it's a balloon. A balloon-blowing-up machine."

"A *simulation* of the expanding fireball caused by thermo-nuclear energy release."

"Who invented the balloon-blowing-up machine? Can you get them in the shops?"

Tappen raised his voice and sternly completed the recitation. The stick-thin boy with the obsession about balloon-blowing-up machines asked how this part of the awesome apparatus was powered and how much it cost. Tappen told him that the information was classified. A plump girl mentioned disdainfully that *all* this was stuff she'd already *read* in old *science fiction* books and didn't the exhibition have anything *new*? Tappen told her the new things were classified. A smaller boy, whose mouth had hung open through this meeting of minds, now began a complex enquiry about the location of what appeared to be unmentionably vital defence installations. "It's classified," Tappen snapped just before it became clear that the installation in question was the toilet.

"This is a simulation of the nuclear explosion itself ..." From the corner of his eye Tappen saw the noughts-and-crosses sideshow next door was doing cheeringly badly. Though it had attracted numerous pasty-faced boys with pebble glasses, these were loudly deriding the antique computer, the feeble display, the fuddy-duddy Victorian – if not Dark Ages – noughts-and-crosses software itself. All the kids had far superior computers in their own bedrooms, and the cowering SO's excuses about NUTC budgeting were greeted with scorn. A particularly pimply thirteen-year-old mentioned how much he himself was earning by writing infinitely advanced arcade-game software. Tappen would have relished the sight of a Scientific Officer going green and clamping his jaws tight shut, except that the figure was actually more than a grateful government showered on Senior Scientific Officers such as Tappen.

"The nuclear explosion is triggered by ludicrously inequitable distribution of wealth," he heard himself say, and hastily started again.

The twitter-beep of digital watches sounded for three o'clock and much later for four. Tappen sweated in the sticky, moist air and parried routine questions with routine answers; less probable ones he evaded, or ignored on their own merits. His brain thus disengaged, he was able to consider the secret countdown to approximately five, when almost anything would be rather more likely than not to happen.

"This is a simulation of the nuclear explosion itself ..."

Researches into his and Llewellyn's memories indicated that anonymous blue-grey Transit vans were most often to be seen leaving NUTC a little after five, a little before the major lemming-rush for the gate. You were supposed to call the latter "outmuster", balancing the morning "inmuster", like delicate euphemisms for nineteenth-century ailments.

"No, it is not a rubber johnnie. It's a balloon simulating the expanding fireball caused by the collapse into supercriticality of Robinson Heath canteen sausages within the tortured digestive systems of its employees ..." (This after a sudden inner pang. None of the kids seemed to think his words out of the ordinary.)

"How big? The central plutonium bit is a hollow sphere about the size of – that's classified, actually, but it's bigger than a gerbil and smaller than a pig."

Anonymous blue-grey Transit vans tended to leave by the northeast gate, the Bogley gate, very convenient for Bogley and shops in Bogley, another straw's weight of confirmation for Tappen's conspiracy theory of the MoD Illuminati.

"No, if you work here you can get into *terrible* trouble saying that. 'Kills people and leaves property untouched' isn't right anyway, what they do is kill a lot more people for the same property damage – only you mustn't say that either, a friend of mine put it in a *New Scientist* article and they had him on the carpet for writing propaganda and gutter journalism. What you're supposed to say is that n-bombs don't knock quite as many houses down for a given number of dead people, which is of course a totally different thing ... look love, there's no need to cry, it's a *deterrent*, which means you never actually use it, see ... oh bloody hell."

Blue-grey Transit vans passing outward at the critical time were known, in at least one case, to trigger the gate r/a detectors, by a mindboggling coincidence just after an officeload of junk including old r/a sources had been cleared.

"Oh, you've been round SPERA ... you don't really swim in it and the blue light is Cherenkov radiation ... caused by particles going faster than light in the water ... like sonic booms when Concorde goes faster than sound ... I *know* Einstein says you can't go faster than light, only light goes slower in water so you can ... sorry, Mr Science Fiction, this does not mean spaceships can travel faster in water than in space ... where was I: *this* light represents a nuclear fireball at a temperature of hundreds of thousands of degrees, expanding to lay waste whole cities as part of a peaceful programme of nuclear deterrence under the auspices of NATO ..."

Alf Rossiter declined to search sinister blue-grey Transit vans which did the sinister blue-grey things already featured in Tappen's intermittent thoughts.

"Only very, very, wicked and cynical people call it Britain's Independent Detergent. Who said that to you? ... Oh, ah, that must have been a slip of my tongue ... Well, what the rude cynics say is it's because it glows whiter than white, cleans off soiled foreign countries and is kind to what it leaves of your hands..."

The contents of Bogley Surplus Stores spoke for themselves.

"This is a simulation of the nuclear explosion itself ..." Tappen felt like a drunk who knows the first line of a song and no more, but is undeterred. Only this time he was deterred, perhaps even independently, as a small girl with large blue eyes told him in triumph: "You said that *before!*" The realization that some of the kids were going round twice made Tappen feel doubly foolish, no longer a high-minded imparter of wisdom but a comedy routine whose audience knew all the punchlines and greeted them with yawns of delight.

"Piss off," he murmured; and then, in louder and more fatherly tones, "Special tour at ten to five, starting just outside the doorflap. Tell your friends."

Since the little darlings had already been given a chance to drown in the seething radioactive waters of SPERA, a gaggle of them wandering northward to the gate should cause little comment. Of course they might be shot as an entire horde of midget Soviet infiltrators, but in for a sheep, in for a lamb, however the proverb went. (Into a sheep, into a lamb? Reminded him of Welsh-valleys jokes.)

A new and oversized schoolboy appeared before Tappen's dimming eyes. He took a deep, sighing breath and began the litany. "This is a simulation of the nuclear explosion itself ..."

"Looks like it's got a puncture," said the squeaky voice of ace reporter Green. Tappen blinked and looked. Sure enough, the balloon was barely tumescent and hissing gently through a pinhole. Sabotage, no doubt – some junior sceptic had adjusted matters to his own version of a likely British fireball. He wasn't that far wrong, Tappen brooded momentarily.

"I'm glad to see you, Steve," he said heartily and almost sincerely. With the moment of untruth so near, Tappen kept wanting to vanish forever, live in a cave and eat bats. "Everything's under control here, and if this comes off you should see corruption happening before your horrified eyes." You bet you will, he thought. "Though of course there could be a big cover-up that kills your story, like with Watergate in the early days ..." You bet there will, he thought.

"Lead me to it," said the ace journalist, beginning to draft what Tappen supposed were searing sentences in his notebook. ATOM BASE "ROBINSONGATE" SHOCK!

"Ten to five just outside the entrance," Tappen said.

Green made an O with finger and thumb – a most unBritish gesture picked up from low journalists, Tappen suspected – and went to conduct investigative journalism on the computer stand. Here one of the pastiest of the infant programmers had won a £5 bet with the doomed SO, by successfully creating a playable PacMan game within an hour. Green promptly joined the queue to play it.

"Special tour at ten to five," Tappen said to a random selection of passers-by, choosing older kids for preference. "See the living security men. Be appalled by brutal police methods. Be amazed by the astonishing 1950s perimeter defences. Ten to five outside the entrance ... roll up, roll up!"

Instinctively his voice dropped as imagination took a hand in the announcement, until at the last he was almost whispering: "Ten thousand security drum-majorettes in a massed nude spectacle! Mixed MoD policefolk, animal mineral and vegetable, present a new twenty uses for truncheons, culminating in universal Fellini-style fellation! Special rates for children and OAPs..."

Then 4.50 pm approached, and with a curious numb feeling of walking the last few paces to a vasectomy clinic, Tappen threaded his way to the exit. The main obstacle was a crowd of kids making scatological comments at a disrespectful distance from Health Physics' urinalysis display. Outside, after the shady marquee, the sky held a soggy grey dazzle like floodlit porridge. Tappen squinted to count the haul in his net: twelve mutinous schoolchildren, or thirteen if you counted Green. Tappen, who was most emphatically not superstitious, decided at once to count himself as well. They headed for the gate in a disorderly rabble, discreetly trailed by a security policeman who perhaps hoped to seize Green in the act of sketching some classified clod of Her Majesty's soil.

The plumpest of the girls prattled somewhat nervously about a display Tappen hadn't seen, where a big grey man with a scraggy little beard had talked forever about how awful radiation poisoning was and made her blood run cold. Also he'd stressed the interesting statistic that one could build and maintain the whole extensive British nuclear defence force for less than the cost of feeding one underprivileged child. Tappen thought he recognized the erratic eloquence of Roger Pell.

"Running all over the place you'll see these enormous pipes," he announced by way of subject-change, indicating the two-foot-diameter monstrosities that criss-crossed and encircled Robinson Heath like the Midgard Serpent trying to fit into low-rent accommodation. "Would anyone like to guess what these triumphs of nineteenth-century engineering are used for?"

"High-energy particle accelerators," said the tallest lad intelligently.

"Speaking tubes."

"*Nerve gas* pipelines," a small girl suggested in chilling tones.

"Airconditioning, you crawl through it to escape," offered a boy who'd plainly watched too many Bond films or episodes of *Mission: Impossible*.

"You put animals in them and do horrible experiments on them."

"Obviously transport pipes for contaminated radioactive sludge," Green murmured, all too visibly the investigative journalist from whom there were no secrets.

"All wrong," said Tappen. "That's NUTC's central heating system you see there. If you know the MoD as well as I do, you'd have guessed this from the clouds of steam escaping from the joints a little way back, and also from the clever way in which radiant heat losses have been made as large as possible by painting the pipes black ... And here ahead of us is the desirable bijou hutette of

Northeast Gate security police, with the gate situated artistically just beyond." He speeded his pace, heart suddenly pounding like the underfloor noise of mating rabbits, as a blue-grey Transit van rattled and bumped towards the gateway. It whizzed through with the headlong speed of a Members' pay-rise zooming through Parliament, and was gone. Tappen slowed again, thinking complicated thoughts.

The young MoD policeman Tappen had met before seemed uncertain of how to cope with the advancing mob; he stepped back into the hut, and Alf Rossiter at once came jovially forth, brushing globules of tea from his moustache with a suave gesture.

"Afternoon there, Roy, didn't know you was a family man."

"These young folk are from the exhibition, Alf: I brought them round here so they could see the trained, picked security men they might one day grow up to be – unless they go straight pretty soon. Thought you could tell them about the famous detector system and all that."

"Fine, fine, fine. You come along with me, kiddies, and we'll show you how the boys in blue look after scientist blokes you can't trust out on their own." A wink and cock of the thumb in Tappen's direction. "See here, this box on the gate's a neutron pickup: got no idea how the ruddy thing works, pardon my French, and I don't want to know and neither do you, but when you get down to brass tacks like–"

Since Tappen's conscientious attempts to treat children as equals never seemed to work and usually let him in for derision, it was maddening to see Rossiter going down as an uproarious success despite his condescension. He was the epitome of black-sheep uncles who turn up on Christmas Day to be disapproved of by all the family but the kids; he told mildly off-colour jokes, pulled scientific legs and looked ready to organize games like Postman's Knock if not restrained. A slight crack in his joviality did appear at the information, from the tall, repellently knowledgeable boy, that the MoD-issue gun at his belt had long since been superseded by (if Tappen heard correctly) the flintlock.

Green lurked with ostentatious furtiveness, and Tappen hoped he would pass without explanation as a teacher. He looked up from his notebook: "Is this it? Is this the guy? Corrupting them? Is he going to offer them sweets and lure them out onto the Heath? Doesn't look the D.O.M. type but you never can tell."

"No no," Tappen said. "It isn't that sort of corruption at all. There's no such thing as an MoD Police issue greasy raincoat ... though it does set you thinking, M.O.D., D.O.M., an entire new world of palindromic speculation opens out before us."

"What?" said Green, looking alarmed.

"Just wait." Sweating small ice-cubes, Tappen scanning the horizon for looming Transit vans, by now almost glad of Rossiter's popularity. He'd had uneasy visions of standing here, in heavy, puzzled silence, dredging excuse after feeble excuse from his mind in a ragged attempt to stay plausibly close to the gate until ... He consulted his watch. Ten past five. Soon, very soon, the victims of Wednesday-Evening Wanderlust (an affliction related in its symptoms to Monday-Morning Malaise and Friday-Afternoon Fever) would be flocking through, driven by insatiable need to be somewhere other than Robinson Heath. A clogging sense of failure began to stir in the region of Tappen's appendix.

Then a blessed blue-green Transit came bouncing along, and Rossiter called, "Move back, move back, kids," even as Tappen moved forward, and was this it?

Yes. Bells, sirens, falling barriers, a major screech of brakes counterpointed by a minor screech from a startled young girl.

"You're in luck today!" cried Tappen with synthetic enthusiasm. "Now you'll see Sergeant Rossiter exercising the tight security controls which protect Robinson Heath from all manner of spies and thieves, and have made his name a legend in the underworld. Ah, it's not every day he catches someone in his cunning nets and snares like this –" He poked an elbow into some soft part of Green, as a hint to pay attention.

"Must have been a false alarm, mate," Rossiter said rather too hastily, and made as if to slip into the hut where the alarm override controls were. But already Tappen had moved cheerily to the back of the throbbing, impatient van, saying, "Gather round, children," in tones he was horrified to recognize as those of a Cub leader he'd long ago known and loathed. The van's rear doors were magnificently unlocked. He threw them wide, with the words, "I'm sure Sergeant Rossiter would love you all to help him search this van for contraband items, now, wouldn't you, Sergeant?"

All that could be seen inside the capacious van was a battered filing cabinet, two of its drawers protruding in an unbuttoned and licentious fashion. The labels on the four drawers read: USE OTHER DRAWER. DO NOT OPEN THIS END. THE LABEL ON THE DRAWER BELOW IS TRUE. THE LABEL ON THE DRAWER ABOVE IS FALSE. Tappen had always known there was something about computer people.

It appeared that the mild radioactivity of thickly-spread luminous paint was quite enough to set off the detectors.

With deep concentration Green was writing in his notebook; his lips moved in a faint murmur of "Sergeant Rossiter ... would ... love ... you ... all ..." He paused and contemplated the result with suspicion.

Rossiter's complexion had gone a simmering puce. Hastily Tappen pressed on: "Ah, it's only a filing cabinet, no doubt being sent out for routine repairs ... you have to change the oil every 10,000 miles, you know ..." (Rossiter was modulating from puceness to puzzlement.) "But just as a formality, why don't you search it in case it's stuffed with atomic weapons. See if you can do as good a job as the Sergeant's trained men!"

Three or four of the youngsters climbed rather hesitantly into the back of the van, taking turns to throw dubious looks backward. Perhaps they had Tappen cast in the role of Green's dirty old man, poised to slam the rear doors and let them be carried off to a death worse than fate. With further backward glances they poked about the floor, slid the cabinet's drawers in and out, rummaged halfheartedly inside ...

"Ooo, I've found something," said the plump girl, with excited little tugs at an unseen object apparently fastened to the cabinet's inner wall. There was a rending sound, as of sellotape tearing loose. Tappen stepped forward with bland innocence written all over his face in forty-foot neon capitals. He'd been afraid he'd have to find it himself and strike another blow against Tappen credibility.

"Good heavens," he said, taking the slim xeroxed booklet from her pudgy fingers with badly simulated shock and horror. "You deserve a medal, probably two medals. Look at this! UTTER TOP SECRET/ATOMIC. UK EYES ONLY LIST 1AAA ... and a *very* exclusive list that is, too, I don't think they let the Prime Minister on it. Nuclear Catastrophe Analysis, no less. Heads are going to roll for this; and all thanks to your cleverness, young lady. As the highest-clearance person here" – until Monday – "I think I'd better take this very important document in charge." He thrust it into the inner jacket pocket where he kept important science fiction paperbacks.

The girl looked up at him with huge, soulful, mud-coloured eyes and an expression of overweight ecstasy. To his left he heard scribbling and the snapping of Green's second pencil. To the right ... he paused, putting off the awful moment of looking at Rossiter, for fear that by now the sergeant would be giving off destroying radiations whose merest touch would convert Tappen to the stuff you can never quite clean out of ashtrays.

Here near the high point of success, he felt an inner chill, stomach like a cold and floppy bag of mercury. As though through the wrong end of a telescope Tappen saw himself standing and bluffing like a B-movie confidence man. In a moment, it seemed, Green and Rossiter and all the kids must erupt in hysterical laughter at the funny man with his amateur theatricals. Silence is golden but speech is expensive plutonium with ruddy great diamonds stuck all over it, he told himself desperately.

"Do you think the driver's in on it?" said the tallest boy in a low voice, indicating that purple-faced miscreant with a surreptitious thumb.

Tappen managed to launch an intercontinental ballistic chuckle of considerable heartiness and second-strike capability, and found himself talking on in a technicolour haze. "Only a dupe, I daresay. Sergeant Rossiter will hammer it out of him in the interrogation chamber ... won't you, Alf?"

Rossiter said nothing. His arms hung at his sides, knuckles increasing and decreasing their whiteness in a fascinating slow-motion rhythm.

"Gosh," said Tappen in a froth of false enthusiasm," this will be a scoop for Mr Green, won't it? Oh, I haven't introduced you to Steve Green: he's with the *Redbury Chronicle*, and I'm sure he'd love to interview you, you'll get a marvellous write-up for your daring interception of the document that could have betrayed NATO's inmost secrets to the teeming Eastern hordes."

Green was longhanding furiously, and had reached his fifth pencil.

Rossiter opened his mouth, emitted a significant silence in the later manner of John Cage, and closed it again. He closed his eyes and by way of artistic variety opened them again. He fixed his tormentor with a look of such deadliness that Tappen saw tiny cross-hairs in each pupil.

"Roy," he said with the mildness of a homicidal psychopath whose sedatives might wear off any minute, "I reckon we ought to have a word about this private-like, straight after work –"

In blinding self-realization Tappen saw that deep down, he'd expected to be arrested, denounced or even shot at this stage of the negotiations. For a long moment he could only stare, and nod with foolish enthusiasm.

Green looked up from his reconstruction of Linear B in the notebook, and fired the first salvo from an arsenal of probing questions calculated to rip the lid off. "Er," he said, "how do you spell Rossiter?"

Twenty Three

"My treat: what's yours, Roy?" said Rossiter in carefully neutral tones. Rossiter never offered to buy the first round. It was a special occasion.

"Brandy, please, Alf." Tappen never drank brandy. For this special occasion, though, he felt he needed something more or less traditionally medicinal.

The MoD Police Club inhabited a wasteland beyond the NUTC sports grounds. Large, charmless and sterile, its interior was surprisingly like that of a police station. A long bar replaced the usual counter, the inverted bottles behind it put Tappen in mind of truncheons, and the grim doors which promised cells or third-degree chambers led to the toilets and squash court. Dark blue uniforms were everywhere, making Tappen feel like the traditional piece of china in a bull shop. He was still riding high in waves of fantasy, the intrepid agent who'd penetrated to the heart of enemy power, nerves of tempered steel taut in readiness for the icy-calm confrontation with the insidious Fumanchuski of SMERSH, holding up his sleeve the fatal card which would complete the vast jigsaw of strategy to checkmate the opposition in the first over ...

"One bleeding brandy for the connoisseur," snapped a voice, and Tappen's tempered-steel nerves sent him six inches into the air. A glass containing what might have been a thin film of machine oil was clunked on the table before him.

"Cheers," he said, sniffing cautiously.

"Time for a bit of a heart-to-heart, eh, Roy?" said Rossiter, not looking Tappen in the eye. "Ah, what story did you tell the kids, if you don't mind me asking?"

"Oh, on the way back to the exhibition I explained to them that the whole thing was so desperately secret and hush-hush that the savage, fascist lackeys of the police state (that's you, I'm afraid) would subject them all to the death of a thousand cuts plus extra homework every night for a year. Oh yes, and you personally would glue D-notices over their tender young faces until they all looked like the Man in the Iron Mask. I left them trembling with fear of the frightful Sergeant Rossiter who for years hence will haunt all their dreams."

Though seemingly not a hundred per cent pleased, Rossiter relaxed visibly.

"Well ..."

"Of course it's going to be much harder to convince my reporter friend Mr Green."

A mild convulsion: beer foamed onto Rossiter's jacket, forming an interesting symmetry with the dried tomato sauce from lunchtime. He glanced around him, either seeking moral support from the other blue uniforms or terrified of being overheard by them. The foursome at the next table took no notice, engaged as they were in loud denunciation of the unfair limits placed on their jurisdiction, so that outside the NUTC fence they were cruelly hindered from roaring up and down the roads shooting at people like real policemen.

"Want me to die of suspense, is it, or old age? Let's hear the rest, Royo."

"Well, I thought the best thing to say to him was that all this was a big practice manoeuvre done partly to test the gate security – you know, I'd never realized the detectors could be tripped by TOP SECRET stamps, isn't science wonderful – and partly to put on a show for the kids."

"One-track mind you've got ... but that'll do fine." Rossiter looked faintly puzzled.

"I didn't think of that story till afterwards, though, in the general excitement and surprise of all those, er, unexpected events, but I did suggest that Green shouldn't file his big story about espionage and corruption at the heart of Britain's nuclear defence system, not until I'd had another word with him. Of course I'll set him right as soon as I can, wouldn't want our wonderful MoD policemen to look silly ... but I don't know when I'll have time to phone him up since I have some little domestic problems."

Without visible transition they were now talking the same language, it was clear. Rossiter nodded the serious, concerned nod of a solicitor who hopes to collect huge sums for one and a half sentences of expert advice. "Problems, Roy? Maybe I could give you a bit of a hand, like ... always ready to help out me old mates, eh?"

"Nothing much really. I must admit it would be handy if one of your colleagues were to accidentally lean on the override switch for those detectors for a few minutes, say tomorrow morning, when I bring my car in. Er, I've been having a touch of stomach trouble this week, and the sirens give me acidosis, so it would be nice to be sure just *one* morning that there wouldn't be a false alarm when I drive by ..."

But Rossiter was shaking his head, the slow and sadly smiling headshake of a solicitor whose client has revealed a touching belief that torts are baby reptiles. "Now what would you be wanting to smuggle in, that your Uncle Alf mustn't see, then?"

All right! Cards on the table! Let him have it full in the face! Er, on second thoughts: "Oh all right, it's a couple of r/a sources, harmless things really ..."

Rossiter's slow wink indicated rapid linking-up of this factoid with things like home-made dummy pits constructed to cheat in gigantic smuggling manoeuvres.

"... Only Lizzie can't bear to have them in the house, *that's* why she moved out for now, she's got a Thing about r/a the way people have things about hairy-legged spiders or great slimy slugs or security – home security, that is. But I can't sneak them back in here with you and your detectors on the job: you're too clever for me, eh?"

"Oh Roy, you've been a naughty boy, I don't think. Bugger me down dead, is *that* all that's got your knickers in a twist? Some people. Drop by early, let me have the stuff outside the Main Gate, and I'll slip it through for you – special delivery to your own office."

Hell. No matter how he worked it, Rossiter would catch on when he found the two "sources" were the size and shape they were. There was only one dummy in 334 area and Alf might know that ... Argh. "No need to go to all that trouble, Alf. My way's less work all round, and in the wonderful Civil Service it's practically the first commandment that you don't do any more work than you can get away with. OK?"

Rossiter shook his head again. "No, Roy. See, I've got my pride in my job – oh, I know, but a few perks for the lads is neither here nor there, wouldn't you say? No mucking around with *real* security, that's my rule. Just you do it my way."

Tappen wanted to hide behind the brandy-glass and think, but it was too small. It was entirely in keeping with the present Tappen horoscope (*This month you are doomed. Do not get out of bed except for essential bodily needs*) that his newest, Mark XXVI master plan should founder on this one solitary outcrop of integrity in Rossiter's entire personality. He opened his mouth to tell all: and closed it again. A sudden vision of Rossiter Triumphant, of handcuffs and gleeful swoops on the 33 Rutland Gardens arsenal, of Tappen's feeble mutters about Security peccadilloes dismissed as the writhings of a master criminal on the hook, of Lizzie wringing her hands as the red judge assumed the black cap. He daren't even show Rossiter the weapon cores. He might hold them together, or suspect the truth when after the first favour Tappen asked a second and identical one ... oh, sod it.

"That's what I wanted to know," he said with what he hoped was a knowing smile but felt from the inside like the deathly rictus of lockjaw. "I wanted to make absolutely sure you still had your priorities right."

There is nothing more soothing to fallible human beings than the news that they've been obscurely tested and have triumphantly passed. Rossiter smiled, and almost preened himself. Then a tinge of bewilderment coloured his features, as though deep inside him a forgotten doner kebab was making its salmonella-laden presence felt.

"So ... So there isn't any little favour you'd like doing when it gets to brass tacks? Put in a word for you somewhere, eh, Roy?" His eagerness had a haunting familiarity; Tappen traced it back more than twenty-five years to a schoolmate belting the infant Tappen and then anxiously whining, "Hit me, go on, hit me back, hard as you like" – anything to wipe the slate clean and settle things on a secular level without the awful High Justice of the schoolmistress ...

"No," Tappen said sadistically. "I'm getting along just fine, career going like a bomb. – Let me get you a drink," he added by way of heaping coals of fire on Rossiter's liver, and felt in an inside pocket for his anorexic wallet.

His fingers encountered a crumpled paper. Not the all-potent *Nuclear Catastrophe Analysis*, now safely locked away: it was the notice of a vacancy at that tidal research place on the idyllic south coast. He smoothed it out for Rossiter: "Of course, if you should happen to wield such influence over the powers that be that you could get me this transfer ..." As well ask for the moon, with several desirable residential asteroids thrown in.

"No trouble. Just you leave that to me," Rossiter said, brightening.

"Surely, Alf, surely, After which I'd like a Nobel Prize, the next vacancy for Aga Khan, and ... do you think you could swing the Miss World judging panel as well?"

"Sceptical little bugger, aren't you. Like to risk a fiver on the side? Be doing myself a favour, shifting *you* out of Redbury before me and the missus get round to moving there."

"But, Alf, it's NUTC *policy* to hold onto physicists by the short and curlies because there aren't enough to go round, not now the kids don't dare take science degrees in case it's 'Piss off, you're overqualified' when they end up trying to be bus drivers or saggar maker's bottom knockers. *You* know. You have to be really popular at Robinson Heath to fiddle a transfer, it's worse than parole boards, and my name's mud."

"So it's taking lollipops off kids, you winning this little bet, eh? What say we make it fifty quid, Roy, make it more interesting." Rossiter smiled fascinatingly, and his voice held the eerie persuasiveness of an insurance salesman or perpetual-motion machine inventor.

"You're on ... for twenty-five," Tappen blurted, suddenly doubtful of all the foundations of his universe. As if in a dream he saw himself filling in the application-for-transfer on the back of the paper, passing it to Rossiter, nodding helplessly at the elaborately casual, "Oh, and you'll see to that Green twerp, eh, Roy? Can't have him getting the wrong idea about us, can we now..."

"Actually it's going to be difficult to find time for a *tête-à-tête* with the famous Green while I'm still in a state of anxiety and turmoil about my future career," Tappen managed to say as a postscript to the nod. He dreamily realized that the world was still turned upside down, for Rossiter merely made affirmative noises and of his own volition went for more drinks. Two rounds in succession bought by Sergeant Alf Rossiter: it was a portent on the same order as blue moons, eclipses, assistant scientific officers born with two heads, or sheeted dead squeaking and gibbering in the Robinson Heath canteen.

An hour and a half later he sat with Lizzie amid the noxious red vinyl and synthetic Tudor of the Station Hotel, both of them struggling with awkward distinctions of texture and taste between the chicken and the basket. Cruelly she was wearing the favourite yellow skirt and blouse whose effects usually sent them stampeding hand-in-hand to a convenient bed.

"It's what we've always wanted," he said moodily. "Down there in Milford-on-Sea with the gulls crying and verdant fields sloping down to the shingled beach suffused with the gentle wash and murmur of a sapphire-like sea aglitter beneath the golden sun. Also the pay is better."

"Prose like that, darling, is a radiation hazard. And speaking of which, I suppose from the crypt-like tone of your voice that there's no chance that we're now, um, not all there upstairs?" Her hands traced the outline of a filing cabinet, her eyes behind the enormous glasses began to flash small DANGER signs complete with the trefoil emblem of r/a hazard.

"No chance," Tappen said, slumping further into the chair and wiping his fingers on a paper serviette slightly larger than a postage stamp. You couldn't even be heroically tragic when smeared to the eyeballs with chicken fat ... He ran through edited highlights of the day's merry japes.

"We're doomed. I've given up all hope. Not a single cosmic master plan left in the cupboard. Either I get myself arrested for giving the damn things back and never see daylight again, or do horrible unforgivable things to the environment and God knows who else by dumping them, or I go through the rest of life with them hung round my neck like bloody great twin albatross eggs. Probably you'd better divorce me before you get to be an accessory after the fact; or maybe I should exonerate you in a lengthy suicide note explaining the whole situation, or ..." He lapsed into morbid silence, feeling a deep spiritual oneness with the small slug which chose this moment to peer from the folds of lettuce in his basket.

"Nonsense," Lizzie said robustly, the subdued light glinting from her small, sharp teeth. "Tomorrow you'll probably wake up with fifty million brilliant ideas to solve all your problems. *Our* problems. Look on the bright side, love, there's the chance of the Tidal Research post, and you didn't actually eat any of that lettuce, and ... mmm. Things do start getting a little bit thin on the ground after that."

"Also I'm a security risk because I grope SOs and have strange men in the house and indulge in the perverse practices of the Cities of the Plain to such an extent that my own chaste wife has left home in horror to be where the air is cleaner and the pillar-of-salt hazard less imminent." In a yet more funereal voice Tappen elaborated on this theme, with bitter allusions to AIDS and green carnations.

"Well, you just put the screws on that slimy Alf Rossiter again, and blackmail him into repainting your character whiter than white. Why not?"

"My dear, that would be unethical. I said I'd cloud the mind of S. Green – not that it needs much clouding – if and when this hypothetical string-pulling of Alf's gets me a transfer to the sun-drenched south. I can't ask *another* favour on top of that."

"Why not?" Lizzie repeated with female ruthlessness.

"Well, I suppose I might take unfair advantage just this once ..." But almost immediately he sank back in gloomy contemplation of all his other woes. "Would you say drowning, gassing or a nice overdose would be on the whole more comfy?"

Lizzie snorted. "What you need, darling, is a psychological boost. You need to be taken out of yourself. As an antidote to this wretched self-pity you should pop upstairs and see the revolting squalor in which others like your poor exiled wife are living. Victorian steel engravings on every wall, even."

"What?" said the listless Tappen, the sound bubbling slowly up from several fathoms' depth of despondency.

Demurely Lizzie adjusted the hem of her skirt over a white-tighted knee. "I said, husband, would – you – like – to – come – up – and – see – my – etchings?"

And by and large, and in the main, it wasn't such a bad evening after all.

Twenty Four

(1) Blackmail Government (NB which government? What are usual channels for this?)

(2) Sell for huge profit to nation desiring independent World War III starting capability. (Chad? Upper Volta? Wales?)

(3) Bazooka to provide unobtrusive way through fence. (Army surplus shop?)

Psychologically boosted and topped-up with neurotic energy, Tappen buzzed and twitched about his 150 square feet of office like a bluebottle caught in a ping-pong game, occasionally halting to scribble an addition to the list. This was the way to do science. Put down every idea you have, eliminate the ones which are impossible, and whatever remains, no matter how improbable, must be ... only conceivably nothing might remain, and how d'you get out of *that*, Sherlock?

(8) Swans trained to fly in formation, carry heavy loads? (Early SF story about this, can't remember who wrote it or whether he died a swanpecked husband)

(9) Divert huge lorry off road through fence at dead of night (headlight trick).

The headlight trick was a fiendish notion Tappen had had one night as he drove through the maze of narrow lanes about Robinson Heath, watching formless UFO lights rise in the trees as his headlamp beams reflected from puddles. By dead of night the lights of cars were all you saw. Suppose a few simple electrical alterations to your vehicle, and suppose you're a homicidal loony, and in the dark another car is following you down the lanes, the

194

driver's eyes glued to your tail-lights. Suddenly, har har, you brake! And at the same moment, hit the secret dashboard switch! Your red tail-lights die; in their place, cunningly mounted at the rear, the extra set of headlights comes on; triggered by what seems a suicidally onrushing car out of nowhere, the sucker's reflexes send him swerving and skidding clear off the road, clear through the heavy mesh fence of Robinson Heath, opening the way for you to sneak in while your confederate – er, wife – escapes in the guilty car.

Despite its lack of application to everyday social life, Tappen was quite proud of this idea, as one of his all-time most original scientific notions. He felt, though, he'd prefer something a trace more foolproof.

(13) Power cut. Must be one sooner or later. Take nice winter holiday when electrician's unions declare open season, wait x days till RH lights go out, sail in past barriers. After a fraught pause Tappen reluctantly added: *(Standby generator?)*

This morning he'd abandoned the pretence of working. Fussy little men wandered in at intervals, demanding to check the door and window locks, search the wastebasket for possibly classified notes, and in suspicious tones ask his precise relationship with the photo of Lizzie on the desk: all routine. The photo eyed him critically, and in silence suggested he should pull his finger out.

(14) Daring confederate (Lizzie? Um) puts axe through main and standby power lines with exquisite timing precisely as RT approaches gate detectors.

(15) NUTC boiler house outside secure area: crawl with items through main pipes while system being serviced, and ... and come bursting lithely from an office radiator? Let's face it Tappen told himself in strictest confidence, R. Tappen is incapable of anything involving violent action or risk-taking: too bloody embarrassing to be caught out. He sat chewing a thoughtful pencil, in a long trance of scientific creativity which continued and continued, only broken by the entrance of another site messenger. With the casual sleaz-

iness of a croupier the wizened wreck dealt a letter from the bottom of his stack into Tappen's tray, and passed on. Jolted back into the real world where people sometimes ate, Tappen realized the lunch break had passed into archaeological time, as evidenced by the inward sense that his stomach was an interstellar void troubled by the hollow rumbling of gravity waves. Also the pencil, now nibbled to a fifth of its length, might be playing some part in this discomfort. No matter: he took firm hold of the damp stub and, tongue protruding with the agony of parturition, wrote –

(16) See also (13), (14). Sabotage all gate detectors, r/a luminous paint again, causing continuous false alarms, etc. Make them turn the bloody things off.

He was so enchanted by the brilliance of this that he read it to himself three, four, five times with the loving attention one might devote to a poem of Keats, assuming one were into nightingales. Visiting a joke shop over the weekend for more luminous paint, devising a squirt-system to lay the false trails by the gates like saboteurs' aniseed, practising before a mirror to perfect the needed look of elaborate innocence ... all these small matters were logistical exercises to be left to the student.

Knock-rattle, bang, and Fortmayne was leaning over his desk again, for once without his habitual stare of accusation. His copious grey hair had been rumpled by headscratching into a Patrick Moore thicket, and his eyes were slightly crossed.

"Roy, could you possibly tell me what you're up to with this transfer?"

"Transfer? Oh yes, I applied for the Tidal Research thingy. Don't we all keep trying? Like filling in pools coupons."

With quivering fingers Fortmayne removed the – as Tappen now saw – *sealed, white, typed* envelope from the top of the IN pile and passed it across the desk as though on a silver salver. Determined to be cool and, if feasible, laid-back, Tappen sorted with unhurried clumsiness through his drawer for a pair of minute dissecting scissors (lab use only) with which he attacked a long edge of the envelope in forty-two nonchalant snips.

Admin Central

1 July 10am

The request for transfer by Mr R. Tappen (SSO, SNO) is hereby approved and confirmed by Admin Central, TPRE Milford-on-Sea. The interview requirement has been waived. This transfer takes effect on Monday 2 August.

pp P.T.St.J. Hanratty, Assistant Director

(Distribution as per attached schedule)

"What I'm saying," began Fortmayne by way of verbal throat-clearing, "is, since when have *you* been the AD's blue-eyed boy? Talk about friends in high places. What secret power over him and TPRE, unknown to we mere mortals, do you possess? Have you paid him large bribes, have you kidnapped his children or unearthed the body in his back garden ...?"

The tirade washed harmlessly over the inert and starry-eyed Tappen, who with inner awe was contemplating the beauty and extent of the web of naughtiness linking Rossiter, half the Security force, Bogley Surplus Stores, far-flung bits of the MoD empire like TPRE, and now, well ... He wondered absently whether the Minister for Defence got a cut.

"I think the AD must just like me," said Tappen outrageously. "After all, although it's all *quite* mistaken, it seems the last PV report on yours truly came to some pretty odd conclusions, and who knows? The AD may think of me as a kindred soul. Probably he'll invite me up to the office next, to see his etchings of US nuclear tests."

"I don't agree with what you're ... I don't want to hear any more," said superstraight Fortmayne as he backed away from Tappen's zone of contamination. "I'll be over in Lab Four for the rest of the day, firing neutrons at Jenny Wren, if anybody wants me –" The fast-closing door cut off his voice.

Jenny Wren was an experimental item of Army equipment which might one day be standard Forces Issue, an inflatable lady intended to distract the troops from incidents abroad likely to result in bad public relations and/or interesting varieties of pox. Naturally Jenny couldn't go on general release until proven reasonably immune to neutron bomb attack, since after *that* eventuality the men would need more distracting than ever. Rumours that the MoD (an Equal Opportunity Employer) was investigating a male version codenamed Deadeye Dick were so hotly no-commented as to be very likely true.

Tappen spent some happy minutes totting up his remaining annual leave. Eight days at least; he needn't ever work at Robinson Heath on a Monday again. And with all the rest of the month to play with, a man of his towering genius would have no trouble tackling the piffling little problem of a home whose natural dry rot, subsidence and silverfish happened to be complemented by a couple of medium-sized city-busters. He went to tell Llewellyn the glad news; but Llewellyn was still cowering in his phone booth of an office, emanating the painful goodness of a Little Lord Fauntleroy, and only grudgingly admitted that probably he could keep the plute inventory fiddled until the requested dummy pit arrived from the workshops on Monday to make life easier. (Tappen was surprised to hear the workshops were breathing smoke and flame *re* the demand for dummies this year: what, they asked reasonably, was being done with them all? What dummies?) Poor Llewellyn, it must be awful to be subject to these terrible intermittent spasms of conscience, or cowardice, if there was really any difference here where men were men in the wonderful world of megadeath deterrence.

(16a) Oh God this is really brilliant. Forget all that bumf about squirting r/a paint on the gates through a flower in my buttonhole. This is triumphant British Ingenuity, this is: spread the paint or any old r/a powder, nice harmless uranium salts, on gravel path outside MoDP Club. They all step in it, lunchtime, clumping great size-16 boots with just enough r/a to set detectors screaming STOP THIEF whenever fuzz themselves come close. Poetic justice I tell you, within an hour after lunch they'll have to shut down the whole system – and then – faster than a speeding ICBM – Tappen the Masked Avenger strikes!

He basked in the glow once felt by Einstein, Newton, Galileo, or

God on about the fifth day, before His big mistake. With the detectors dead as last week's NPIWP minutes, they might go mad and commit anatomical dissection on everything that went out, but Tappen's car would be going in. To relieve his high spirits he opened a cupboard door, on which was a libellous drawing of Dr Alastair Staverton covered in what looked like blackheads; taking the darts from the desk drawer, he scored a cheekbone and the number-three chin, five points apiece, and then fifty for a dazzling bullseye up the right nostril. A perfunctory knock behind him speeded his stroll to the cupboard, which with the studied casualness of long practice in Fortmayne-evasion he slammed before turning to see another aged messenger whose corrugated face suggested an intermediate example of the headshrinker's art. "Ar, 'tis old Scrotum, the wrinkled retainer," he noted under his breath, stepping forward to accept an envelope which was once again sealed and white and typed.

For a long while he regarded this with the enthusiasm of one who has been awarded the most noble order of the black spot. Eventually ...

Office of the Director
1 July 2pm
Mr. R. Tappen (SSO, SNO) is hereby suspended from his duties on full pay, until further notice. This suspension is effective as from Friday 2 July. Access to NUTC is suspended likewise.
pp Sir Leopold Bleaney, Director
(Distribution as per attached schedule)

Tappen moaned. The end of all things. Only an hour left of the working day, no time for last-minute car dashes, and no more working days until TPRE. After a while, deciding the condemned man deserved relative peace and quiet as he mounted the thirteen steps, he tiptoed down the corridor and stole the identical envelope distributed into Fortmayne's office as per attached schedule. On the way back he bumped into Pell, who told him he looked like, er, death. Tappen mumbled something about domestic problems, and Pell made sympathetic cluckings, also confiding the earth-shaking news that he was having trouble with the central, er, heating. At this he looked oddly guilty, but Tappen was by now unconcerned with any guilt but his own.

"Oh Roy you shouldn't have done it," said Carol of 334 Admin when he phoned her, voice wavering between due solicitude and gratefulness for Tappen's newest provision of juicy gossip. "Though of course I don't suppose it matters to you now you're being transferred, and I heard tell the Director didn't have anything against *you*, it was those mingy political people that leant on him, you know old Sir Leo wouldn't hurt a fly ..."

"What political people?" Tappen visualized the Master of the Buckhounds beating on Parliament's door with a mace to carry the regal demand that Tappen get it in the neck. The conspiracy theory of history – they were all in it except him – the Director himself had a private helicopter and wine-cellar paid for by the great filing cabinet fiddle – every man's hand was against Tappen for his courageous probe into Bogley Surplus Stores – bloody hell, he'd spill the beans to ace journalist Green yet, if Green hadn't been removed to a psychiatric hospital by the fascist oppressors of Military Unintelligence!

"Oh it's all over the site, Roy, it seems there was someone at the exhibition who was frightfully annoyed with you because you were a bigoted rationalist (that's what he said) and insulted some science book he was ever so impressed by, I suppose you were only joking really but you have to watch your step with these people, don't you, Roy? My horoscope said this week –"

"Thanks, Carol," Tappen uttered, putting the receiver down with abnormal gentleness and restraint if only because the force he wanted to use would not merely smash the telephone but convert his fingers to bolognese sauce. Gently and restrainedly he rummaged through eight piles on his desk until he found the sacred scientific text he required, and with slow calm deliberation he tore out each separate page of *An Experiment with Space*, crumpling each one and hurling it randomly across the floor for the cleaners to complain about. *Politicians.* Finally he skimmed the covers frisbee-fashion at the window (which exasperatingly failed to break), and shrieked introspectively, "FUCK!"

Half a dozen scales of paint fell from the ceiling in a dispirited way.

If he had a box of matches, he could heap up all the crumpled leaves and mounds of computer printout, and sprawl himself on it as a settee, if that was what the Indians called it, a final fiery immolation, taking the whole of 334d with him and a good thing too. What a pity he had no matches and felt too terminally apathetic and pissed-off to pop round and borrow Pell's.

The numb horror of his situation drove him at last to the final desperate resort of civil servants when nothing else remains: he started looking through the pile in his IN tray. Junk mail (computers), junk mail (microchips), junk mail (insurance) ... suggestion from someone at Ukulele (UKAEA) that it would be fun were Tappen to set all else aside and without recompense help this inept someone do his job ... progress reports from dynamic colleagues failing to solve vital questions he didn't want the answers to ... minutes of Energy Usage Working party saying it would be nice if scientists, as opposed to important administrators, did without the luxuries of heat, light and power throughout the coming winter ... flimsy slip from Health Physics mentioning he'd received a dangerous overdose ... staff association newsletter ...

Wait a minute.

He scanned the slip of Health Physics computer-print.

OVERDOSE + + + YOU ARE ADVISED TO REPORT FOR TREATMENT AT HEALTH PHYSICS BLDG + + + DUE TO OVERSTRAINED FACILITIES THIS IS THE ONLY NOTICE YOU WILL RECEIVE + + + CHECK THAT NAME OF YOUR NEXT OF KIN IS ON FILE WITH PERSONNEL DEPT + + +

But. But he hadn't been to the labs at all to speak of, much less in Red or Purple radiation zones. But on the other hand he'd come close to a couple of objects in the 33 Rutland Gardens zone. But on a third hand, surely not *that* close or *that* often. Come to think of it, they hadn't done any tests on him just lately, so how ... Oh, but they had, a urine sample back last Friday. He found himself sweating great drops, possibly even a Symptom. But ... he'd dried up. It was Pell's whisky he'd put in the bottle, he remembered now. Several dozen symptoms of terminal radiation sickness, which had been hovering in the wings twirling their moustachios, departed with cries of "Foiled again!" as this particular bubble of memory rose to the surface.

Tappen sighed, the familiar weight of gloom settling over him: better the gloom you know than the gloom you don't. It simply meant Roger Pell had left his whisky near a big neutron source or something, activated it to a level that probably wouldn't harm a reasonably healthy streptococcus, but was definitely more active than the, ah, exhaust emission of a healthy SSO should be. For a period he lay back glumly self-satisfied, brilliant and inert, like a high-tech Nero Wolfe.

Except ... Pell was a theoretical man, designing experiments but never, never going near the hardware. No loose neutrons littering his office floor. No way the home-made whisky could have got like that, unless, of course, silly idea though it was ...

Tappen sat bolt upright in his seat as though suddenly coated with a thin layer of zinc. The most peculiar clicking and whirring seemed to be taking place inside his brain, a brain he tried to give as much healthy rest as possible but which now appeared to have stripped its gears and to be racing uncontrollably. Pell. Pell's whisky. The central heating, about which Pell felt guilty. Swords and ploughshares. Phenomena noted in Pell's garden, such as wisps of "smoke" and the man himself with his coy fashion parades to and from the house in a frog mask. Pell's underground shelter – what a convenient place that would be for fermenting home-made wine to be adulterated into the sort of whisky they ran cars on in Brazil. Pell's reluctance to show off the famous shelter. Pell's phobias of radiation here and there and everywhere in house and garden, with jolly r/a meters to back it up. Even, come to think of it, a remark of Llewellyn's about what people did with their fallout shelters after building them.

Pell's house was always warm and moist.

"Bloody hell," said Tappen in a long, slow exhalation.

Glowing waves of the most extraordinary smugness began to radiate from somewhere deep inside him, like the happy inner glow of a whisky other than Pell's. Nero Wolfe would have sat baffled on his fat rear. Lord Peter Wimsey would have fled screaming at his first encounter with the home-made paint stripper. Poirot's grey cells would have wrenched themselves in vain, Father Brown's paradoxes fallen flat and Appleby's erudition foundered on what later generations would call the Problem of the Physicist's Plonk. Only Roy Tappen, dashing private investigator, had the needed knowledge to crack the case. Well, only Roy Tappen and about a thousand others at NUTC alone. In the glorious new light of his insight he saw it contained an answer to Tappen's own domestic problem, albeit in a dastardly, underhanded fashion such as only last week he would never have considered. All power corrupts.

"And nuclear power corrupts absolutely," he quoted to himself from a Pell-style pamphlet. In what might be his last phone calls to be charged to the nuclear defence budget, he got through to a Redbury estate agent to make noises about selling, and – after a brutal hand-to-hand struggle with Directory Enquiries – to another in Milford, about buying. He called Rossiter and rudely demanded to be issued a certificate of ungayness before he'd turn off the dreaded Green. ("Eh, you're a right little bugger," said Rossiter on a note of strained admiration.)

He visited Llewellyn and said goodbye – "I leave you my desk, my filing cabinets, my computer printouts and my unfinished projects, you lucky devil." On Fortmayne's desk he placed a typed note reading, in part, *My affection for you has not dimmed, and when I gazed into your eyes this morn I dared to hope that it might be returned. But alas, our love can never be. Farewell!*

Finally he slammed his office door with such enthusiastic violence that something fell over inside, while the underfloor rabbits could be heard stampeding. Peeping back in, Tappen noticed that the far wall of the office, the one with the window and the dry rot, had toppled gracefully out onto the toadstooled grass of Robinson Heath. "I knew that was going to happen someday," he said aloud, lying in his teeth, and scrupulously followed regulations to the last by locking the office door behind him.

The result seemed pleasingly symbolic of Robinson Heath security.

Now for the domestic nuclear proliferation talks, which like charity and overpopulation would have to begin at home.

Twenty Five

Once upon a time number 35 had merely been the bland mirror-image of the semi the Tappens were buying and eventually bought; it acquired Pellish personality as they grew vaguely acquainted with Pell, and developed overtones of fairground Crazy Houses on sight of his domestic disarrangements. As of today and Tappen's great deduction, the place had the evil, throbbing look of Franken-stein's biological research installation in Transylvania, Porton Down or wherever it was. Tappen paused at the gate and swall-owed, the same pause and swallow he remembered from when in the bedsitter days he'd gone to reason with an eight-foot Rasta neighbour overhead, about the aesthetic value of 120dB reggae at three in the morning. ("Come have a drink, mon," had been the jovial reply, and Tappen's claims of gradual but totally effective diplomacy were poorly received when he undulated home at dawn.)

After further halts to polish the unlabelled bottle he carried, to admire the front garden's marrows on which Pell failed to be self-sufficient, and to clean his fingernails carefully, twice, Tappen reached the off-grey door and rattled its knocker. Past experience had taught him to avoid the antique bell-pull, which had to be hauled out eighteen inches against stiff resistance before producing a subdued tinkle: this was another Pell energy-saver, with the huge effort of pulling the knob harnessed to turn a small dynamo and charge up storage batteries, so every passing Jehovah's Witness contributed to Pell's DIY electric systems.

"Er, hello?" Pell opened the door on the chain and peered out with one eye, as enthusiastic as a gay Jewish resistance worker welcoming a stray Gestapo patrol.

Yesterday Tappen would merely have knocked and expected to

be let in. Today, feeling tortuous and complex, he said: "Hello, Roger, I hope I haven't disturbed an important project to harness the mighty tidal energy surging to and fro in your bathtub. And speaking of bathtubs, I wondered if you'd like to try a drop of our own home-made plonk, Chateau Jardins Rutlandières '33, guaranteed to contain no harmless ingredients. Of course it couldn't be as unforgettably *different* as your, um, whiskoid, but let's have a splash and taste it now. How about it?"

A gothic rattling of chains and creaking of hinges, and Pell beckoned Tappen into the dim interior. "That's very, er, nice of you, Roy ..." (Tappen at once felt deeply guilty and treacherous, and had to harden his heart no end.) "Is it, erm, a special occasion or something, then?"

Because he'd, unusually, felt a need to justify a drink and had done several seconds' intensive research at home, Tappen was able to say fluently: "Yes, indeed, the glorious first of July you know, anniversary of the Battle of Marston Moor in 1644, not to mention the setting-up of the Vichy Government in France in 1940, the 1840 Mount Ararat earthquake, all sorts of famous events. Also, and equally joyous, my last day at Robinson Heath."

"Oh ... that's interesting," said Pell with his back turned leading the way down the dim hall. Tappen found himself leaning exaggeratedly this way and that, contorting himself so that as much of him as possible stayed as far as possible from the burgeoning heating pipes. This was difficult: they covered the walls like surrealist prison bars, lending an institutional atmosphere which must make Pell feel right at home, or at work.

The sitting-room's single naked bulb was brightening and dimming fitfully with the wind, like a bad disco light-show. Pell held up the unlabelled bottle Tappen offered him, squinted through it as stout Cortez might have looked with wild surmise at a greasy fingerprint on his telescope lens, and said grudgingly, "Seems to have, um, cleared nicely. Not bad at all, not for a fiirst effort ... though you can detect a faint ... cloudiness, sediment. The trained eye, you know."

"Of course," said Tappen. "By the way, Roger, I never got round to taking you up on your invitation to look round your famous fallout shelter – last year, wasn't it? Lizzie and I were thinking we'd like one, since as Joe Llewellyn says, you can convert it to all sorts of useful things."

"Er, well, that was before ... I mean, it's in no fit state for visitors now." Pell busied himself opening the wine, using a clever little pressure-pump which gave you a sporting chance of being sprayed with wine and glassy shrapnel should the cork not pop out as described in the instructions.

"One of the things Joe mentioned, that would be a real status symbol, was an underground swimming pool. Just think of that."

Pell was filling the grimy tumblers: he convulsed and spilled half a glassful as he thought of that. Tappen wriggled slightly inside his clothes, this being a compromise between casual relaxedness and cavorting about the room in a victory dance.

"Cheers," said Pell hastily. "Mmm, very interesting Roy, a trifle too yeasty and obviously, erm, home-made, but quite respectable. Don't think you could have ... fermented it at quite the right temperature."

"I'm sure I'll do better next time, with good advice like yours: somehow I hadn't noticed until I was put right by an expert." After arriving home on the NUTC bus, Tappen had spent twenty minutes scraping and soaking the label from a bottle of perfectly respectable Niersteiner, all in the name of artistic verisimilitude. The effort, he considered, had been worth it.

"Did you start with potatoes or, mmm, turnips?" Pell continued, becoming more expansive with the conversation running on safer lines.

"Old tea-leaves and cauliflower stalks, mainly. Oh, and quite a lot of orange peel. Lizzie used to watch out for it on the pavements." (Pell studied his tumbler with new suspicion.) "But the trick's in the fermentation, isn't it, Roger? Lizzie gets so uptight about the bath, the airing cupboard, the washing machine, all the obvious places. You're lucky having that extra space out in the garden."

"Mmm, yes," Pell said incautiously, and again Tappen wriggled his wriggle of muted triumph.

"I expect the warmth stimulates the yeast no end, too."

"Ye – no, no, not warm at all – ha ha – what a peculiar idea ..."

"And a little blue background lighting is highly recommended in *Spettigue's Promptuary of Domestic Plonk*," Tappen said in a burst of inventiveness.

"Really? That's very ... that is to say, I don't, um, know what you're talking about."

"Roger Pell," said Tappen on a note of doom, "I know your guilty secret! You it was who committed the crime with the candlestick in the conservatory ... sorry, wrong chapter. With my x-ray vision like what Superman has, I've penetrated the terrible secret of your fallout shelter. I *know all*."

"Oh dear," said Pell. And after a pause during which he rallied himself with a further large tumbler of home-made Niersteiner Gutes Domtal 1978: "You will have your, ah, little joke, Roy. What, er, what could I possibly hide in there?"

Tappen felt he shouldn't be enjoying himself so much in this serious and constructive heart-to-heart, but it was impossible to curb his innate talent for bad acting. "You know my methods, Roger: apply them. What would I expect to find out there? Wine and water. Swords and ploughshares. Something borrowed and something blue." Feeling this to be in the best tradition of cryptic master sleuths, he refilled his tumbler with wine and what he conceived to be an air of brooding menace, regarding the miscreant through half-closed eyelids.

"Oh dear," said Pell. "Roy, I wish you wouldn't make those, mmm, *faces* at me, this is all bad enough already. You must understand that I'm trying to make an, erm, important political and sociological point. Er, you do understand?"

"Stow the gab," Tappen said from the corner of his mouth, conscious of a slight lapse of genres. "Let's see where the bodies are buried. Right now."

"Oh dear," said Pell, conveying the impression that through constant intonation of this rare mantra he hoped for inner calm. Despite his huge, cadaverous aspect, he managed to look so much like a small boy threatened with confiscation of his Dungeons and Dragons kit that Tappen was impelled to say, "Look, Roger, this is just me, I haven't breathed a word to NUTC Police, or the UN

Security Council, *or* the residents' association. I just – well, I've got a little domestic problem too, and a trouble shared is a trouble doubled, and all that. I'll tell you in a minute, but first let's have that wonderful guided tour you promised us so long ago. OK?"

"Oh dear," Pell riposted wittily. He hauled himself slowly upright like some vast articulated device for repairing the tops of cooling towers, and led the way to the rear. In the kitchen, a foul decoction of fungi and dandelion roots glowered sullenly, and the legendary biomass methane-generator welcomed them with ominous bubblings and fartings. While Tappen clutched his nose in admiration, Pell tested one of the ubiquitous heating pipes with a cautious finger and mumbled that it was safe at the moment, as though the proposal was to splash in the alligator-pool but luckily the creatures had just been fed.

Out, then, into the dim back garden, where Tappen tripped continually on the piping and cables he'd thought were all to do with the windmill listlessly twirling at the far end. Something extremely horrid happened underfoot, and huge summonings of courage were needed for Tappen to bend, squinting in the half-light, and find he'd popped one of those malformed vegetables the Americans – with rare feel for words – called a squash.

It loomed up suddenly, a rickety wooden shed not as impressive as the dwarf kiosks from which Redbury Council tried to flog lottery tickets. It looked incapable of withstanding spring breezes or woodlice, let alone heatflash, 40 p.s.i. blast overpressure or neutron showers: but instead of casually kicking it over, Pell undid four padlocks with slow precision, and by careful steering managed to make the door swing open rather than fall off. A 20-watt light came on inside, as though this were an outdoor fridge, and they descended rough concrete steps into the bowels of the back garden.

Twelve steps down, Pell said, "Er, wait here a moment," cleverly stopping first so Tappen could bump into him from behind. There was a tiny lobby designed on the classic architectural lines of a public toilet cubicle, and opposite the steps a steel door sprouting cancerous-looking combination locks.

"Eighteen ... five ... eighteen ... seventy-two," murmured Tappen's guide to the nether regions as he twiddled. "Er, Bertrand

Russell's birthday, you know."

Tappen raised a sceptical eyebrow which was wasted on Pell's back. The heavy door opened slowly out, revealing itself to be a rugged ten inches thick, and moist warmth rolled forward in slow sticky waves from a darkness in which, on the second or third or thirteenth look, you began to think you saw the blue glow of unflickering TV tubes.

"Optimax exposure is about sixteen minutes," Pell said with scientific briskness, and clicked a lightswitch inside the portal. "Actually, er, that's just a guess ... not my strong subject you know ... in we go, then."

Tappen was all set to be obnoxiously blasé about the scene – had he, the great detective, not deduced it from the scantiest of data? In the event it was like the difference between picture post-cards of the Grand Canyon and the dizzying, yawning, soul-sucking appearance of the thing itself. Tappen gaped.

The "underground shelter" was a single cluttered chamber nearly twenty feet square (it must stretch from edge to edge of Pell's back garden), all rough concrete except for the central pool. Llewellyn had hit the target with his guess: it was an underground swimming pool, round and deep, the sort of Hugh Hefner indulgence one would never, never expect from Pell. The pool brimmed with steaming water, and the depths pulsated with gently glowing blue.

Tappen took a zombie-like step closer, and another, unable to believe the accuracy of his guesswork. Spaced over the water like radial strands of a cobweb were eight stout broomsticks, their shoreward ends weighed firmly down by breeze-blocks, the other ends dangling nylon ropes like fishing-rods set to catch efts or axolotls or strange blue-glowing fish of the underground deeps.

Tappen knew what would be on the ends of the lines, though he wished he didn't. He peered through steamy air and simmering water: there they were, near the bottom, precisely spaced in a ring, each cradled in rope and dangling from its own pole, eight dark spheres not as big as footballs. The blue glow of Cherenkov radiation was brightest in the water around them. Tappen closed his mouth but it fell open again. He had to admire it, the preposterous horror of a home-grown, alternative-technology nuclear reactor.

"Actually, Roger, there are other ways of heating swimming pools," he managed to say at last.

Pell took this seriously and, slightly nettled, pointed out the heat-exchanger pipes which circulated warm water through 35 Rutland Gardens' radiators, the ventilation tube which let excess steam escape harmlessly up through the gooseberry patch, the ingenious thermostat which, if the reactor overheated, would shut it down by triggering a big spring and hurling one of the bootleg weapon cores out of the swimming pool ...

Tappen counted the phrase "swords into ploughshares" eight times, and "power for the people" in every other sentence. He found himself backed up against the wall, as far as possible from the hellish pool, while Pell went on into fantasies of nuclear-waste disposal methods and the vibrant new example his reactor could offer to people like CND if only fuddy-duddy restrictions didn't prevent him from flaunting it before the world.

Seeing all this in a back garden rather than an ultra-modern laboratory, or even an NUTC laboratory, full of humming instruments ... it gave Tappen a curiously insecure feeling, as though he'd spent many a day browsing happily in the Zoo only, now, to find the entire contents of the Reptile and Insect Houses wriggling and hissing and chittering their welcome in his bath. Those pits, he told himself feebly, should be somewhere safe where they belong, like in the warheads of Britain's wonderful missile force. You simply can't let dangerous loonies like Pell go mucking around like this; the only thing to do is (after passing him the buck, both bucks, from the filing cabinet upstairs) to tip off Security and have him taken away. But, shaken and queasy at sight of Pell's domestic arrangements, Tappen found his brain churning and upsetting his habit of resolutely not thinking about nuclear nasties in real life.

After all, if Mrs Thatcher and her merry men were actually capable of pressing *the* red button, then letting dangerous loonies go mucking around like this was more or less what Tappen had been doing for most of his working life. He fingered this daringly heretical thought as though it were a promising new pimple just begging to be popped.

Pell was still lecturing while testing the reactor temperature with a thermometer scientifically tied to a string. "You can't mmm, get the fuel, you know," he said, sounding appallingly like Henery Crun. "Ever since they put in those *wretched* gate detectors ..."

Tappen had abruptly realized why the workshops complained of making so damned many dummies. And, come to think of it, why so damned many British underground tests had flopped more than somewhat? "Oh, I think I can give you a hand with the fuel," he said in the offhand tones of a neighbour prepared to be generous about loaning out the Flymo.

"And by adjusting the, mmm, positions of the fuel elements I can alter the criticality and, er, power output," said Pell unstoppably. He must have lectured down here to countless imaginary audiences, far more attentive and respectful than real Tappens.

"I said, I can lend you a few cupfuls of plutonium fuel if you like, Roger."

The spell was broken. Pell stared at him resentfully. "I was saying ... er, Roy, you never said, exactly *how* did you know about my, ah, noble experiment down here?"

Tappen indicated the clutch of fermentation jars going happily *bloop-bloop-bloop* in ideal temperature conditions. "The neutrons get into your wine and whisky, Roger. I – that is, I had a hunch and found the Scotch you gave me was radiating gently. Just one tiny overlooked detail, but enough to bring a wanted man to justice. Mind how you go."

"Piffle," Pell complained. Apparently he had thought of that, had tested his wine most carefully and found it purer than pure (albeit a trifle cloudy). Apparently any stray whisky-neutrons must come not from Pell's backyard reactor but from additives like the Lab Four absolute alcohol as pilfered by Pell, which, come to think of it, was kept a little, er, close to the neutron-source cupboard ...

Abashed to find his outbreak of Great Detection had accidentally reached the right answer by close pursuit of a red herring, Tappen could only say, "Oh, I'm sorry, Roger."

"That's, er, all right, Roy. Now this is the really interesting aspect," Pell said mercilessly, pointing into the pool of wet blue fire and droning on about intricate safety precautions consisting largely of rubber bands eked out with the occasional paperclip.

"Sixteen minutes," said Tappen as a last resort, backing through the doorway and nearly falling over several cables and pipes. Reluctantly Pell closed the steel door on the blue-glowing entrails of his central heating system, and (still lecturing) led the way back to the house and the unfinished bottle of wine, which didn't stay unfinished for long.

Restored but still trembling, Tappen faded politely into the night and presently returned with grunts and a suitcase which felt full of lead. As well as the lead screening it held two large, aluminium-jacketed balls of plutonium, and Tappen commended these into Pell's enlightened care.

"I'm sure they're safer with you than they would be anywhere else," he said unctuously, and in the relief of this long-awaited moment he found himself believing it.

"Marvellous ... I might be able to put in some upstairs radiators, now," said Pell as he cooed over his clutch. "Roy, this calls for, mmm, a celebration. Do join me in a magnum of my special home-made Imperial Tokay. The night is young."

But full of his new knowledge, Tappen made elaborate and confused excuses, to do with his urgent need to visit town and make up the quarrel with Lizzie, a process so complex and fraught that almost certainly he wouldn't get back that night and would be forced to sleep (sod the manager's wife) in a hotel.

In the dim front garden of number 33, an estate agent's board – which hadn't been there when he got back from work – winked at Tappen through the gloom. He patted it affectionately, then climbed into the Volvo and drove away, not looking back.

Had he perhaps been tactless in refusing Pell's final, kindly offer? With enough fissile material at his disposal to raze ten good-sized cities, the older man had confided that, with a little tinkering, he was almost sure he could provide free heating for Tappen's house as well.

Postscript

"And this is the cellar," Lizzie was saying to the visiting Joe Llewellyn, who hadn't yet been allowed to take his coat off and already had the glazed aspect of a VIP being educated against his will.

"This is where the rising damp starts," Tappen put in helpfully. "It rises for about eight feet and then there's an interesting dry zone before you reach the falling damp from the roof leaks. Also down here we have fascinating enclaves of wet rot, weevils and woodlice which you are at liberty to examine more closely."

"Nice place," Llewellyn said. "Much nicer than the old semi."

"Ah, but you haven't yet seen our collection of *Anobium punctatum* or common furniture beetle – I believe the proletariat call it woodworm. Come outside and view the bits that need repointing, refurbishing, rebuilding and general resurrection."

Lizzie said after an interval: "This is the back garden, Joe. Normally I'd expect you to recognize a back garden, being a trained observer and all, but my dear husband hasn't yet found a moment to reclaim it from the jungle."

"But see," said Tappen, "where the verdant gorse and bramble slope down to a shingled beach suffused with the gentle wash and murmur of a sapphire-like sea aglitter beneath the golden sun, all of which would be much more visible if it weren't for the clouds and the unfortunate fact that they built the Tidal Power Research Establishment in the way."

"What's it like there?" Llewellyn asked.

"Much more soothing, Joe, much more soothing than Robinson Heath. There's something restful in knowing that even if I expose myself at close range to several million gallons of tidal power, there's no chance of falling over with all my chromosomes lightly grilled."

"Mmm," said Lizzie, patting his arm. "I keep expecting you to accidentally bring the English Channel home in your briefcase, darling. – I'd show you upstairs, Joe, but it's all wall-to-wall cardboard boxes we haven't unpacked yet, all with dreadful things like Brains Faggots printed on them, what a ghastly name for anything to eat ..."

"They should call them Jumbo Meatballs," Tappen suggested.

"Hard luck on poor old Jumbo," said Llewellyn, and Lizzie pretended to faint. "Roy, Lizzie, I never sussed how you sorted out that pit trouble. What's the story?"

"I wasn't trusting that to the phone, but now you've come visiting at last ..." Pausing only to prepare three gins-and-tonic powerful enough to make a jumbo oblivious of his loss, Tappen related the true and terrible history of Roger Pell's garden pool and the strange denizens thereof. At gratifying intervals, Llewellyn ejaculated, "Bloody hell!"

"The funny coincidence, Joe, was when we sold the house," Lizzie said. "You'd never guess who bought it."

"Who?"

"He *said* he was going to move," said Tappen. "Sergeant Alf Rossiter."

A dreamy look passed over Llewellyn's face. "Him and Roger Pell ... they deserve each other."

"Now how did *you* make out? When I made my famous Houdini escape you were still juggling the inventory to conceal a certain shortage of nukes. From the lack of handcuff marks on your wrists, I brilliantly deduce you got away with it?"

"Ah," said Llewellyn evasively.

"Not *another* fizzled underground test?"

"Ah," said Llewellyn. "No, actually I, well. Had a dummy to replace your second one, yes: and you sent me that postcard with the hint, and I checked the pit store. Four more dummies there."

Tappen shrugged. "I knew Roger had to have got his somewhere. So – *five* test flops? Must have had them rushing through an Act to amend the laws of physics."

"Not exactly. Not that many tests, you know that. Had to get them assigned somewhere all the same, somewhere they wouldn't get checked. You see that." Llewellyn seemed fascinated by the toes of his shoes, which he shuffled compulsively to and fro on the carpet. "Lucky it was Chevaline replacement-and-upgrade time of year. So I changed things round and they're all out of the way. In Polaris warheads."

There was a lengthy pause, punctuated by a rude heckling of gulls outside.

"Well," said Tappen at last, "if you don't tell the Soviets and neither do I –"

"Or the Americans," said Lizzie caustically.

"– it's still a jolly good Independent Deterrent, isn't it? With a built-in safety factor now, for when the Cabinet gets drunk and falls on the red button while trying to balance the budget. Really they should give us medals, if you look at it the right way."

"Or tie pits to our ankles and drop us in Roger Pell's swimming pool. If you look at it the wrong way." Llewellyn shivered and held out his suddenly empty glass. "Gawd. How d'you keep on grinning, knowing all the things you know?"

"Effortlessly. It's what we aged and cynical scientists learn to do all the time." Stretching luxuriously and trying to veil his growing unease with things nuclear since they ceased being common objects of the IN tray, Tappen added with one eye on his wife: "What you need is a dose of healthy exercise to take your apology for a mind off these morbid notions. It so happens that the paperwork of moving here has sort of swamped my storage: maybe you can give me a hand with this filing cabinet I have my eye on, down at the Tidal Power station ..."

He ducked as Lizzie hurled her shoe at him. It whizzed overhead and hit the wall with a harmless flop, just like the Polaris they accidentally fired at Stockholm three weeks later.

The End